An
ATOMIC
ROMANCE

An

ATOMIC
ROMANCE

A NOVEL

Bobbie Ann Mason

Bobbie Ann Mason (signature)

RANDOM HOUSE

New York

Copyright © 2005 by Bobbie Ann Mason

Published in the United States by Random House, an imprint of
The Random House Publishing Group, a division of
Random House, Inc., New York.

RANDOM HOUSE and colophon are registered trademarks of
Random House, Inc.

LIBRARY OF CONGRESS CATALOGING-IN-PUBLICATION DATA
Mason, Bobbie Ann.
An atomic romance: a novel / Bobbie Ann Mason.
p.   cm.
ISBN 0-375-50719-1
1. Nuclear fuel plants—Environmental aspects—Fiction.
2. Plutonium—Environmental aspects—Fiction.   3. Nuclear fuel
plants—Employees—Fiction.   4. Radioactive wastes—Fiction.
5. Women biologists—Fiction.   I. Title.
PS3563.A7877A88 2005
813'.54—dc22   2004061458

Printed in the United States of America on acid-free paper

www.atrandom.com

2 4 6 8 9 7 5 3

Book design by Dana Leigh Blanchette

For Roger

She is the fairies' midwife, and she comes
In shape no bigger than an agate stone
On the forefinger of an alderman,
Drawn with a team of little atomies
Over men's noses as they lie asleep.

Romeo and Juliet, I.iv

An
ATOMIC
ROMANCE

1

*R*eed Futrell still went camping in the Fort Wolf Wildlife Refuge, but he no longer brought along his dog. One spring evening, after his shift ended, he raced home, stuffed his knapsack, loaded his gear onto his bike, and headed for the refuge. He was in one of the enigmatic moods that clobbered him from time to time, and when it struck—the way a migraine hammered some people—his impulse was to hop on his hog and run. Last fall, when one of these moods grabbed him, he rode hundreds of miles, to Larimer County, Colorado, where—in a hot-tub at a spa—he came to his senses and felt like turning back home.

"Good boy, Clarence," he had said to his collie-shepherd combo as he left the fenced yard and fastened the gate. "Lay low now. And be sweet—unless anybody tries to break in. You know what to do, killer."

During the five-mile ride, he ignored the industrial scenery and the suburban tableaus and the trailer havens. He escaped the desolation of the outskirts quickly, pretending his hog was a Thoroughbred stallion. As he approached the wilderness, Reed tried to imagine that he was seeing the place for the first time, as if he were entering the unfolding present of the opening of a movie. He was watching, curious to see what might happen.

What anyone notices first about this vast, flat landscape is the fantastical shapes of rising white clouds—plumes and balloons and pillows of cloud, like fleecy foam insulation blown from a hose. When Hollywood filmed a frontier drama here, the source of the clouds remained just outside the frame of the Cinerama panoramas. A radiant green extended for miles, and the great mud and might of the river seemed unlimited. Even now, if you saw this landscape from a sufficient distance and you didn't know better, you might imagine an untouched old-growth forest. The billowy puffs seem innocent. They are so purely white, it's as though only dainty, clean ladies' drawers could have been set aflame to produce them.

But now as the camera zooms in closer, you see that the green is crisscrossed by linked electric towers leading to a set of old gray buildings of assorted sizes—including Quonset huts and prefab mobile units. They are unprepossessing except for the largest two, which appear ample enough to house a fleet of C-5 transport aircraft. These two buildings, in chorus, emit a low roar, like the sound of a waterfall.

Now, the close-ups. The row of gleaming scrap heaps. The gate with the DANGER signs. The small building brightly decorated with yellow signs and festooned with yellow tape. One rusty pile of smashed barrels and girders and coils staggering to the height of a two-story building. From this mountain of metal, a ditch threads into a lagoon, where the still water is green and shiny. Other small lagoons are outlined with yellow ribbon.

A parking lot is filled with large metal canisters painted a pretty aqua color. They resemble gargantuan Prozac capsules. Thousands of them line the pavement. They are parked in geometric rows, like patient pupae waiting to become worms. Beyond the six-pack of cooling towers and the twin smokestacks, two tall construction cranes rise from a clearing on the edge of the wilderness, where a scrim of temporary fencing conceals a new act in an ongoing drama.

Reed's motorcycle plugs along a gravel road, skirting the security perimeter, passing the tall scrap heap, then leaving the gray, humming village and easing into the solace of the woods, where campers and hunters, with their dogs and deer rifles and picnic coolers, have pursued the natural life for years. Boy Scouts have their roundups and jamborees here. Coon-dog clubs hold their field trials.

The wilderness sprawls toward the river. The road leads into the heart of this sanctuary, away from the string of high-voltage towers and the dancing plumes. Even the crash and gurgle of the invisible waterfall grows distant. But the luminescence of the place remains, brightening with the growing dusk.

*R*eed Futrell wound through a labyrinth of gravel roads, stirring up a dusting of memories. He had been coming to this place all his life. His uncle Ed taught him to fish here in the large ponds, long before the water began to turn strange colors. He killed his first—and only—buck here. He hunted squirrels with his cousins. He went on church picnics, although he belonged to no church. He probably had camped in this woods three hundred times.

He decided to camp near the levee, where he could hear the blasts from the tugboats towing barges of iron ore and coal. Leaving his bike near a clearing, he lit out through a stand of river birches. He followed his glimpses of the immense metal bridge that spanned the river. At the top of the levee, he squatted and let the last of the sunset happen, imagining it was coming out of him, that he had the power to make the sun go down. If the sun, flaming orange, was like the inferno inside him, the burning blaze of fear and desire, then perhaps he could drop it over the horizon as casually as a basketball. He rose to attention as the sun's top rim sank. A haze of thin clouds spread above the horizon. A cool tinge in the air brushed his skin. A coal barge was gliding along, and he could see the tugboat captain on his perch. Reed had considered that way of life for himself at one time, a means of living without moorings.

At the levee, he was always aware of his maternal grandfather, who had worked with the Army Corps of Engineers building the levees and preparing the way for the marching towers of electricity that fed the gaseous-diffusion plant. Somewhere along the levee, Boyce Reed had been working on an erosion project, laying willow matting along the banks, when he fell ill with pneumonia. Whenever Reed came here, he was gripped by the vision of his grandfather suffering from fever and congestion while lying in his tent by the riverbank. He had been in the tent for three days before anyone realized how sick he was. He died in 1951, before Reed was born. Reed knew little about him, a pale man in a portrait on his mother's mantel, so coming here was like a ritual connection. Reed did not have a line of men he was close to. His father, Robert Futrell, had died young, in 1964, when Reed was only six, in an accident at the plant. It was up to his uncles to teach him how to be a man. "This is the way your daddy always baited his hook," they would say. Or, "He was the champion when it came to muzzle loading." And "The Almighty broke the mold after he made Robert Futrell." Reed felt he couldn't live up to his father's reputation, and it took years for him to realize that his uncles meant nothing personal.

In the growing darkness, he hiked briskly through the woods back to the spot where he had left his bike. He made his camp methodically, laying out one of his tarps on the ground and stringing the other among some tree branches for an overhead shelter. Then he smoothed off a place for his tent. Slamming the pegs with satisfaction, he anchored the base corners, then wormed the aluminum tubes through their little fabric tunnels. His pup tent sprang open like a flower unfolding on high-speed film.

He constructed a small fire and heated some beans, then unwrapped a chicken focaccia sandwich and snapped open a can of beer. He ate, watching the fire swell and turn colors. The warmth was pleasant. The air still held the mellow spring daytime smells of bloom and decay. The light from the plant blotted out much of the night, but he could see a faint smattering of the Milky Way and a few of the brighter stars. He thought he could make out Sirius. He liked to imagine dying stars, their enormous fires imploding or exploding. He tried, as he often did, to grasp the idea that the present moment did not exist in some star a million light-years off. It was not now there. Not even on Mars was it now. If that was true, it could be reversed, he thought. He and his fire and his tent did not exist from the vantage point of the star, or on Mars, at this moment—whenever that might be.

Viewing the stars, he always felt privileged to witness ultimate mystery, to be in it. The universe tantalized and affronted him, ripping him out of his own petty corner. As he ate, hypnotized by the fire, he listed in his mind all the things in his life that were good. His kids had jobs and weren't in trouble, his ex-wife was satisfied, his mother was nestled in a senior citizens' home. His dog didn't have fleas.

But he had not seen Julia in six weeks. She came out here with him a couple of times, most recently on a freakishly fair day on the last of February. They picnicked in a meadow beside the ruins of Fort Wolf, the old munitions factory that had operated during World War II. It was one of his favorite places. The hulks of the ragged concrete walls were like the forlorn remnants of a castle. Two water towers, their brick and mortar crumbling, stood like bookends without books to hold. He cavorted with her, half-naked, shouting, "It can't get any better than this!" In the sunny afternoon they wallowed around lazily on a flannel blanket. At night they snuggled in the pup tent (his double-pup tent, he told her when she questioned its size) and shook up the wilderness with riotous sex.

Still gazing at the fire, his sandwich now gone, he wandered into a reverie about Julia, trying to create a Top Ten list of sex-dates with her. But none of them could be relived in his mind. He couldn't remember what she was wearing the last time he saw her. She said, "I can't loiter. I've got an immunogenetics seminar to go to." And after that, she did not answer the telephone messages he left.

Julia, who worked at a cytopathology lab, planned to save the world from sinister infectious diseases like Ebola and anthrax. Early in their relationship, not realizing how ambitious she was, he had suggested she go to nursing school. She good-humoredly dismissed his idea.

"I can stick people," she said. "But I'd rather be in charge of a mental hospital than have to do a Foley or a rectal."

"You'd rather hear about their cracked minds than look at their cracks," he said.

She thought for a moment. "A cracked mind—I like that."

Julia was from Chicago. He loved to hear her talk. Her sweet Scandinavian-Irish-Polish twang. Her sharp, precise sounds, her back-slanted *A*'s and rounded *O*'s. He missed her vowels. He missed her lip gloss. She used flavored lip gloss habitually and sometimes smeared it straight across, instead of following the natural lines, so that her mouth was a wide, glistening swath.

He would get his blood tested if she could be the one to stick him. He hadn't had a complete physical in five years. He was a notorious procrastinator—with tinnitus and a thrumming lust that ran like a refrigerator, kicking on and off automatically.

The tree frogs were peeping a cacophony, in which he heard raucous machines and anxious melodies. He draped a blanket around him and fed the fire little twigs. He picked a tick from his scalp and dropped it into the flame. The sky was gathering clouds, and the stars were fading. The clouds moved swiftly. He couldn't even see the Dippers. He had been to the Smoky Mountains one August during the Perseid meteor shower; it was dazzling, like fireworks, like the Big Bang. He tried to remember it now, but it was like trying to remember sex; you had to be there then. If there was no now now, then there would be no then there now either.

Inside his tent, he sidled in and out of sleep, dreaming that Julia was with him. He dreamed that she telephoned a pizza parlor, and a machine voice told her, "Your call is important to us. Please stay on the line."

A sound penetrated his sleep. In his semiwakefulness he thought he heard himself fart—a muffled, explosive blat that projected over toward the levee, as if his bowels were practicing ventriloquism. But he hadn't heard himself fart that loudly in years. As a gentle rain began to fall, he sank back into sleep, with the soothing and hypnotic shush of the raindrops on the leaves.

In his dream, a car pulls up nearby and the engine shuts off. The headlights go off, but an interior light stays lit. The car seems to huddle between the shadows of the ancient water towers. The moon climbs high, but the driver of the car does not emerge. With spring peepers screaming out their courtship messages, the night seems welcoming. Hours pass. Then, near midnight, the car door opens once briefly, and a woman—indistinct in the dim light—slips out of the seat, shuts the door, and squats on the ground for a few minutes. Then she reenters the car, starts the engine and lets it run. Radio music blares. The car does not move from its spot in the shadows. The engine keeps running, with the dome light shining and the music playing until the car runs low on gas and begins to sputter. The engine dies. The light goes out. And the blast of the gun splinters the night calm. In a while, rain begins to fall softly.

Reed tries to awaken, but he feels paralyzed. He struggles fitfully, and then eases deeper into dream as his muscles release and he floats toward the car. He glimpses the ice-blue metal, burning like candles, between the water towers. He approaches cautiously, noticing that it is a luxury sedan, a nice city car, not the kind of vehicle a camper or hiker would be driving. Slopping his way through puddles, he reaches the car.

He stares through the broken window at the shattered face. She has fallen toward the wheel, but he can see half her face is ripped away, leaving a reddish-brown spaghetti sauce. She must have hit her temple at a slant. He does not need to open the door. He can see the revolver on the floorboard, a .38 special, its handle decorated with floral decals.

On the dashboard, fastened with tape, are pictures of children. Two boys and two girls. All of them little, smiling, in Halloween costumes, the least one in a bunny outfit, with long, erect ears.

Moaning, Reed reels away. He streaks through the woods—crazed, stupid with disgust and horror. He calls out. He runs and runs, but he feels he is traveling at the speed of a shrimp trawler, which he imagines as a slow boat to Ethiopia. But then the shrimp trawler zooms across the Gulf of Mexico, where he awakens, in a sea of sweat.

His mind had given him a private screening of a horror film. Who was the woman? Why would she come out here to kill herself? He could not fathom a woman killing herself when she had four small children to care for. He turned and stretched in his musty, oversized sleeping bag. Was it so simple to go mad and kill yourself? He didn't believe it. What if she wanted to spare her children from something? An illness. Maybe the woman believed herself inadequate to the task of raising them. He wondered if her husband would ask the same questions he was asking. Over and over he heard the shot muffled by the rain, saw the faceless woman, someone he would never be able to recognize. The Halloween costumes raced ahead of him as he relaxed again into sleep.

Rain awoke him at the brink of dawn. The dripping rain made a sound like someone pounding in a fence post. Leaving his camp undisturbed, he pulled on his slicker and zipped up his tent. Guided by his flashlight, he began slogging his way through overgrown brambles and wet vines toward the shimmering light of the plant, until he spotted a certain metal scrap heap some two hundred yards away. He didn't go closer. He could see eerie blue flames licking the metal junk, with tongues of fire nearly a foot high. In a gentle rain like this one, mysterious blue flames often erupted, flickering delicately like a gas fire on artificial logs. The flames were lovely yet terrible, another of those elusive phenomena—like a solar storm, a starburst—that you strive to grasp but can't. They made him think about quasars, those distant blue lights in the firmament.

The rain was slacking up. He tramped a different route back to his camp, following dirt-bike paths and small lanes, avoiding the briar patches. The ruins of the munitions factory lay ahead. He reached the clearing where in his dream he had found the dead woman. In the dream the setting was visually more of a museum than a wilderness, but his mind had placed it in this space. It was the exact spot where he had romped with Julia among the slag heaps and ruined buildings. They had played hide-and-go-seek in the bunkers, chasing each other around the towers. That was before she accused him of betrayal.

When he reached his camp, he quickly collapsed his tent, rolled up his wet tarps, and crammed his gear into the carrier. Then he kicked the motor to life.

*W*omen were always after him to get a cell phone. If Reed had really needed to call the police about the dead woman, it would have taken him half an hour to find a telephone. The dream had been so real that as he swerved through the back roads, he seemed to be dreaming still. He imagined going to the police station to report what he had seen. He harbored a slight worrisome thread of paranoia. What about his footprints at the site? And did he touch the window? No. He knew nothing. She was a stranger.

The scene had been so desolate. No one had heard the woman's last utterances; she was like a tree falling in the forest with no one around to hear. His own ears were nearly dead from the decibels at work.

Reed was normally a confident guy, given to bursts of pleasure and celebratory blasts of energy. He wasn't afraid of much, he knew how to protect himself, he could deal with almost anything. Being neighborly, he once rushed into a burning house to save a ninety-seven-year-old invalid. "Slow down," his former wife, Glenda, had often said to him. "You'll burn yourself out." Now in his forties, he still aimed to charge through life with youthful zeal. But for the last couple of years, a deep pain welled inside him occasionally and confused him. He supposed it was simply chemical—if chemistry was ever simple. But as bitter as his moods had sometimes been, he had never entertained a suicidal thought. The dead woman couldn't have represented Glenda. She was too much of a schemer, a master of coupon organization. And the dead woman was definitely not his mother. Although she had high cholesterol and arthritis, her life force had the strength of the *Saturn V.*

And she wasn't Julia. In no way was she Julia.

He skirted the construction site east of the plant. It seemed forsaken without the row of blue portable toilets, which were removed the day construction was halted. The cranes posed for still lifes.

Reed rode all day, through several counties, following no particular route. The dream wouldn't fade out. If he had really found a dead woman, people at work would approach him, curious and agog. They would want to hear his story over and over. It would be like receiving congratulations for something extraordinary he had done. Over and over he thought of her last hours. The way she lined up the photos on the dashboard—how long did she stare at those pitiful pictures? Did she talk to them? Did she put off her act until she had said everything she wanted to say?

He let the wind fly through his hair as he swirled around the narrow roads, the sun winking through the leaves like a strobe light. He loved the patterns of sun and shade in the woods on either side of him. Wildlife fled from his mighty engine. Reed Futrell did not know where he was going. He rode along a precipice. He was a mechanized Road Runner, rushing along, but watching himself too, knowing that if he leaned too far in one direction or the other he would pancake down a canyon. His fatalism annoyed Julia.

"I've been living with that stuff so long my insides would be neon green if you opened me up," he had told her. "If I've got it, I've got it."

"But if you don't, wouldn't it be a relief to know?"

"Can't you do the blood test for me?"

"No, it's against the rules. The paperwork would screw you up."

"Won't you stick me, honey?" he said, running his hand down her back.

"Can't do."

"I'd like to stick you," he said.

Julia could not know his work history. He hadn't told her. He wouldn't.

His mind always meandered while on the road, or lying on the tarp in the woods, or inside the patched pup tent he'd hauled around for years. But now he observed that he was surveying his whole life as though it had a pattern, passions and frailties that connected together.

Reed had grown up reading the *Encyclopedia Americana* and listening to big bands. He always had dogs. He loved shooting targets. He loved women. He loved being married for the first fifteen years, before he and Glenda began fighting. He realized that when they married, they didn't understand each other, that they were too young to understand their own natures, or their differences. Glenda had always been picky, and then she sometimes demeaned him by calling him boorish and overly macho. Their counselor began harping on passive aggression, which Reed understood to mean that Glenda blamed him for her own bad behavior. She said she had to go away so she could grow as a person; Reed said that was ironic for a person always on a diet. The divorce was simple, and she finished raising the kids, Dalton and Dana. Now his children were young adults whom he saw only once in a while. They treated him decently. They seemed normal. He was lucky.

His kids bounced along with the scary optimism of youth. Dalton, with ambitions of becoming an architect, worked at a design company in North Carolina. And Dana, who didn't quite finish college, worked with a producer on Music Row in Nashville. She sent him CDs, sickly pop stuff that you would call gruel if it were food, Reed thought. One of the songs Dana was so proud of had a line, "Carry the gospel to them all," which Reed persisted in hearing as "Carry the gospel to the mall." He often kidded her about that song, even singing it on her answering machine.

In a titty bar somewhere on the edge of a river town, Reed ordered a beer. A jejune band was playing country-pop drivel, and he had to listen to half a dozen songs before the girls came on, swinging their fringed anatomies—fringe flying from their tits, fringe hanging between their legs like a collie dog's skirt.

Reed kept himself fit. Every day he stretched and pumped and jacked up his heart rate. He considered himself sexually attractive and had no trouble getting women. He enjoyed women, made new conquests easily, flirted shamelessly. He'd tuck his finger inside a woman's blouse and playfully tug her bra strap, or he'd reach down and play with the hem of her short skirt. He would do that even before he knew their names, and they would giggle and swoon. Reed had a certain cockiness, and the way he moved seemed to thrill women. He had simple urges—always present, it seemed, throbbing like a hurt toe and keeping him on high alert, like those power lines humming into the plant.

Sitting at a table near the door, he stayed through two beers, but he did not tip these girls. Tonight he did not feel like folding a five-dollar bill and tucking it under a G-string. He left the titty bar and whisked through the night.

As he crossed the bridge over the river, his mood shifted. He gunned his bike, knowing that just a little slip on a pebble could send him flying. He was eager to check his telephone messages.

His street was quiet and the moon was high when he arrived at his old bungalow, a relic from the 1940s with a pyramid roof and a pillared porch. He left his bike and gear in the garage and went to the backyard where Clarence was in an uproar. The dog was overjoyed to see him, nearly knocking Reed over as he entered the gate. Clarence lunged into the house with him, and Reed hugged him and let him slobber on him.

"Yes, that's exactly what I'm saying," Reed said to Clarence. "Woof woof. We're in total agreement."

The answering machine held nothing significant, nothing from Julia. He sat on the dog-abused sofa with Clarence and read the newspapers, to see what had happened in the world during his absence. Same old thing, he learned quickly. More commotion at the plant, troublemakers demanding more investigations. The wider world in chaos. Clarence rested his head on Reed's lap and ate corn chips with him.

"Clarence, it says here the cops found five bags of marijuana at a yard sale." Reed laughed. "Probably antiques."

He was glad to be home. It was comfortable here now with Clarence. Reed read the obituaries, noting the ages. On the page of personal funeral notices, a guy named Jack, a construction worker, had died at age sixty-eight. Reed said, "Come see Jack in the box, visitation two to four p.m. Sunday." Reed laughed. Jack could have waited all his life for such a moment and then missed it.

The telephone rang. "Go, killer," Reed said, opening the back door and shooing Clarence out. He answered the telephone.

"Hey, Reed. This is your Prayer Warrior, calling with your ten o'clock prayer." It was Burl, his best pal since high school. "Hey, man, are you up?"

"Up? Why wouldn't I be up? Do you mean Big Reed or Little Reed?"

"No, man, wake up. Listen. This is urgent."

"What?" Reed settled himself against the wall.

"A while ago I had a heavy, heavy notion, Reed, that you were in need of prayer. I need to pray for you."

"Pray away, Burl." Burl could be a Prayer Warrior or a pagan dancer. It was all the same. Inevitably, he was drunk.

"Are you all right, Reed? Was your little trip good?"

"Yeah. I saw the blue flames again."

"No shit! I wish I'd seen them."

"Next time."

"But you shouldn't hang out at that place."

"I was way over by the river. That's O.K."

Reed told Burl in some detail his dream about the dead woman. "It was so vivid," he said. "I'm still thinking about it."

"Write that down, Reed. You could win the Pulitzer Prize."

"Win what? The tulip surprise?"

Burl chortled. "You need a hearing aid, Reed. I said *Pulitzer Prize*!"

"You don't have to yell! I was making a joke."

"I'm praying for you, Reed."

"O.K."

"That business out at the plant is like the butterfly effect," said Burl. "One thing leading to another."

"Sure." What *wasn't* involved with the fucking butterfly effect?

"Did you get that test yet?"

"Oh, Burl, go on back to Xanadu, and let me get some sleep. I'll see you tomorrow."

"O.K., but I'm praying for you."

"That's nice, Burl. Thank you. I'll pray for you too."

There was no way to pray for Burl, even if Reed were a praying type. Burl was like an asteroid that made periodic close encounters, but never quite came to earth.

Although Reed was tired, he sat down at his computer. As usual, he had a hard time getting past his screen savers, a dazzling variety of galaxies and nebulae, photographs from the Hubble telescope, gliding silently toward him, changing at twenty-second intervals. They shifted before him, unbelievable, colorful close-ups of outer space—galactic clusters, hot clumps of nebulosity, supernovas, spiral galaxies. The universe. When he stared at these pictures, his mind seemed to empty out. He changed the pictures frequently in order to retain that fresh astonishment.

Finally, he checked his e-mail. He wished Julia had e-mail, but she refused to waste her time with it. He found dozens of new answers to a personal ad he had placed on the Internet. Curious, and with a pleasing sexual stirring, he ran through the responses. His ad had been simple: "Strong, good-looking guy looking for smart, sensitive woman with sense of humor and curiosity. Sex not a requirement. Let's just hang." He left his zip code and moniker, "Atomic Man."

He dumped all the messages with distant zip codes. He read the remaining one, from a zip code near his own, someone calling herself Hot Mama.

"Your ad is too vague. You don't reveal anything about yourself. Why should I be interested? Your ad seems intended to reel in all women indiscriminately. Who would confess to being insensitive, without humor or curiosity? Sex? Screw you."

"Goddamn," Reed said aloud. "I can't deal with you tonight, Hot Mama."

He stared at the message until his screen saver came on; the shifting images of the cosmos were hypnotic, and he began to feel sleepy.

Exhausted, he fell into his stale sheets. Sleep wouldn't come. He was too tired to sleep. He rose and dashed off a message to Hot Mama. "I'm sensitive, with a sense of humor, and I'm loaded with curiosity. I don't stick to the everyday. I fool around with the *cosmos*. My favorite poem is 'Kubla Khan.' I have a scar on my wrist that resembles a rat's ass. Why am I telling you all this?"

He sent the message, felt better, then went easily to sleep.

2

The Easter tree in the lobby at Sunnybank seemed as fresh and fecund as it had on Easter Sunday, three weeks ago. Its machine-decorated plastic eggs still seemed newly laid, Reed thought. His mother never celebrated Easter in any special way—except the time she went to a sunrise breakfast at a park on the river. He remembered her saying that since the park was on the east side of the river, the staging was all wrong for the resurrection.

Today was Mother's Day. Reed's mother, Margaret ("Peggy") Melinda Reed Futrell Sisson Daly—name tags for husbands no longer valid—lived at 115 Willow Court. Willow Court was a wide, sunny corridor carpeted with pink cabbage roses. Last year Reed had talked her into moving to Sunnybank Assisted Living so that she wouldn't be alone. He became concerned when he found a blob of stainless steel—a former saucepan—welded to a burner on her stove and found her eating from a plastic container of purple gelatin a neighbor had brought her a month before. Her refrigerator was nearly bare. In the freezer compartment, he discovered dozens of little packages—tidbits of hamburger twisted in foil. He asked her what she was doing—making chipmunk packs? He ordered her a pizza and stocked her refrigerator. After she moved to Sunnybank, her mind improved, and she resented her displacement, insisting that she should not be kept with the toothless and feeble, like a helpless old donkey in a stall. She was forgetful, but not incapacitated, she said then. She withdrew into her apartment, where she read romance novels and worked with her paint set, copying the old masters from an art book. Aides came to remind her of social activities, but she went only on occasion.

"This place is full of incompetents and nuts," his mother said now, greeting him and his spray of supermarket flowers at the door of her apartment. "Elder abuse, too. I can document it."

But she was grinning, happy to see him.

"Happy Mother's Day," he said, planting a kiss on her cheek and hugging her.

Her steely curls were springy, like the metal coils on mousetraps, and she wore a lively complex of cosmetics. Her place was sunny and spacious. Reed's sister, Shirley, had fixed it up to resemble home, with family photographs and knickknacks. A bowl of plastic Easter eggs rested on the dining table. Reed recalled a woman he had gone out with who decorated her Easter eggs with swastikas. Where did he find such women? he wondered.

"If I had stayed home, I could be growing my own bouquets," Reed's mother said.

"Probably so, Mom," said Reed. "And maybe you could get a job driving a bus, too."

"Don't make fun of me."

"I didn't mean to." Reed still felt guilty that he had uprooted her from her home and plopped her into this glorified way station. It was supposed to be a resort, not a last resort. Maybe he would have moved her back home, but her house belonged to someone else now, a couple who had installed a volleyball court and free-range chickens. The court was enclosed with chain link, and the chickens ran in the street.

Stooping with only slight difficulty, she found a green vase under the sink for his cellophane shroud of blooms. Reed glimpsed a standing army of green florists' vases in the cupboard.

Her bird clock signaled the hour. It was the woodpecker's Morse code.

"My birds are screwed up," his mother said. "It's supposed to be the cardinal."

"They need to be readjusted," he said.

She ran water into the vase, and he plunked the flowers into the water. He set the vase next to the Easter-egg bowl on the small dining table. They situated themselves, Reed on the sofa and his mother in her recliner.

"The food here is getting worse," she said. "The dietitian is overweight, and I think I see everybody gaining a little."

"You're not. You look good."

"I'm not gaining weight because I won't eat that slumgullion they concoct here. I fix myself a little something here in the room. I microwaved popcorn last night and watched *An Affair to Remember.* Did you ever see that, Reed?"

"Probably. I've forgotten."

He listened to her summarize the story. He liked to watch her animated hands, which followed the enthusiastic, girlish trills of her voice. It made him feel better to know that she always made the best of a situation.

"Have you seen Julia again?" she demanded.

"No. She's still mad at me."

"Haven't you apologized?"

"I guess."

"I know you—you'll fool around and she'll get tired of waiting. You always did put off what needed to be done."

"It's not that easy." Reed took a deep breath.

"Go after her! You'll fool around and lose her if you don't."

"Any more orders?"

Abruptly, she inquired about his work. "Reed. Listen—are they going to cancel the new plant?"

"Don't know. We'll have to see what the D.O.E. says about how long the cleanup will take."

"I'm so afraid we'll lose the new plant. We need the jobs."

"Oh, we won't lose it unless the D.O.E. makes the whole place a Superfund site."

"I doubt if they would take that much interest," she said, twisting a curl between her fingers.

Seizing an opportunity, Reed said, "Talk to me about the good old days, Mom, when toxic waste was what you found in the cat litter pan."

"Ha! Good old days! That's the biggest fallacy in the kingdom."

He didn't know how much she knew about the current troubles, and he didn't want to worry her. He didn't see a newspaper anywhere in her crowded living room. The family pictures covered several surfaces. His eyes rested on the photograph of his father. He was handsome and clear eyed, a confident man in a tweed jacket and striped tie. Reed recalled his parents dancing to their favorite instrumental from the big-band era—Artie Shaw's "Dancing in the Dark." They glided across the hardwood floor of their small living room as if they had all the space in the world.

He said, "I thought you were pretty happy when you started out—when I was little and my dad was alive."

"That's true." She smiled. "He loved his job. It was so important to the national defense."

"Everybody was fighting the Communists."

"I don't believe we ever saw any," she said with a laugh. "We just believed they were there, like elves."

Reed had often heard the old-timers tell about how the bomb-fuel plant was the salvation of the community after the Depression and the War. The plant was shrouded in secrecy then.

"Maybe things seem a little different nowadays, Mom."

"I'm afraid of what they're finding out," she said. "I'm afraid it'll kill the new plant. Will it?"

"I doubt it," Reed said to reassure her. "They've stopped construction while they do site assessment—that's what they're calling it. But I don't think it'll take long."

She roused herself from her chair to reach a garment from a table.

"Look at this crazy thing," she said, laughing. It was an apron she had made in crafts. It had at least a dozen pockets.

Reed said, "I could use one of these at work."

"It's just silly!" she said. "They think we're going to lose everything. They think we're liable to lose our heads."

"Looks to me like you could put insulation in those pockets and go to the North Pole," Reed said. "Or carry your camping gear. You'd be prepared for anything."

"I'll have to carry my head in this side pocket," she said, laughing.

Whenever she laughed, Reed felt heartened. He laughed with her, and he stood up, swinging the apron around his shoulders like a cape.

"Look! Up in the sky! It's a biker! It's a maintenance engineer! Yes! It's Atomic Man!"

3

*R*eed drove his truck to work early, to beat the rush. He followed Constitution Avenue past the Jewish temple, the
medical-supply stores, the farm store with a forest of spring bushes
and hanging baskets outside, a line of auto-hardware stores, then a
fast-food strip. He dipped under the viaduct just as a train trundled
overhead. The sunrise at the end of Constitution flashed in front of
Reed as he emerged. A soft luster surrounded the sun.

At work, the buzz of the day was beryllium. Lately, it was one
alarm after another. The morning TV news had reported that over
the years a number of workers at the plant had been exposed to
beryllium, which could cause a lung disease. Reed, whose TV had
broken a year ago, had missed the latest revelation. A group of his
coworkers in the main process building were talking about it, but no
one seemed especially concerned except Teddy, an instrument me-

chanic who had been there for only ten years, fewer than most of the guys.

Teddy followed Reed into the process workers' break room. "I've got all the symptoms," he said. "It's in my lungs. I wheeze and spit."

"I thought beryllium disease was an allergy," Reed said. "Not everybody gets it."

"I never even heard of beryllium before."

"It comes from emeralds." Reed released coffee from a spigot into a foam cup.

"How do you know that?"

"Chemistry 101."

"They say you have to breathe it." Teddy coughed for emphasis, and his coffee dribbled down the side of his cup.

"It's spring," Reed said. "It's pussy willows."

"Aw, Reed, you're not taking this seriously."

"If I've got it, I don't want to know about it."

Reed tasted his coffee. It resembled sewage sludge and tasted worse. He stored his sandwiches in the refrigerator and his cap and keys in his locker.

"Don't worry, guys," said Jim, the shift superintendent. He entered the break room, with his newspaper rolled into a tube. Jim was a small, pale-skinned man with a prissy little goatee that Reed never could match with Jim's congeniality or complexion. Dispensing reassurance like baby oil, Jim said, "We don't have enough beryllium to be scared about, and even if we did, by God"—he used his newspaper like a light-saber to stab at the air—"if we did, we'd kill that snake dead."

"Is it radioactive?" Teddy wanted to know.

"I wouldn't think so," Jim said. "Not like the scrap piles."

He distributed the work packages containing the permits and other paperwork for the day's jobs. Reed went out to the floor. A bunch of guys were laughing near a supply office.

"Hey, Reed, how hot did you get that last time?" said Kerwin, one of the guys Reed had worked with for years.

"Don't remember. I didn't pay attention to the numbers," Reed said, sounding like a politician insisting that he ignored polls.

"I've been hot four times," Alberto bragged. "Hell, the numbers were higher than the stack, but I thought, hey, what the hell."

"I figure the company will take care of us," Kerwin agreed. He was writing on his work papers, turning them sideways to write marginal notes, as if he were writing personal commentaries.

"The union will," said Alberto.

"You get more in a year from doctors than from what we do here," Jim said, hurrying past. "X-rays. Dental stuff."

"Oh, hey, Jim," said Alberto. "We figure you're watching out for us."

Jim waved his light-saber, grinned, and walked away.

*R*eed dismissed beryllium, as if it were an annoying insect. But he liked knowing it was derived from emeralds.

He changed into pale-green doctor scrubs and whammed his clothes into his locker. After chugging a cup of water, he ascended to the second floor, where it was at least a hundred and ten degrees and eighty-five decibels. It sounded like jets taking off. Although the fourteen-acre building was probably large enough to fly a plane in, it could be claustrophobic—with the rows of cells, the overhead maze of Freon piping, the noise, the dusky light, the swirl of dust, the giant fans.

Reed was a cell rat. On the second level of the largest process building he crawled inside dark, dusty enclosures to repair machinery that yelled in his ears. When he worked on those risky jobs, he wore his yellow astronaut suit. He liked working in the outfit, with its fire-retardant coveralls, plastic socks, and rubber shoe scuffs. To top it off, a cloth hood with a long cape and a respirator with an ultraview plastic face protected him. It was his job to help keep the vital enrichment system, the Cascade, going flawlessly, and he always approached the task like a surgeon with an unwilling patient. Even though the enrichment technology was somewhat antiquated, and dealing with it was tricky, Reed was still awed. It was astonishing, really, that the system could separate out radioactive uranium isotopes like forty-niners panning for gold. But it was a colossal operation. Liquid uranium hexafluoride was fed into autoclaves and heated to a hundred and fifty degrees to change it into a gas. Powerful electric motors sent the gas spinning and shooting through hundreds of axial-flow compressors and into converters, where barriers with tiny holes filtered out the heavier isotopes. The tumult of hot gas hurled through all the stages hundreds and thousands of times until the final product could be drawn off into cylinders. This was the system, his friend and his enemy, the multiplex of little cascades forming a giant Cascade. Reed, armored in his moon suit, felt he was the master.

When the out-of-state reporters began snooping around last fall, there was general suspicion throughout the workforce. They weren't local, and no one knew their motives. The reporters—in khaki pants and plaid flannel sport shirts—had been in and out for over two weeks, following workers, poring over documents, roaming around the junk piles. They were friendly, professing amazement at the operation, admiring the intricacy and grandeur of the Cascade with its miles of piping, empathizing with the employees who worked on the high-risk jobs. So it was like a criticality-warning siren when the news reports eventually emerged about toxic leakage from secret landfills out in the Fort Wolf Refuge and contaminated scrap heaps inside the plant's fences. The out-of-state newspaper had assembled a tight, explosive little package. Code words for fear floated out of the paper like thought balloons. Radioactivity. Uranium. Cancer.

Those reporters were hunting their Tulip Surprises, Reed thought now. If the situation at the plant were a movie, he thought, some superhero character would save the whole place from a meltdown. Here, there was no nuclear reactor to melt down, but the movie would have one, photographed from sinister angles. A shiny actor-hero in a magic military chem suit would seduce an energetic blond FEMA investigator in the swank downtown Palace Hotel. Then a resplendent special-effects earthquake along a conveniently located fault line would magnify the nuclear havoc. The greenery of the wilderness would capsize and sink into muddy soup, with the animals screaming in panic. Throngs of refugees fleeing. Hogs swimming. Big turkey stranded on a roof.

A bird was flying above him, its flight meandering and desperate. Birds slipped in under the eaves and often couldn't find a way out. The bird's wings fluttered silently. It crashed against the ceiling and the walls. Now and then it perched on a girder. Birds died here, delirious in the heat. The heat desiccated them, sucked out their juices and kept them preserved like mummies. Or beef jerky. Reed had a pet dried bird he called Eisenhower. He had found him lying atop the asbestos housing of a cell. The bird was handsome, with black feathers and yellow streaks on his wings and face. He was a little thin, but with those crazed eyes he seemed fully alive.

Eisenhower stood on Reed's toolbox, his feet taped down. He was upright and realistic, with a mortician's grin. For verisimilitude, Reed had added a few white spots of caulking beneath the bird's tail. Everybody on the floor knew Eisenhower.

Reed took a deep breath and cut off his oxyacetylene torch. Big-band music filled his head, but the melody was indistinct, vapors of wandering sounds within the howling of the Cascade. He resumed his welding. Even though the plant no longer enriched uranium for bomb fuel, but instead supplied nuclear-power plants, Reed was still proud of doing this dangerous kind of work. In college he had majored in chemistry, after a guidance counselor steered him away from astronomy, saying there was little money to be made in that field and that he would need graduate school to go into research. After college, Reed had to earn a lot of money quickly, so that he could marry Glenda, whose expectations included a king-size bed and fancy vacations. New jobs were opening up at the plant, and the money was exceptional. He was following in his father's footsteps, and he had grown to love the work. Now Glenda was gone, their kids grown, and the same stars were still shining in their mysterious canopy.

But it was Julia he wanted now. In the deafening noise of the Cascade, Reed heard her name whispered over and over. Her name was always near his lips, the song bearing her name a deep undercurrent in his being. With her perfect self-possession, she always seemed to know clearly what she was doing. She never overindulged. She wasn't overweight. Her moves were so graceful they seemed unconscious. It was a discipline she learned from tai chi, he was made to understand.

Julia had the casual air of a fashion model, the kind of person who would look good even in a tow sack and kneesocks, but she didn't seem to need to shop or complain about her hair. She seemed self-guided, like one of those museum tours with headphones. She was the opposite of most women he had known—dolls with every hair pasted in place, the skin paved like asphalt with brilliant makeup, the gestures calculated and coy. Julia possessed a kind of aloofness that self-confidence produces—she was never beseeching, needful, weak, or self-conscious. Even when dressed in her lab wear, with aqua cotton pants and sneakers, Julia was cool.

Usually women simply disregarded things about him that didn't appeal to them, such as his interests in quasars or chemicals or asteroids. But Julia would cheerfully study anything, like a forensics expert with a lapful of dirty bones. When he showed her his Hubble slide show—hundreds of stars and galaxies on a CD-ROM—she was astonished, gasping at the Starbirth Region of Nebula NGC 604 as if she were witnessing it at an IMAX theatre. With Julia, he ranged through the Cat's Eye Nebula, the Eagle Nebula, the Crab Nebula, and the Horsehead Nebula, fading then into the diseased-looking Cone Nebula rearing its phallic sea-worm head and belching out stars.

"Here comes a supernova," he said, ducking. "A star on its deathbed."

"We need 3-D glasses," she said.

"If you let your eyes go out of focus a little, you can imagine you're inside."

She squinted and stared. "Very nebulous," she remarked. "I see what you mean."

Together, they traveled light-years through the universe. She began to recognize the repeats. She liked the dense, busy print designs of millions of stars.

"Oh, there's a face in that one." She pointed out the beady eyes, the mustache, and the chin at the center of a nebula. "My ex-husband," she said.

"Burl says it's God."

She laughed. "My ex-husband thought he was God."

"I get lost in these," Reed said, moving the cursor to click a new folder.

"Close-ups of disease germs look a lot like this," she said. "Under a microscope, a lot of them are like impressionist paintings. Anthrax is really pretty."

He pointed out a spiral galaxy, its arms flung out as if trying to grasp the whole universe.

"Everything spins," she said. "Doesn't that seem to be true? Galaxies, planets, people's lives?"

"That must be why the record industry is so big," he said.

That was months ago, early in their relationship. But now she was angry with him for taking her out to Fort Wolf that sunny day in February. He never meant to deceive her; he would never take her anywhere dangerous. But he was afraid she was making excuses. He was afraid they were worlds apart.

Reed needed a break to chill. He loved the luxurious moment when he emerged from the cell and burst out of his suit like a butterfly. He was dripping wet. He always told people he took saunas because he felt as if he had just stepped into a Nordic climate. Leaving his yellows inside the contamination zone, he went to an air line to blow off until he was dry.

He grabbed the handholds on the man lift, a little platform on a continuously moving belt. It shot him down through the hole in the floor, and he deftly stepped off at just the right instant on the floor below. It was like knowing when to go in and out of the window of a turning jump rope, he had told his daughter when she was a child. He could do it with his eyes closed, he boasted.

*R*eed's uncle Ed, his father's brother, who had retired from the plant a few years before and moved to a Florida condo, had often told him that the chemicals they handled were safe. His loyalty to the plant was absolute. Although his uncle's slow, old-timer manner made him impatient, Reed decided to telephone him about the developments at work.

"I've heard some of the news, but I don't know what to make of it," Uncle Ed said.

"They've stopped work on the centrifuge building till this gets straightened out," Reed said. "Most guys at the plant are more worried about their jobs than what's out in the woods."

"I would be too. I heard that new plant's going to cost two billion."

"Ed, listen. I was wondering if you ever knew anything about beryllium being there."

"I heard about that berry stuff they found. What did you say it was?"

"Beryllium."

"They said it on CNN, but I still can't repeat it. What is it?"

"It's something that's been here all along, but it just didn't come up before as a topic of conversation."

"I don't remember any such thing."

"It's used in nuclear reactors to make bombs," Reed said. "So how did it get here?"

"Beats me. What are they telling you?"

"They don't know how it got there. They just say don't worry." He explained about beryllium disease. "They're probably nervous about whether anybody's going to file a claim."

Ed cleared his throat. "I don't really believe all they're saying on the news. Everybody was real careful, and management took care of us. I wouldn't worry about it, Reed."

Uncle Ed had started work at the plant in 1960, when it still processed uranium hexafluoride on-site, mixing black uranium dioxide and hydrofluoric acid to make greensalt and then burning that with fluorine. Ed scooped piles of greensalt into hoppers—sometimes with his bare hands. He breathed black dust and even got it in his mouth. He always said it tasted terrible.

"Uncle Ed, remember when you used to come home from work all covered with greensalt?"

Ed laughed. "Hell, we were all green back then."

"I've been wondering, Ed, what did your first wife think about that?"

"Do you remember her? Lucy?"

"Just barely." Blond? Wore hats?

"Sometimes I can't remember her either. She moved off to Akron, Ohio, after we divorced. She was a good woman!" Ed spoke in a sentimental voice. "When I used to come home from work green—and the next morning the sheets were green—that scared her."

"I was wondering if she was afraid of the stuff."

"She'd say, 'I can't sleep with you if you're going to turn the sheets green.' I'd shower at work, and I'd shower at home, but I couldn't get rid of it. I even spit green."

"Lucy probably liked a clean house."

"She was the best woman. But I put my country first. Now I'm sorry I did. I never should have let Lucy go."

Reed had been working days, but now he was swinging to the night shift, which meant fooling around with his caffeine intake. Burl gave him a few whites—he called them "speedies"—to make it through the transition. Reed was off Tuesday, then he was due to go in Wednesday evening at seven. That day he ate an early lunch, then took a sleeping pill to get some rest in the afternoon before the first evening shift. He had just gotten settled in his darkened nest when the telephone rang. He had forgotten to turn off the ringer.

"Hey, Dad?" It was his daughter, Dana.

"Yeah. Hi, babe." He could visualize her in the pink tutu she wore when she was a child taking ballet lessons.

"I didn't expect you to answer," she said. "I thought you'd be at work. I was going to talk to your machine."

"I'm on nights now. So you'd rather talk to the machine than to me?"

"Did I wake you up?"

"Not yet."

"I just wanted to know how you were. Every week or two I hear about something awful going on at the plant."

"Don't worry, sugar. They're talking about legacy waste, stuff from ages ago. They're cleaning it up. It's safe now."

"I'm praying for you."

Reed didn't want to know what perversities his kids might be into. It was simpler that way. Still, he was moved by his daughter's concern. He didn't want his kids to think of him as diminished, like some gutless victim. But when did Dana start praying?

Reed lay in the dark, waiting for sleep, Julia on his mind. It was a fine spring day outside, and he thought he could hear birds chirping, but it was only imaginary music in the white noise of his box fan.

4

*I*n retrospect, Reed knew he should have expected his
mother to have a stroke. But he was thick-headed, oblivious,
and too immersed in his own problems to monitor his mother's
health. About ten days after his camping trip, a Sunnybank aide
called to tell him that his mother was in the hospital. It was seven-
thirty a.m., and Reed had just arrived home after a twelve-hour
shift. In a whirl, he threw food at Clarence and without showering
or changing clothes, he flew his battered blue pickup to City Hospital. She didn't seem to recognize him. She tried to speak, but her
words rolled around in her mouth like marbles. Although her right
hand was limp, she managed to point to her leg. It was a two-by-
four, Reed understood her to say. He hadn't known that tiny warning strokes called T.I.A.s had been puncturing her mind like BB
shots for some time. She hadn't complained.

Reed, in a daze of disbelief, took off work to stay by his mother's bed. He spent the first two nights in her hospital room trying to sleep in a recliner chair, which realigned his spine with seemingly murderous intent. Her I.V. drip bag made him think of a douche bag, but he didn't know why, since he had little actual familiarity with douche bags. Each morning, the doctor—on his five-thirty rounds—woke her up to check her responses and wrote on her chart that she was confused and disoriented. "She's dreaming," Reed told him. "I'm dreaming myself at this hour." She was drugged to the eyebrows, he thought. The notion that she could die made him feel angry and helpless.

When he telephoned his sister, Shirley, in California, she told him she couldn't come unless their mother took a turn for the worse. Kids, career. "Sounds like she's over the hump," Shirley said.

"Everybody asks where you are, Shirley," he said. "They say what does a son know about taking care of his mother?"

"Let's face it," Shirley said. "She'd rather be around you than me."

The edge in her voice was slight, like a faint lisp, but it stung. He felt alone. His mother's scattered relations had put in ritual appearances, but they were all busy with their own lives and he could not ask any of them for help. He had not heard from Julia. Burl was his main support, but mostly on the telephone. Burl visiting the sick was similar to an excitable terrier gate-crashing a board meeting.

Burl dropped by the hospital room early one morning on his way to a painting job. Reed had just arrived. He had returned to work, thanks to some potent speed, and he was at the hospital early, after his shift ended. He was helping his mother with her breakfast. Her right hand was weak, and she dropped the spoon. Her speech was improving, though she was still addled from the drugs.

"That sausage looks almost good enough to eat," Burl said to her teasingly. "And is that eggs? Hen products? Why, this place is a veritable spa! Who would have imagined?"

With some difficulty, she told him, "I felt hydrophobies in my

stomach all night." After eating a bite of cereal, she said, "A camouflage fell across my eyes."

"I've had those too," Burl said. "If not one, then the other."

Reed could tell that his mother was glad when Burl left. Burl
seemed to know, too, that he shouldn't stay long with her, because
he fidgeted too much and talked too loud, so he waited for Reed in
the family lounge down the hall. A little later, Reed found Burl pacing by the window. Burl was wearing paint-splattered jeans, an im-
maculate white T-shirt, and a greasy, stained cap he had worn for
several years. A man in blue work twills was asleep in front of a television set, tuned to the Golf Channel.

"He watched the Golf Channel all night long," a pudgy woman
in pink pants said to Reed. "His daddy had triple bypass yesterday."

Reed joined Burl at the window and they watched cars in the
parking lot.

Burl said to Reed, "Don't forget I'm your Prayer Warrior."

"Weren't you my Prayer Warrior *before* she had the stroke?"

"I'm not God."

"I thought you had a direct line."

"Maybe yes, maybe no." Burl tilted his hand back and forth in the
sign for uncertainty.

"I wish I could call Julia and tell her about what happened."

"Why don't you?"

"I'm afraid to. I don't want to make her feel sorry for me."

"Won't she want to know about your ma? Didn't she like her?"

"She'll know. The hospital admissions are in the newspaper."

"But she might not read it."

"She'll know somehow." Reed rose from his chair and flexed his
biceps. He felt stiff. He needed to work out. "I'll call her. Just as
soon as the time is right."

"I'll say a prayer on that."

Burl's faith was a quixotic, fluctuating matter. Reed, not knowing
when to take him seriously, often teased him about it. Burl had
thrown rune stones, practiced meditation, gone to a snake-charmer

fortune-teller, tested out every charismatic leader in the area, even slipped into the large uptown Presbyterian church only to pronounce it the dullest and least inspired of the Christian denominations. Burl liked to say he had a searching soul.

Reed's mother had given him a deliberately unconventional upbringing. She took him to a variety of religious services, although she was not a believer and did not expect him to be. She told him, "It's refreshing to see how the other half lives." They cruised Jewish temples, Catholic churches, and several black churches in an old part of the city where most white people at that time were too scared to go. And they dabbled in the Protestants. He thought the Baptists were more fun than the Methodists, but his mother found the plodding placidity of Methodists hysterical. Reed and his mother had attended church only sporadically. Most Sundays after church, they went to Captain Mack's, a home-cooking eatery that featured liver-and-onions. On Sunday mornings when they didn't go to church, she lounged on the wicker couch on the sunporch in her robe, sipping coffee and working crossword puzzles. "I'm a lady of leisure today," she would say.

She didn't keep liquor in the house, but on his eighteenth birthday she brought home a pint of bourbon and poured him his first drink—the first one she would acknowledge. Reed had tried everything from amaretto to zinfandel by then.

"This is your initiation," she said. "If this generation of the family still lived in Ireland, your father would take you to the pub, and all his friends would celebrate your manhood."

"This is the first I've heard we're Irish," Reed said. "When did we get to be Irish?"

"Oh, it doesn't matter," she said. "Pretend."

Not long before, she had buried her second husband, Mort—after a long illness—and she was on grief leave from her bookkeeping job. That day when Reed pretended to take his first drink and pretended to be Irish, he felt, curiously, as if there were no secrets between him and his mother. A long, dark bedside vigil was over, and she was free. Reed was free too, free of the stepfather whose lackluster presence and long dying made it necessary for Reed to wreck two cars, fail trigonometry, and cause one girl to have an abortion. His mother always claimed she loved Mort, but after he died she let loose like a rocket. "I'm not even fifty," she told friends. "I'm going to have a good time." They all said she deserved to have a good time.

5

Every time he rode the elevator in the hospital, Reed thought achingly of Julia. He had met her a year ago in one of the elevators here when she was attending a conference. After visiting a coworker who was recovering from colon surgery, he had headed for the basement cafeteria. He was alone in the elevator when she boarded at the fourth floor. She stabbed the B button, even though it was already lighted. Her name greeted him silently from the photo-I.D. laminate on her lab coat. Julia Jensen. Her glance acknowledged him—as though he were a decent person, not a stranger about to accost her. The elevator—or perhaps his heart—seemed to stand still.

"This feels like we're on Einstein's elevator," he said.

Her eyebrow shot up. She half smiled. The door opened and they both aimed for the cafeteria. He was aware of her flitting around the food stations, picking fastidiously but decisively from the salad bar, while he loaded up on meat loaf, gravy, mashed potatoes, and carrots. They emerged from separate checkout lanes simultaneously, and he followed her to a table halfway down the room. She parked her food and sat down, facing him. He said, "Would I be in the way if I sat in front of you and gnawed on this meat loaf while I admire your hands?"

"Be my guest."

He sat and waited for her to arrange her napkin, doctor her tea with artificial sweetener, squeeze in the lemon.

He was studying her graceful hands—no rings—when she said, "*So.* What do you think of Stephen Hawking's explanation of space-time?"

He was quick. "It's turtles all the way down," he said.

She burst into laughter and choked on her tea. The tea splattered on him. She crumpled her napkin in front of her reddening face.

"I don't know many people who have read Hawking," she said, gasping.

"I can't say that I have, exactly," he admitted. "About every five years I try to bone up on Einstein and learn about time and relativity all over again. You think you've got it, and then it escapes again. And then along comes quantum mechanics, and I just beat my head against the wall."

"And what about string theory?" she asked, a glimmer in her eye.

He laughed. "String theory's too deep for me."

They chatted long past the meat loaf. He hadn't meant to be that funny. He was just repeating the punch line of the anecdote at the beginning of Hawking's mind-smashing book: a woman had declared that the world was flat as a plate and resting on the back of a tortoise; when asked what the tortoise was standing on, she said, "It's turtles all the way down."

"You're not from around here," Reed said, listening carefully to Julia's accent.

"Chicago," she said.

He liked her sound, the clipped spurts, hurried words yet precise and polished, like pretty pebbles.

"Where do you work?" she asked.

"Atomic World—or that's what I call it. The gaseous-diffusion plant. But that doesn't reflect on my character. I'm not a gasbag."

"You've got a wit," she said.

"I need it to do what I do."

"Is there anything funny about working with uranium?"

"Oh, uranium is hilarious. It's pretty funny for a fissionable element."

"Enrico Fermi was at the University of Chicago," she said.

"The father of atomic energy? My main man?"

She nodded. "The very one. There's a plaque on campus."

"Really?"

"There's a big sculpture too," she said. "Right on the very spot where he split the atom. I probably went past the thing a thousand times."

"What's it like?"

"Like a skull, but it's supposed to look like a mushroom cloud too."

They shifted the subject. Reed hadn't used any pickup line of distinction, but she had snared him with the best pickup line he had ever heard. He marveled over it from time to time. The way she said "*So*" echoed in his mind even now. *So. What do you think of Stephen Hawking's explanation of space-time?* She scared him a little. But a woman with smarts had reached out to him as an equal. After that, they often bantered about science, tossing at each other tidbits that teased their minds. It was flirtatious, like foreplay. Burl laughed at them when they tried to spin his head around with quantum mechanics. Yet it wasn't just intellect that turned the key in the ignition of his relationship with Julia; it was erotica amidst the mysteries— and maybe microbes. She was crazy about diseases, he learned. Julia, the cytotechnologist. She had loved diseases since she was a small child. But she had no kind words for nuclear energy. She told him soon after they met, "You know, when Fermi was laying that atomic pile, he could have blown up Chicago—or the world. Nobody knew where that experiment was going." She implied that the same was still true, as if she expected the world to self-destruct at any moment.

The first few weeks with Julia swirled in his memory like the puffing plumes from the cooling towers. Reed and Julia were like kids with no skates on a frozen pond. They were easy together, willing to be adventurous. With her, Reed seemed to forget the block of pain that he usually carried inside him. She had a way of letting go, embracing the moment. She had married very young, divorced early, raised two daughters while eking out a college degree, and now, with her daughters grown, she seemed to be grabbing a second chance. Reed felt they were young lovers—in a way that young lovers never got to be because their youth made them stupid, except in the movies. She had an eye for ironies. They sat on a bench at the center of the mall and watched people. ("That woman with the stroller of twins has identical bruises on each bicep," she observed.) They ate popcorn in the park, danced at a roadhouse across the river. They watched their money float away when they went on a gambling-boat excursion. They saw a cartoon festival at the drive-in theater. He introduced her to barbecue. She taught him to like wine. They tried wine with barbecue, which both insisted was unheard of. She made him feel more sophisticated than he really was. Glenda had been purely suburban, but Julia brought in intriguing layers of urban textures, like a magician's scarves.

But even when they were together, from last June to February, Julia had kept some distance between them. She told him, "I've had a bad marriage and a few disappointing love stories that you don't want to hear."

Divorced after only three years of marriage, she had left Chicago and brought up her two girls by working at a hospital lab, then advancing to the cytopathology lab. Now one daughter was attending the state university on a scholarship and the other had a partial scholarship with a student loan. She spoke of them like women friends, not children. She gave her older daughter a book on how to achieve an orgasm—a book recommended by Oprah, she said with a laugh. Julia's pride in her daughters was part of her radiant self-assurance, Reed thought. About Oprah's orgasms, he wouldn't care to speculate.

"Why can't I meet them?" he asked her. "You met my kids."

"I don't want them looking you over like you were a stepfather candidate. It's really none of their business."

"But their orgasms are your business?"

She had to think quickly for a comeback to that one. "Well, I wouldn't want my girls to meet your kids. What if Lisa and Dalton hit it off and wanted to get married?"

"Would that mean we couldn't double-date?"

They laughed. That was one sweet warm day last fall when he took her to the levee and they watched flocks of migrating birds, whose honks and shouts merged with the barge horns. She showed him pictures of her daughters, Lisa and Cassie. He could see the resemblance to Julia in the curve of the cheeks, the pale eyes. The daughters seemed real enough.

6

Two social workers waylaid Reed in the doorway of his mother's room to say that the hospital wanted to send her to a nursing home in a couple of weeks, when she was discharged—for physical therapy. Her right leg had to be retrained, they said. The social workers—attractive women with fashionably severe haircuts—stood before him with clipboards. He didn't trust people with clipboards. He knew guys at work who carried clipboards around just for effect—low-level managers inflated with self-importance because they didn't actually labor.

"We don't have any openings on our transitional-care floor here, and we feel she needs physical therapy from a qualified facility." The blonde continued to state her case, her recitation dry as a streambed, until Reed interrupted.

"You'll have to take her in a straitjacket," he said. "She'll refuse to go to a nursing home."

"Let's ask your mother," the other woman said, her voice soaring like a hostess or a salesclerk working on commission.

"I'm too young for a puppy mill," his mother said to the social workers hovering by her bed. They kept using the phrase "transfer to a facility." Her speech was only slightly slurred. Her right hand worked in slow motion. He suddenly noticed his own hands—the rough-textured skin hiding crumbling bones.

Reed spoke briefly with the doctor, who made a pop-up visit after lunch. Briskly, the doctor, while writing his notes on the chart in the nurse's station, told Reed that his mother's health would likely deteriorate over time and that she could continue to have little strokes. "But she's improving," he said. "For the short term, she can probably regain most of her function. We'll see, once we get her in a nursing facility."

Reed met Burl in the lounge at the end of the corridor. Burl was pacing, his thumbs crooked in his jeans pockets. Reed could tell that Burl's mind was flying in a hundred directions. Burl was brilliant in an oddball way, with so much creative energy he couldn't contain himself. When Burl's mind went into freewheeling mode, Reed would often glide into his slipstream, just for the ride.

"Hey, Burl, how are you doing?"

"Oh, I'm day to day. How's your mom?"

"The doctor said she'll probably get better, but then she'll have more strokes later on." Reed sat down in a vinyl armchair. "They want to send her to a nursing home."

"If I know your mom, she'll tell them to piss off."

"It's not good news. This can't all be happening, Burl. I can't get my mind around it."

"I don't know about your mama, but I know what you might need," Burl said. "Colonic irrigation."

"I will if you will. End of conversation."

"Well, they say it takes the poison out of your system."

Burl's motto was "Happy to be anywhere." Once, he had joined a troupe of entertainers on a riverboat. But he jumped ship before they reached landfall—he said he got river-sick. He had a license from a mail-order church, the Infinite Love Circle Church, to marry people. Burl himself had never been married. He couldn't keep a woman interested because of his drinking. So when a woman ditched him, he drank more, or took speed. He attracted women easily enough, but then he mooched dinners off them.

Burl was dark haired and stocky. He wore his hair long, and he often sported a two-day growth of beard for several consecutive days. Reed wondered how he achieved that—and why. Both Burl and Reed spurned fashion. Reed wouldn't wear a T-shirt with words on it. Burl did, because so many T-shirts that had ads on them were free.

When Burl was eleven, his father kidnapped him from his mother—after a custody battle—and took him to Detroit. It was two years before his mother found him, and she kidnapped him back. But his parents worked it out somehow and even got back together briefly after Burl's mother took a liking to Detroit.

"What's going on out there at Atomic World?" Burl asked, sitting in the chair next to Reed. It was early in the day, and he was sober.

Reed grunted. "I just do my job. I don't know anything. I've got too much else to think about." In truth, he realized, he was almost glad that his mother's illness was diverting him from workplace woes. He said, "Julia probably thinks I get about ten rem a day just by going in the door out there."

"How are you coming along with string theory?" Burl asked, playfully slapping Reed's knee. "She'll probably want to give you a quiz."

"I'm studying it. But it's like a magician's bag of tricks."

"A string bag?" Burl made Reed laugh.

A few months ago, Julia had challenged Reed to read the sequel to Hawking's book on time. She said it was easy to browse around in it, and it had pictures. And she gave him a couple of other books on quantum mechanics and string theory.

"Ever hear of Schrödinger's cat?" Reed asked. "Schrödinger was one of those quantum mechanics. He said put a cat in a lead box, then drop a capsule of cyanide in the box and seal it up. Now we don't know if the cat is dead or alive, because we don't know if the capsule broke, so technically it's *both* until you open the box and find out which."

"Won't the cat suffocate anyway? Or starve?"

"You don't wait that long to open it."

"Well, then you might get a whiff of cyanide too."

"That's not the point!" Reed was trying to remember the point. "It's subatomic stuff—something about how a particle can be in two separate states at once. Or, it's about how you can't pin down the subatomic stuff. It's all indeterminate."

"This is the kind of shit Julia's jerking you around with?"

"It's O.K. It keeps me from thinking other thoughts."

Burl jumped up and bounded toward the vending machines. Then he turned to Reed. "You know it was scientists meddling with the atom that got you in the trouble you're in at the plant."

"Well, so what can anybody do about that now?"

"They tampered with Mother Nature!" He sawed one index finger against the other in a "shamey-shamey" gesture.

Burl found a couple of quarters and pinged them into the soft-drink machine. Reed shook his head no when Burl asked him if he wanted something.

"You know, I'm sure Julia's blaming the whole fucking nuclear industry on me," Reed said. "I kept telling her people have to have jobs."

Burl opened his can of cola. He said, "If we don't get the centrifuge this town will be going to its own funeral." He pointed to the telephone cubicles. "Call her," he said. "I dare you. It won't hurt."

Reed did. If he had waited any longer, he would have thought too hard about it. He got Julia's answering machine, and he left a brief tongue-tied blurt of need.

The Comet Hale-Bopp blazed westward, trailed by a twelve-billion-year-old star cluster and a young cluster of blue stars. Behind the stars were more stars, behind the galaxies more galaxies. Reed never tired of the Hubbles on his screen.

In his daily life, Reed's frustrations could send him to the wilderness with a pistol to shoot targets. But when he contemplated a spiral galaxy or a massive globular star cluster, or even something as common as a comet, he swelled with imagination. In some miraculous mode of transportation that transcended the speed of light—the Reedmobile, that little ego-cart of a vehicle his mind had possessed since childhood—he wandered through the gas clusters and nebulosities, a tourist cruising the cosmos, protected by a radiation-proof shield, with windows. The time would be now wherever he was. Somehow, he thought that if he went on such a voyage deep into the universe, he would never feel lonely.

7

$\mathcal{A}$s his mother slowly improved, Reed got more sleep, but he still went to the hospital to see her every morning after his shift. In the early light, as he drove along the bypass from the plant toward the hospital exit, he had a clearer view of the changing city. It was growing, smothering and ingesting cornfields and pasture-land. A large farm that once sold its produce in a roadside stand had, in the last two years, transformed into a poultry-processing factory. Its water tower, a pale sphere on a tall stem, pressed against the sky like a painted moon. Dead chickens often littered the shoulder of the highway. Today Reed counted four white leghorns. Did they fall from the delivery trucks? Or did they escape from their coops at the factory, flapping and screaming in their short, hopping swoops toward the traffic? The dead chickens were becoming familiar, like icons on his computer screen. He considered scooping up a chicken for Clarence. But he didn't stop.

A bundle of bones topped with a red wig—a scarecrow—had shared his mother's room for the past two days. In the bright light today, Reed realized that the wig was actually the woman's own hair, bleached strawberry blond, the roots a gray shadow. The woman sat upright, open eyed, impassive. She looked at least a hundred, but yesterday Reed had learned—through eavesdropping—that she was only seventy-eight.

"Is that you?" his mother asked, stirring from her sleep.

"I just got here," Reed said, giving her a quick kiss. "How are you feeling, Mom?"

"Terrible. They keep poking me with cattle prods. I just get off to sleep and here comes another one. Is that candy over there?"

"No. Mouth swabs." They did resemble lollipops. He offered her one and she took it eagerly. "Did you know there'll be an eclipse of the moon this week?" he asked.

"I don't care if they go to the moon," she said, sucking on the swab. "If there's not any grass, what's the point?"

Her speech was clearer and her color improved. Reed cranked the bed so that she slowly rose into a sitting position. Bunches of her frizzy silver hair aimed in several directions.

"You look pretty today, Mom," he said.

"I'm not ready to head for the pea patch yet," she said. "Hand me some water."

Her right hand flailed, tubes dangling from it like fringe. He removed the swab and held the plastic cup for her. The bend of the flexible straw was segmented like a hard-shell centipede. She took a few small sips, then eased herself back against the pillows. "Don't you need to be at work?" she said.

A lab tech with a lab tray interrupted, and Reed stood aside while his mother's blood was drawn.

"You're going to feel a little stick, darling," the girl said amid her procedure. Reed thought about Julia, in her lab coat. He longed to call her again but knew he shouldn't. He had not heard from her. He knew he shouldn't have called her.

He made some small talk he was not sure his mother heard, and the aide finished her work, withdrawing the tourniquet with a snap and slapping a piece of cotton on the wound. Another aide arrived and replenished the plastic water pitcher. The TV was tuned to the House and Garden channel, but not loud enough for Reed to hear. In a while, his mother was asleep again. He studied the lines in her face. She had on no makeup, and age spots speckled her skin like the camouflage pattern on a quail. It did not seem possible that she could have grown so old.

His chair fit in the meager space between the bathroom and a metal cupboard with two drawers. A drawer face was loose; the soap dispenser on the sink had lost its plastic cover. At the bottom of the drape on the window, a long string dragged the floor.

He stared out the window. He had a wide view of the plant, several miles distant. The weather had been cool and the steam clouds were well defined. He watched the steam rising, rolling and accumulating into marshmallow clouds on the horizon. From this perspective, he could see his life tamped down by the sky, with its illusory lightness and fluff. To the far right of the cooling towers, the twin smokestacks, skyscraper tall and fishing-pole thin, were puffing a precise line of gray smoke trails—as if the Cascade were exhaling its dragon breath. He observed the necks of the construction cranes rising above their dark hole. In the foreground, gas-station signs rose on high stork legs; a brick office park occupied a large portion of the near view. The highway interchanges and access roads and ramps cluttered the view below the hospital and across the parking lot. An S.U.V. was leaving, and as it drove out the exit lane, the orange mercury-vapor lamps along the street turned off, one by one, as if the vehicle were deactivating them as it passed.

He stood frozen at the window, his mother perhaps dying behind him, his future blowing before him like smoke rings. He tried to imagine what an astronaut would see, peering down on that patch of green earth with its gray scar, the earth still steaming from its little wound.

*H*is mother had not been strict with him, as she had been with Shirley. He had spent his childhood looking for trouble, and he had found his share. Foibles. That was his mother's term for his failings—foibles. It was a gesture of forgiveness, he thought.

He remembered the time he went to see her just after her third husband walked out on her. When Reed arrived, buzzed on a little weed, she offered him some Old Crow, and they watched a tape of an old musical-variety show. He remembered her kick-stepping along with the June Taylor Dancers, a group from the days before aerobics classes. In the middle of her dance, the telephone rang and she answered, "Rainbow Room." It was her nosy aunt Willoughby, who told her she had seen Danny Daly, the wayward third husband, with a woman at the mall. The woman was wearing a dog collar above her knee like a bracelet, and they were shopping for camping gear. Reed's mother, radiant with the bourbon, spouted to Willoughby, "I guess they plan to shack up together, if you can do that in a tent." She giggled. It struck Reed that his mother was astonishingly sexy, with a streamlined figure and bouncy, tennis-ball breasts. He could see how a man would fall for her and couldn't see why Danny would go for a woman with a dog collar on her leg. Reed had an impulse then to make everything up to his mother, but all he could do was mumble and pull a joint from his shirt pocket. To smoke a joint with one's mother seemed to Reed at that moment the height of sharing.

That was years ago. Reed was still angry at the living ex— "Danny Boy," now a retired freight agent. Reed had always thought Danny Boy was a con man. He exuded false charm in proportion to the scheme he was promoting. One plan was a mobile unit—like the bookmobile—that offered appraisals of antiques and heirlooms; another was organized trips to the casinos in his van. Reed imagined a produce truck packed with illegal immigrants.

Reed hung around the hospital all morning. He meandered down the corridors. Every time he passed the door to radiology, the yellow radiation-warning sign jolted him—a safety reflex from his training. When he spied a tower cart of lunch trays in the hallway a few doors down from his mother's room, he decided to get her meal and help her with it. The staff simply plunked down the trays in front of the patients (who could be helplessly supine or asleep), jerked the metal domes from the plates, and vanished.

Each meal was identified with a room number and menu selections on a pink slip of paper. He found hers on the bottom tier. When he stood up with it, he heard "Hello, Mr. Futrell" behind him.

Reed had been avoiding the social workers, who he imagined were stalking him with their clipboards, but here was the pretty blonde. She had been looking for him, she said. She wanted to know his decision about the nursing home, and she told him again that his mother needed physical therapy. "Speech, walking, and occupational rehab," she added.

"She doesn't need occupational rehab," he said. "She's retired."

"Occupational means help with grooming, dressing, transferring. There are six life-activity criteria—"

"Oh. I thought you meant learning welding or something." He waited for her smile but got nothing.

"We would be glad to fax out to the nursing homes in the area," she said, brandishing her clipboard. "Do you want us to fax out?"

"I'd like to fax you out, baby."

"I beg your pardon?"

"My mother loves irony," he said, knowing he wasn't making sense.

After helping his mother with her lunch, he drove to a Mexican place and bought a pair of hot tamales, a chimichanga, and a twenty-ounce orange drink. He ate in the truck with a big-bands medley blasting on the CD player, but he hardly heard it. His mind was a blur. He knew his mother wanted to be cared for by her family, not by a SWAT team in hospital scrubs. But what could he do? His natural pursuits involved machinery—motorcycles, old trucks—although he didn't care for the typical stuff like tractor pulls and NASCAR. He wasn't a gearhead. He was a stargazer, and it probably showed in his off-kilter personality. He felt helpless to deal with his mother. He wasn't a hand-holder. Still, it bothered him that women attributed so many failures to men: men couldn't show feelings; men didn't know how to plump pillows or select place mats. It was wrong that his sister was in California while he was here. Yet he doubted that Shirley could care for their mother any better than he could. Shirley, married to a systems analyst, managed a small balloon-delivery company. She didn't clean her own house or go to flea markets or bake.

He longed for Julia's company. She was serious, but not like his sister, whose thoughts came boxed, with instructions. Julia would listen with deep delight to any fool thing he said. He remembered her tickled gasp when he told her about the praying mantises that used to collect in the filter rooms at the plant.

"We'd find hundreds of them stuck in the filters. That was before the safety standards got uprated." He exaggerated a little. "I got a trophy mantis that barely fit in my lunch box."

"Does the safety manual tell what to do about a praying-mantis invasion?" She was teasing.

He laughed. "Probably. I don't see many around anymore."

"They probably heard the Rapture was coming," she said.

Her hands swept the imaginary swarm of praying mantises into the sky.

8

*R*eed, trying to catch up on his sleep, had been dumping the responses to his ad, along with all the junk messages. After the rebuke he got from Hot Mama, he soured on the notion of a blind date. Then he noticed—among dozens of bogus alarms about anatomical size—that she had written again.

"At first I was going to write you off, but then I decided I'd give you another chance. Our zip codes are touching and nuzzling. We've probably passed on the road a hundred times. We may as well meet and say hello sometime. It was 'Kubla Khan' that did it for me. A man who would like a poem is unique in my world. I like Whitman's 'Leaves of Grass' as well as pie. I Sing the Body Electric. Do you think men and women stand a chance together? Have you met others in this manner? Actually, I think we should get to know one another a bit on the Net before we go through with it."

Hot Mama went on for two or three screens. Reed skimmed. Apparently *Leaves of Grass* expressed her soul. But she offered few specifics. Reed clicked another reply to his ad. And he laid eyes on Jennifer—melon curves, apricot hair, apple cheeks, grapefruit boobs, cherry lips. She had sent her photograph, with a teaser, "Hey, Atomic Man. What do you think?" Reed fired back a reply and by the next afternoon he had met Jennifer at a coffee place downtown near the hospital. Atomic Man to the rescue, he thought.

She was young, with a short butter-blond bob and brownish lip-stick. She said she was just out of college and had a job at an invest-ment company downtown. She had on dark office-wear, with a plunging neckline that revealed her soft breasts. Sipping her iced mocha, she told him about her trip to Cancún her senior year.

"It was the coolest time of my life," she said, playing with her straw. "You know, the kind of thing you know you'll never have again unless you like work at it and really *try*? I can't tell you how cool it was."

"Try," Reed said.

She prattled about some of the memorable things she and her roommate did in Cancún, as if nothing they had done was either stupid or trite, or there had never been a spring-break movie.

"My roommate got TMJ—that pain you get in your jaw?—from sucking cock." She didn't avert her eyes from his. "There's this bar, the Happy Top. And after everybody's been through a couple of pitchers, a row of guys like holds on to a sort of bar overhead, and the girls line up and do blow jobs on them. The last guy to keep holding on to the bar wins."

"Wins what?"

She slapped his arm playfully.

"Did the guys have their pants on?"

"Bathing suits."

"Damn, I missed a lot in college," he said.

"You could probably get a cheap ticket to Cancún," she said.

"Yeah, they'd see an old guy like me coming and call the police."

Reed's erection could have levitated the table. But it wilted. He realized suddenly that he knew who she was. The lift of her eyebrows, the lilt of her voice—he remembered a sulky teenager sprawled in front of the TV. Reed used to fuck her mother on winter afternoons, and on one occasion the children came home from school early. In a moment he would remember the mother's name. He remembered a velvet parting beneath loud-colored underwear—lime, orange, bright pink. Sue?

Reed bowed out of the coffee shop—gracefully, he thought, and unrecognized, he thought—paying for their coffee and buying Jennifer a poppy-seed muffin with caramel icing to take home with her. Nice to meet you.

Julia. Julia. It had surprised him that someone so brainy could enjoy sex so much. He was used to women whose minds dwelt on clothes and schedules and recipes. Their heads were all wound up with intricate little rules, and sex was somehow an elaborate concoction, a romantic idea that was supposed to take shape the way an extravagant gourmet creation did on a TV cooking show. But not Julia. No matter how involved she was in some theoretical problem in her books, or a messy case of administrative incompetence at work, she seemed able to be right there in the moment. She would gaze straight at him and smile. They would be looking *at* each other as they jockeyed into position. Some women just wanted to close their eyes. But Julia had treated him like a rare individual, and she made him feel that she was thrilled in every way to be with him— their bodies, their minds, their hearts, their histories, their memories, their dreams. Maybe he had never been truly in love before. Entirely immersed in her, he had spun through shifts at work like a weaver at a loom, unaware of repetition, feeling outside of time.

9

Reed tiptoed past the sleeping redhead in the bed near the door. A basket of lilies with a tag sat on her tray table. A curtain separated the two women in the room.

When Reed gave his mother a peck on the cheek, she whispered, "She's not getting any better. The doctor said she had the dwindles."

"I believe it."

"Find my tweezers," his mother said. "I want you to pluck out this hair on my chin."

He found the tweezers among her personal things in a drawer, along with a plastic tray of toiletries provided by the hospital. The toothpaste tube appeared to be unused. He didn't have his reading glasses—despised and clumsy and slightly effeminate—with him, but after redirecting the light, he located the stiff white hair on her chin. When he gave the hair its liberating tug, she winced. He pulled out a few more, aware that he was jerking them too roughly.

"I need to get you a razor, Ma."

"I don't want to shave every day."

A young aide flitted in with a small white paper cup. "Time for your medication, sweetheart."

"When did that start?" Reed said to the aide. Her collar hid her badge and he couldn't see her name.

"I'm sorry?"

"Sweetheart. Everybody is sweetheart. Or sugar, or sweetie. Or darling. Where did that come from?"

"We like a little personal touch." She flipped a quick smile at him and turned to his mother. "This here's a horse pill, ain't it, hon? Do you want me to cut it in two?"

"No, that's O.K."

Reed's mother swallowed the pill and lay back on the pillow, closing her eyes. As she shifted her legs, her gown fell open, and he glimpsed between her legs. "Oops! I took your picture," she said, with a little titter.

"Bye, sweetheart," Reed said to the aide as she danced away.

He stared through the doorway a while, holding the image of her blue-clad butt twisting out of sight. Then he turned to his mother.

"Did anybody comb your hair today, Mom?"

"No. Nobody was here."

"Did they give you a bath?"

"No. Maybe they did."

He wet a washcloth and rubbed her face. It felt odd to touch his mother's face—her skin so soft, her cheeks curved like breasts, her mouth hanging open. He got a whiff of her breath, like onions and fish souring together. The dead woman in the dream still invaded his thoughts from time to time. He found himself measuring his life—and his mother's life, and everything he held dear—in terms of the imagined woman who chose to die. But he always believed his mother had the strength of a steel cable hauling a train up a mountainside. She was the fun in funicular, he thought.

"You're good to me," she said, touching his arm.

"Hang in there, Ma," he said. "I've got you covered."

That was what the TV evangelists said: the Lord has got you covered. If you lose your credit card, he's got you covered. If you get cancer, he's got you covered. The cover-your-ass school of theology, Reed thought.

Later, in the lounge, a wide-bodied family gorging on three gigantic pizzas offered him a wedge of pizza.

"Go ahead and eat some," they urged him. "There's plenty."

He shook his head, thinking he would go home later and have some leftover carry-out spaghetti carbonara with a glass of burgundy, if his mother didn't need him again tonight. His shift wasn't until seven the next evening, but he couldn't think that far ahead—how would he cover his ass if he took off from work another night? Maybe God could cover for him, if he wasn't too busy.

When he returned to his mother's room, he met a male nurse and a lab tech wheeling an ultrasound contraption out the door. Reed was always surprised to see a male nurse.

"Radiology just scanned her bladder," the nurse explained after Reed identified himself. "She doesn't need the catheter anymore."

Reed saw that the scanner was equipped with an enormous black plastic ultrasound probe. Reed thought of aliens kidnapping people and scanning them on their intergalactic operating tables.

He said, "Could you please see that her teeth are brushed? She has a bridge, and I don't think it's been out once since she's been here. She'll be growing a garden in there before long."

"One of the aides will be around later."

Reed hammered down a sudden surge of anger. He had no confidence that his mother's teeth would ever get brushed. The nurses and aides changed like runners in a relay race. He did not recognize this nurse. There was no one watching out for his mother except himself. Grimly, he set about the task of brushing her teeth.

"I'll do it later," she said. "I'm sleepy. Go away and let me snooze."

He drove home, aware that he ought to investigate the nursing homes the next day. A few years before, he had gone with his mother to visit her aunt Willoughby at a small rest home. The smell of urine assaulted them at the door, and as they passed the kitchen, he saw the cooks frying bologna. He remembered a scrawny man wheeling up to him and pleading, "Find my glasses!" Maybe the other places weren't that bad, he thought. He would not call his sister until after he had seen some of them. Shirley would be all for a nursing home, he felt sure. Or at least, she would be all for leaving the problem up to him.

It was a bright, full-moon night. He remembered that the penumbral eclipse was coming soon—maybe minutes from now. He kept glancing at the moon during the drive, but it still shone brilliantly. The ancients believed the moon was the eye of God. Who would worship a god with only one eye? Cyclopsians? Cycloppers? He parked in his weed-thronged driveway. He had bought this weathered old place four years ago, after he relinquished the brick ranch house to Glenda, so that she could sell it and buy a farmette in her home state of Iowa. Now she was raising Nubian goats, of all things. As Reed jumped out of the truck, Clarence roared with joy. Reed opened the backyard gate and let the dog jump on him.

"Come on, boy, let's go see about this moon."

The eclipse should start any minute. The moon would turn blood red. He thought he saw a faint red rim around the moon, but he decided his eyes were playing tricks. He walked down the street, glancing upward every few steps. Clarence frisked along, pausing to nose aromatic spots along the edges of the lawns. Reed didn't leash him unless people were around. At the end of the block, they reached a large vacant lot, an open field, with an unobstructed view of the sky. Clarence raced around in extravagant figure eights for a few minutes.

"Hey, Clarence! Aren't you supposed to bay at the moon? Bay before it's too late, boy. Bay!"

Clarence barked. "I didn't say bark, Clarence. I said bay. Oooo—ooo." Reed tried to howl at the moon.

The rim of the earth's shadow had reached the moon, clipping off a sliver of the round white disc. Engrossed, Reed forgot to watch his footing. He was vaguely aware that he had stepped in dog shit. But he stayed out in the field for a long while, while Clarence romped around him and the penumbra slid gradually across the moon, at last engulfing it. The moon was the color of terra-cotta. He could see through the shadow onto the patterned surface of the moon. The moon had a lace curtain drawn across its face.

10

The morning newspaper threw another front-page zinger. Technetium-99 that had been found in an underground plume of water was flowing toward the river at the rate of a foot a day.

"Shit," said Reed aloud.

He read on. The radioactive metal had been found in a vegetable garden near the plant; rutabagas, tested a year ago, contained technetium. Reporters had teased out the data from piles of obscure technical reports. Technetium was also found in white icicle radishes. Reed remembered the volunteer tomatoes that used to grow near the sewage tank at the plant. And more volunteers sprang up in the compost behind the cafeteria. The cooks had used the fresh tomatoes from their cafeteria garden and had even planted cabbages and carrots, which grew to an enormous size. Everyone kidded the cooks about their radioactive vegetables.

A box on the front page announced a public meeting that night at the school near the plant. A representative from the Department of Energy would answer questions about the toxic-waste cleanup, medical compensation, and current safety, but would not address the future of the centrifuge.

The telephone rang. "Got your television on?" Darrell, a co-worker, asked when Reed answered.

"It's busted."

"Oh, I forgot about you and your war on television. Well, you probably didn't hear the latest."

"I take the paper and hear the radio. You mean technetium in the plume?"

"Yeah. We need a bookmaker to bet on when it'll get into the aquifer. Are you going to that meeting?"

"No. I'm on shift tonight. You go and tell me about it."

"I don't know if anybody from the plant ought to be going. We might get in trouble. I can't afford to lose my job."

Darrell got on Reed's nerves because he was always suspicious, filled with resentment about virtually everything. He complained all night at work—the long hours, the cost of roofing, his wife's demand that he go with her to the mall on weekends (quality time together, she called it), the rotten weather. Something was always happening to Darrell: stolen wallet, kid who needed orthopedic surgery, mother-in-law with cancer, car with dead battery.

"Some of us need to go just to provide a sense of humor," Reed said. "You know, to show the funny side of nuclear catastrophe."

"We could forklift a rusty canister of worn-out UF_6 over to their meeting," Darrell said.

"And lay it sweetly at their feet," Reed said. "Now you're talking."

He hung up, finished reading the newspaper, then called the hospital. He waited on hold for some time, listening to a rolling message about hospital services. Local news on the radio mentioned the public meeting but not the technetium. Finally a nurse reported that his mother had eaten a good breakfast. "She's asleep now. There's nothing new on her chart from the doctor."

"Did somebody brush her teeth?"

"That wouldn't be on her chart."

He had vowed to visit some nursing homes today. He had had plenty of sleep and felt he could last all day and through his night shift. But he wasn't eager to begin the mission. Although his tank was still a quarter full, he drove out of his way to get gas at a mini-mart that was his favorite place for filling up. From time to time since his divorce he had gone out with an ex-stripper who worked there. Rosalyn still looked good, although her butt was flattening somewhat, Reed had noticed. She had had a few nips and tucks—and a Botox-frozen forehead—and appeared much younger than her age, which he thought was over fifty.

When he went inside the mini-mart to pay for his gas, Rosalyn pointed to the lead story in the newspaper splayed on the counter. "Who around here grows rutabagas?" she asked him.

"Isn't that another name for hooters?"

"No. Rutabaga sounds dirty—like hogs." She laughed.

Reed thought he should spend more time with Rosalyn. She was probably the nicest person he knew, always sweet-tempered, large in spirit. She had raised four children as a single parent.

"How's your mom doing, Reed?"

"Better. But they're wanting to put her in a nursing home, and I know she won't go." He explained about the rehab.

"That's a hard one. I'm really sorry about that. But they can probably help her."

"Yeah."

She folded the newspaper. "Reed, you watch out what they're doing out at the plant," she said, with concern. "There doesn't seem to be any end to this."

"Oh, they take good care of me," Reed said.

"I see guys come in the store to cash their checks, and it's pitiful what they make at some of these places around—like the sock factory and the plastics place? But at the atomic plant they always made really good."

"I can't complain. I worked five twelves a week last month." He grinned. "With time and a half, I'm rolling in it."

She was regarding him apprehensively.

"Got to finish paying off my kids' college," he said.

"Are you going to that meeting tonight?"

"No, I'm on tonight. Anyway, I don't think anybody can get a straight answer out of the government."

He gave Rosalyn a twenty and a five for his gas. She gave him a dollar and eighteen cents and dropped his receipt into the waste can. He pocketed his change, wadding the dollar down into his jeans.

"I hope your mom is feeling better, Reed," she said as he backed out the door with a wave. "Don't eat any rutabagas!"

Technetium could be used to keep iron from rusting, he thought as he turned the key in his car. He knew about the technetium. It had been there for years, and he didn't want to think about it.

At the light, an eighteen-wheeler was making a turn through the intersection, barely clearing Reed's front end. Reed hit the horn a glancing blow, a slight warning bleep.

He stopped at the Handy Gunner, a collectors' gun shop, located in a basement below a dry cleaner's. When Reed entered the shop carrying an army-issue pistol he wanted to sell, the owner, Andy, raised his hands in mock surrender.

"I give up," he said with a large grin.

"I got you covered, Andy," said Reed, laying the pistol on the counter. "How's it going?"

Andy's girlfriend Brenda was in the shop. She was wearing a pink filmy top with clusters of tiny feathers knotted to the yoke. He knew she loved to shoot, and he had gone out with her and Andy once to the old munitions works to shoot targets. She never got angry with Andy about it the way Julia had with Reed. Now she was examining a small pistol, testing its weight and the texture of the shaft. She caressed the little barrel. Her long fingernails were polished pink.

"I wish I had a pearl-handled pistol," she said. "A little thing to put in my purse."

She set the pistol down and picked up the one Reed had brought.

"What's that for?" she asked, running her finger along an orange stripe that was painted on it.

"An eccentricity of the guy I got it from," he said. "He does it to all his guns. He said it helped him zero in on the sight better."

Reed had bought the gun years ago from a guy named Wade at the plant. Now Reed had decided he was no longer interested in collecting more handguns. Only the historic weapons that had belonged to his grandfather Futrell were worth keeping. They were heirlooms.

"Well, it's an idea," Brenda said, laying the gun on the counter.

"Are they laying off out at the plant?" Andy asked. "What's going to happen?"

"Don't know. Everybody's waiting for the other shoe to drop."

"I don't think it's going to amount to anything," Andy said. "It's all blown out of proportion."

Brenda said, "My brother was in the big scrub-down in '87 when there was that leak. Were you in that, Reed?"

"No. I was at Disney World."

Brenda said, "Tony came home laughing about it. He said it was like being in the movies."

Reed turned to the video section at the corner of the counter. Andy rented action videos and sold snacks. Reed studied some of the movies.

"Did you ever see *The Delta Force*?" said Brenda. "I'd like to see that again. I haven't seen it in years."

"I don't think I ever saw that."

"I love to watch those guys in action," Brenda said, with a side-long glance at Andy.

Reed left the pistol with Andy, who promised to try to get a good price for it.

11

*R*eed peeked into two nursing homes but didn't wait for the guided tour at either place. Quick glimpses sufficed: cramped rooms; metal wardrobes like school lockers; gnarled, half-dead creatures lying in narrow beds, with their oxygen tanks tethered like pets. He vowed to ride his bike off a cliff before he got old.

He wandered through another place that he had been urged to visit. It was different. Reed had heard someone remark that Green Haven was so classy it should be featured in *House and Garden*. This high-tech home was long and low, with several wings radiating from the center. Reed glided down a brightly lighted corridor lined with metal handrails on glaring white walls. He passed X-ray rooms, rehab rooms, offices, sitting areas with floral-patterned upholstery, birdcages, and hanging plants. He paused at the open door of a room labeled AQUATIC REHABILITATION. It was empty, but he could see a whirlpool bath, which had a lift harness like those used for horses. He imagined his mother's roommate at the hospital—a naked old bag of bones being lowered into the whirlpool. *Now sweetheart, let's dunk you in this tub. It'll be good for you.*

As he waited at a nurse's station for a guide, he tried to imagine his mother here. She would find the lights too bright. She always closed the shades in summer to keep the house cool. He remembered playing gin rummy with her in a darkened room on hot summer afternoons. He did not know if she would be able to play cards again.

An aged woman tottered toward him, waving a piece of paper at him.

"I need you to explain this," she said. She was trim and thin, with a white shock of thick hair.

The paper was a flyer—CAR WASH SPECIAL. Reed remembered that his truck was dusty.

"It's about a car wash, ma'am," he said. "Does your car need washing?"

"We're studying it," she said.

"I'm afraid I'm not the expert," he said. "I'll get somebody."

The woman snatched the paper. Then she seemed to be running backwards—taking small, mincing steps, then two fast ones, then two faster ones. Reed's impression was that she was entertaining herself, as a child might do. Suddenly, with seeming deliberation, she threw herself onto the floor, falling flat on her back. An aide and a nurse rushed forward.

"Miss Kitty!" they cried, squatting around the woman, who appeared to be conscious.

"What happened, Miss Kitty? Can you raise your leg?"

Reed hadn't been close enough to catch her. He stood by, useless.

"Did you trip, Miss Kitty? Do you hurt?" the aide asked as she massaged the woman's legs.

Miss Kitty managed to lift her legs, one at a time. The women helped her into a wheelchair, and the aide wheeled her away, saying,

"Now, Miss Kitty, you were having a pity party, weren't you? And something got into you—you had a wild hair, didn't you?"

"I'm so sorry!" the nurse said to Reed. "Welcome to Green Haven!"

"I see you offer gymnastics," he said.

The nurse let out a string of bubbly laughs, and her name tag bobbed alongside her cleavage: LINDA. Linda's uniform fit tight all over. Reed hadn't really meant to be funny, but as he explained his impression that the woman had deliberately thrown herself down, he quickly imagined a convenient dalliance with Nurse Linda while visiting his mom here.

"If I'd realized she was going to try out for the circus, I would have tried to stop her," he said. "I hope she didn't hurt herself." In his confusion, he found himself trying to be charming.

"She has spells," Linda said, waving his concern away. Linda wore a nursing cap like wings of a bird alighting on her crown. Reed liked this old-fashioned touch.

Nurse Linda said, "Follow me and I'll show you the bed we have available."

"I'm ready for anything," Reed said, smiling.

He followed Linda through a large lounge. An orange-and-white round-faced cat feeding from a blue bowl glanced up. The cat appeared to raise an eyebrow at the sight of Reed.

"We have several animals on the premises," Linda said, as she turned down a corridor. "Our guests seem to appreciate their furry friends." She paused at Room 121. "This is a semiprivate," she said to Reed as she knocked on the open door. "Miss Minnie? Sweetheart, are you decent? This gentleman is here to see about letting his mother share your room. Won't that be nice?"

The room was bright, with pink rose-patterned drapes and white metal furniture. A crone curled in a bed by the window slowly rotated toward them. In a wavering voice, she said, "I'm keeping that other bed empty. I'm expecting my husband."

"We know, darling. But this new lady won't be in his way."

"What about when he comes back?"

"I tell you what, Miss Minnie. When he comes, then we'll let him have the bed. We'll just tell the new lady that your husband is here, and she'll have to go to another room."

"Well." The woman turned away from them and pulled the covers over her head.

As they left, Linda whispered, "She thinks her husband is Don Ho, and she says he's off on a musical tour."

Nurse Linda was still talking as Reed hurried down the incandescent corridor in a state of abstract inanity.

At the smoking station outside the hospital, a middle-aged man in a hospital gown was puffing a cigarette. He held his I.V. drip like a ski pole.

"Out for some fresh air?" Reed said to the guy.

"It's healthier out here than it is in there," the guy said, blowing smoke.

Reed's mother was asleep. He sat in the recliner beside her tray table, then noticed a note with his name on it propped against the water pitcher. He unfolded it.

"Hi, Reed," the note said. "I stopped by this afternoon. Your mom and I had a lovely little visit. Sorry to miss you. Julia." Reed bolted out to the hall and strode up and down, carrying the note, wondering what to do. She was *sorry* she missed him! He would apologize to her in a thousand ways, he decided. He would promise her anything. *Lovely*. Only Julia would say that. It sounded so sophisticated. He would assure her that the atomic plant had helped to protect America just as he would protect her. But she would shoot some little atomic barb at him—*Technetium!*—and he would have to justify atomic weapons to her once more. *There you go again*, she would say.

Reed's mother grinned when she awoke and saw him standing by her bed.

"There's my baby," she said sleepily. "Come here and let me love on you."

"I'm just a big old baby," he said, clumsily trying to embrace her along with her I.V. tube.

"I was asleep in a cabbage cluster," she said, a blissful expression crossing her face.

"In a what?"

"A cabbage cluster," she said. She moved her mouth, as if searching for some alternate words caught between her molars. "I was sleeping in a cabbage cluster!" She sighed.

"I need to do a word search on my computer for you, Mom," Reed said.

"What I mean is—" She groped again for words. "A cabbage cluster."

"Do you mean a garden?"

"I'll be all right when I get home," she said. "I want to plant the garden."

He started to say that she didn't have a garden at Sunnybank, and that she must be recalling a scene from childhood, but he caught himself. He realized argument might not be relevant. He and his mother were entering a new configuration. In time to come, Reed imagined, she might enter yet another phase, where she was the child and he was the adult; the normal paths of recognition were being swept clean.

Sipping a cup of coffee filched from the nurse's station, he sat with his mother for a while. He tried to read a science book he had brought—Julia might quiz him on string theory!—but he couldn't concentrate on his reading. Some of Julia's stray molecules probably lingered in the air. He inhaled deeply. He longed to ask her what he should do about his mother. He could not consign his mother to any of those places he had seen. She needed her family to care for her, not Nurse Linda.

His mother was growing wakeful. Squeezing Reed's hand, she

tilted her head to the voices behind the curtain separating the two beds. The scarecrow's son was talking on the telephone. "They tell me Mama ate a hundred percent of her dinner. She eats for Donny, but she wouldn't eat for me. She wouldn't eat till he got here from Denver."

Cooking. He hadn't thought of that. He couldn't cook those complex casseroles and fancy ladies' luncheon salads she liked. But he'd think of something. He could envision the scene—his mother in his house, banging around with a walker, while he concocted some pathetic dinner to please her. He wondered how she would like spaghetti carbonara from Mr. Como's. Frozen dinners were the answer. But Julia would help him, he thought.

His mother scrunched her shoulders against her pillow and reached for her water. He guided the straw to her mouth.

"You're going to be all right, Mom." He realized that Julia must have helped her with her hair, and even some makeup.

"Was Julia here, Mom?" he asked.

"Your lady was here."

"Was it Julia?"

"She didn't stay long. She had a—I can't think of the word."

"Lip gloss?"

His mother lay back on her pillow and smiled. "When I get back home it might take me a little while, but you just wait. I'll be pegging daisies again before you know it. I don't want you to have to do it."

"You won't catch me pegging daisies, Mom," he said. "Whatever you mean by that."

When he last lived with his mother, she was caring for his stepfather, Mort. Reed stayed away as much as he could during Mort's last days. But he remembered times when she cleaned up vomit and driblets of shit from her shag rugs, without complaint—the same as she had done when Reed was a baby. A shudder rolled through him.

Later, in the telephone booth downstairs, he told Shirley about the nursing homes. She was enthusiastic, as he expected.

"How can we do that to Mom?" he asked.

"But they can give her rehab," said Shirley.

"She'll be so bewildered there. She'll hate it."

Reed shifted his weight in the telephone alcove. Was it his imagination, or did he suddenly have arthritis in his knee?

He said to Shirley, "She always said the very thought of nursing homes gave her the fantods."

"Well, what else can you do?"

"They can do the therapy at the hospital, but they don't have a bed available, so they want to ship her out." He paused. He shook his knee. "I could take her home with me until they have room at the hospital."

"How would you give her a bath?"

"I'll get help. There are people who do that for a living."

"It'll cost a fortune."

Reed went on, "She's a little confused in the head, but wouldn't you be nuts too if they gave you Xanax and then tried to carry on a conversation with you at five-thirty in the morning? Her speech isn't so bad. Her hand is a lot better. She just needs therapy on her leg. She's dragging one."

"Slow down, Reed. You can't be serious. For one thing, you'd have to kiss your social life good-bye."

"I'm working twelve-hour shifts, so I'm home a lot of days—sometimes three or four days in a row, if I don't work overtime. A therapist can do home visits."

Reed sensed the easing effect of distance. From California Shirley must see the situation as not quite real—vague scenes without the particulars colored in. The bladder scanner, the scarecrow, the whirlpool with the horse harness.

Reed said, "Right now, I think she'd be better off in the back end of my truck than she would at a nursing home." His knee still hurt. He wondered if he needed a knee brace.

As he cruised upward in the elevator, he realized that Shirley still had not inquired about the plant. It had made the national news, but apparently she hadn't noticed. She had California on her mind, he thought.

In the hallway, he ran into the clipboard twins. He caught the two women off guard—in casual conversation, as if they had been discussing some new exercise for their abs. They said they had been looking for him.

"I went to Green Haven," he told them. "Man, it's state of the art."

They beamed at him. Sunflowers orienting themselves.

"It's got the equipment, the medical support," he went on. "It's five-star accommodations! It's got all the toys, the stuff. And it smelled good. They must have a pee neutralizer that NASA developed for the space shuttle. They should sell it for cat litter boxes. You name it, they've got it." He babbled on for a moment, watching their rapt faces. Then he paused for effect, enjoying his power over their attention. He said, "It also reminded me distinctly of the Chicago airport."

He liked the question marks on their faces.

"What do you mean?" the blonde said, lowering her clipboard.

He imprinted their dumbfounded expressions onto his mind like a photograph, one of those prize-winning battle photographs that captures a revealing moment in the conflict.

"A terminal," he said. "Busy, busy, busy. Big and impersonal and bewildering. People rushing every which way."

The pretty blonde gestured with her clipboard—almost a bow— as she wiggled toward the elevator. His knee felt a little better. He needed to go dancing, stay limber. His mother would want him to get out there on the dance floor. She used to love to dance so much she would jitterbug by herself in the kitchen while Mort watched wrestling on TV in the den and drank himself into a stupor.

Reed tried to imagine Miss Blond Clipboard boogying at the Boots and Saddle dance club he liked to go to. She had an appealing curve to her bangs that paralleled her breast bulges. The clipboard could be a prop, something a stripper would use. *The Dance of the*

Seven Clipboards. If his mother could see him dancing with Miss Clipboard—he in his cowboy boots, with knee braces beneath his jeans—how she would jump and clap! She would applaud his foibles away.

He really was an idiot.

But it was Julia he wanted to dance with. He tried to conjure up her slim, white legs.

12

Reed, sinking into sleep, screamed silently, *Oh, no!* as if he harbored a monster that came alive in the dark. He tried to name the fear as he surfaced into consciousness, still fighting the hollow dread. He awoke, the phrase *black hole* humming in his mind.

Potty chair. She'd need one—sooner or later—if she came to live with him. He had not prepared a room for her in his house. The spare bedroom was full of exercise equipment and piles of magazines and storm windows. An air compressor and the works of a vacuum cleaner occupied the bed.

Julia would know what to do. But even though she had left him the sweet note on his mother's tray, she still wasn't answering his calls. Earlier in the evening, he sat poised by the telephone, about to ring her and ask her for an old-fashioned date, with wine and a corsage. But he knew she would be suspicious when she learned that he needed help caring for his mother.

Now wide awake, he switched on the gooseneck lamp and tried to read about superstrings, the Theory of Everything—T.O.E. Superstrings might have p-branes that flipped into ten or eleven dimensions, all wound up tight. The book said all p-branes were created equal.

Hallelujah, Reed thought, closing the book. He pulled on a pair of sweatpants and flip-flopped into the den, where his Hubble show was blithely sailing around the computer screen. He sat down to peer a dozen billion light-years into the past through the Hubble telescope, a time machine of sorts. *In times of trouble, I turn to Hubble*, he said to himself.

Centaurus A—a collision of galaxies—floated forth, gushing fire, with murky gases hiding its central black hole. The Cartwheel Galaxy was next, another galactic collision. He liked the purple color, the red star aiming at its center. It was more peaceful than Centaurus A. The Cat's Eye Nebula was beautiful—symmetrical and charged with hot color.

For Julia, an equally fantastic journey lurked in microbes and even farther down in the subatomic. Was there a limit in either direction? Or was there infinite regress in both directions? Was one the mirror of the other? He entertained himself with thoughts like these, thoughts that made him spin with wonder until he could feel himself beating against the bars of his cage. He didn't have the focus needed to study astronomy seriously, but Julia had told him he could crack that field with one hand. It was never too late, she insisted. Diseases, of course, were far more urgent. She said, "What if the plague suddenly shows up? We're not ready. We barely had enough flu vaccine this year. How could we halt smallpox?" Evidently she expected someone to drop a suitcase of germs in a town square. At any moment she might recite a paragraph of information on emerging viruses and other deadly diseases. She pronounced their names almost lovingly: cholera, Ebola, hanta, Puumala. She was especially big on hemorraghic fevers.

A spiral galaxy was cruising by. With a touch of one key, the up arrow, the cosmos disappeared, and he checked his e-mail. Hot Mama! She had written, "I totally understand and respect your line, sex not a requirement, because I totally know if we met each other and either one of us was turned off, it's good to have that shield between us, so we don't *have* to do anything. That is *cool* with me, and who knows, we might hit it off. I have twelve years' experience dealing with the public—as a waitress and therapist. I like to fish. I cure my own hams (and double-smoke them). I love Beethoven. I like to sit on the porch in the rain and just enjoy the freshness of the air. I love collecting. I own a complete set of Blue Ridge pottery, which I've chased down at every flea market and antique store in this part of the world."

Reed, in his fancy, flitted through a lengthy meeting with the mystery woman, in which they screwed five times and gorged on double-smoked ham, and he was about to reply in the affirmative, but he read her message again. She was becoming more intriguing. But no, it was too complicated. This woman wanted a relationship. The Blue Ridge pottery gave her away.

He stared at the e-mail until the screen went dark and his Hubbles appeared. He could always count on the Andromeda galaxy.

He had to sleep. He adjusted the curtain to shut out the daylight, then got in bed and read about dark matter. *Dark Matter in the Afternoon*, he thought, as if he were doing something illicit. Dark matter and dark energy involved MACHOs and WIMPs. MACHOs could be black holes. WIMPs could be neutrinos. Nothing was for sure.

13

Rumors were flying around like lost neutrinos. The newspaper one morning early the next week reported that radioactive scrap metal from the plant was being recycled commercially and might end up in such items as barbecue grills and tooth fillings. Outside the maintenance shops Jim told a knot of his workers not to talk to the press.

"They haven't proved anything," Jim said. "They're just trading in rumor and innuendo."

"A roomer with a Nintendo?" Reed asked.

Jim didn't laugh. "It's a game the press plays," Reed offered. "How many radioactive elements can you find in this picture?"

"People will see things that aren't there when they have them on their mind," Jim said, turning to the work permits he was signing.

His hair bushed out today, as if he had forgotten his conditioner, but his face was grim and shadowy.

"I wonder if you could get a knee replacement made out of recycled radioactive scrap metal," Reed said. "That would put a spark in your step!"

He became conscious of the fillings in his teeth, imagining they were radioactive. What a clever invention—a built-in flashlight in the mouth! He didn't have an opportunity to say this. Guys around him were wandering away. Jim was talking on his cell phone. When Jim finished, Reed spoke up.

"Hey, Jim. Seriously—what's going on here? If we've got that much stuff spread around, we won't get cleaned up by the next millennium."

Jim clipped his phone onto his belt and gazed at a girder. "Reed, I wouldn't lie to you. It's a hell of a mess. But it's not enough to put us out of commission. And if the D.O.E. comes in here wanting to start up a new phase of production, we can be ready."

"You're talking nuke talk, Jim."

Jim grinned. "If it comes to that, they're going to need us, and toxic waste be damned. Whatever the D.O.E. wants to do, I think we can handle it." He stroked his hair. "You know the talk around about new start-ups—and I don't mean just power plants."

For some time, they had been hearing about research on a new type of bomb. And at a couple of sites workers were replacing the aging plutonium triggers on nuclear bombs. A trigger was a bomb in itself—just the right size for a little job, Reed thought.

Jim's phone was ringing. Before answering, he said, "Once we get the new centrifuge, we could turn this operation around and do weapons-grade enrichment."

"If you say so, Jim," Reed said.

Up on the cell floor, he hitched his industrial half-ton toolbox to a tractor tow and hauled it to the job site. He opened his toolbox carefully, so as not to disturb Eisenhower. The bird grinned at him foolishly.

"You know something, don't you?" Reed accused the bird.

He hung his lanyard of I.D. badges, including his rad permit and his TLD—the thermoluminescent dosimeter for detecting radiation—on the toolbox to get it out of his way. Then he began removing some of the particular tools he would need for replacing a control valve in the converter piping—an air grinder, a crescent wrench, and a chipping hammer.

Kerwin the old-timer and a sometimes belligerent guy called Double Ass worked with him, but they said little in the cacophony as they prepared the site. Even though the job could be done by one person, safety required three, with one as monitor outside the C-zone. That was Double Ass. Reed didn't trust a lard-ass in the cells.

Two days before, operations had shut the gate valves to the cell, taking it off-line, so that it was cool enough to work on. A couple of health-physics techs arrived to swipe samples on paper swatches from the area and check them with their rad rods. While they strung the yellow boundary rope around the work site, Double Ass hauled in the wagon that held the bagged anti-C clothing, and Reed and Kerwin geared up: yellow coveralls, plastic booties over their boots, scuffs, thin glove liners, long rubber gloves. With a magician's finesse, Reed wrapped his wrists with duct tape.

Today's job was routine process work, nothing out of the ordinary. Yet something had shifted slightly, Reed thought. It was like being in a story where nothing was what it seemed, where anything in the scene might transmogrify, spontaneously shifting shape—into a dragon, maybe, or an alien life-form reminiscent of the squid.

At a signal from one of the HP techs, Reed pulled on his cloth hood and adjusted his respirator. The suit wasn't state-of-the-art, like a military-issue chem suit, which he coveted. Without an impermeable inner layer, it wasn't even a Haz-Mat suit.

Double Ass was goofing off, pretending he was throwing a bowling ball down the painted lane, then hooking a basketball up into the crane bay. Reed remembered a wild yellow cloud spewing from a pipe—the cloud so thick he couldn't see the crane operator thirty feet above. Reed and a crew had been hammering on a troublesome pipe, trying to loosen it. Suddenly UF_6 hit the air and hydrofluoric acid leapt out, with invisible tongues of fire that could etch glass. It left a residue of yellow powder. Thick clumps of it, like cornflakes, landed all around, way beyond the C-zone.

Now, in the murky bowels of the hell-hot cell, with Kerwin as his lookout, Reed—wedged in a tight space—was painstakingly scarfing out a flange with his burning rig. He concentrated hard, to keep his attention from wandering off the hot flame of the scarfing tip he was using to melt the weld on the flange. The heat in the cell was so intense it seemed to roar. He had learned to time his stay so that he did not pass out or cook his mind. He was aware of a harmonic vibration beginning on the west side of the building; then one began on the east side. They rolled like waves toward each other, and with a crescendo they overlapped. Reed could hear patterns inside the noise. He could feel the vibrations surfing through his body. He was so used to the sound of the machines running—in him and around him—that he always noticed any subtle changes. He could tell by listening if anything was wrong.

Reed went for a long ride on his bike. The rush of air was soothing, the landscape variations abrupt and arbitrary. Afterward, he could not have reconstructed the route in his memory. At loose ends, he stopped at a house in the Hawthorne subdivision, where Burl was running his baby earthmover, called a Bobcat. Burl had learned refrigeration at a vocational-technical school, but primarily he worked on construction crews. After he bought his own Bobcat, he was able to earn up to sixty-five dollars an hour, as much as a custom dozer with a much larger machine.

From the driveway, Reed could see two Mexicans on aluminum stilts, sanding drywall seams on the ceiling of a new garage. Outside, at the controls in the air-conditioned cab of the Bobcat, Burl was moving dirt in quick, successive front-end shovel loads. He turned and pivoted and spun the thing like a kid driving a bumper car.

When he saw Reed, Burl braked to a halt and cut the engine. He called out, "I'm moving the mountain to Mohammed."

"Hey, Burl, you were hot-dogging it there. You looked like a teenager in a dance contest doing some dirty dancing."

"Dirty dancing! That's me. You see here seven loads of river-bottom dirt trucked in this morning." He emerged from the Bobcat, stretched his hamstrings, and opened the cooler in the cab of his truck. "Want a beer, Reed?"

"No, that's all right."

He chose a guava soda instead. Burl picked a soft drink too, saying he was dehydrated.

"What's up?" he asked.

"I just wanted to watch you work your Bobcat. I wish I had one to play with."

"I wish I could just drive it down the highway. I'd sell my truck and take off."

"That's an idea." Reed leaned against the Bobcat, surveying the house with its imitation redwood decking and gas grill, and the yard with its lily pond and sculpted shrubs hugging the perimeter of the house. The swimming pool was sunk into a ring of fiberglass rocks arranged to resemble a rocky stream with a waterfall. The curved deck bordered the pool. The treeless front yard had pea gravel instead of grass and was scattered with what appeared to be heavy boulders from one of Jupiter's moons.

"Isn't this place the biggest pile of shit you ever saw?" Burl said.

They laughed together, enjoying the warm June afternoon. Reed felt improved.

He was leaving the ringer on these days because of his mother. Just after he had descended into successful sleep late the next morning, one of the social workers telephoned to inform him that a bed on the transitional-care floor at the hospital was available. His mother could get physical therapy there and not have to move anywhere for a while.

He wasn't sure what he said. He felt delirious—confused, re-lieved. The woman jabbered on through the bureaucratic switch-yards of Medicare. He wasn't sure which of the social workers she was. Their names and voices had overlapped in his mind.

Reed didn't know if it was night or day.

*I*t didn't seem like a nursing home. It was just another hospital floor, but the rooms in transitional care had decorative touches, such as plastic bouquets and colorful posters and tulip-bordered wallpaper. Reed knew his mother was too tired to notice, or she would have said something sarcastic.

Glad that she was no longer lashed to an I.V., he rolled her down the corridor in her recliner chair. "We're flying too fast," she protested.

"What's going on in your head, Ma?" he said.

"You wouldn't want to know," she said.

She didn't ask about his kids, and Reed didn't mention them. Their indifference to their grandmother pained him. Dalton, who kept in touch by e-mail, had sent him pages and pages of Internet mumbo jumbo about nuclear doom. After receiving one particular nuclear-winter scenario, Reed shot back an e-mail: "Dalt, if I'm gonna glow, at least you'll be able to find me when the lights go out." Reed no longer mentioned his mother to either of his chil-dren, because they never inquired about her, even though they knew she was in the hospital. Reed would have admonished them for their neglect except that he knew he had done worse with his own grand-parents. Now that they had been dead for years, he felt wistful about them, wondering what they had known that he needed to know now.

In the lounge, which was equipped with a mega-TV, game tables, and a kitchen nook, Reed paused before the aquarium so that his mother could see the parade of yellow sunfish kissing the glass, but she was nodding sleepily. Parking her there, he stepped across the room to the window. He was on the seventh floor, so he had a broad view of the plant, with the plumes rising out of the gray area. The rest was green. Green from ear to ear, he thought. He felt bolted in place, with his mother behind him, this expanse before him, and Julia nowhere in sight. Even though he apparently had been spared, for now, the impossible job of caring for his mother, he felt anxious, suspended. His mother was here now, alive, but anything could happen. This was one of those moments of clarity that visited him from time to time, when he saw himself in context. Sometimes it was frightening.

14

At the food court in the mall, Reed bought a calzone smothered with tomato sauce. It was lunchtime on Saturday, and the place was crowded. He found a tiny table, with a wadded napkin and a smear of ketchup on it. A family sat down at the table next to him—a small girl and boy, parents. The children snatched at their burger bags, but the father firmly held them out of reach.

"You can't have them till I get the prizes out," he said. "I'm going to kill somebody if this doesn't stop. Now sit down. Let me have those bags."

Reed cringed. He could remember being in the same scene, when he had young kids.

The man's temper had sulled the wife into silence, Reed noticed. She calmly laid out her napkin, her knife, her fork, and opened her own bag of food. Her husband rummaged in the children's bags, removed the cookies and the plastic toys, and then handed the bags to the children. "You can have these if you eat all your hamburgers," he said.

The children didn't seem to notice their father's murderous temper. "I wanted a ladybug, but I'll get the tiger," the little girl said to no one. "Do we get to stop at the slides?" the boy said.

Nobody answered. The man said, "Not one more peep out of you. I'm going to see some good behavior here or nobody's getting out of this state alive."

Reed could have been watching a movie of his younger self. Dalton and Dana were always testing him, whining. He didn't know what to do except play the stern father.

The man munched his sandwich. He had sandy hair and a thin mustache. The wife had straight bleached-blond hair pulled back severely above her ears and tied in back with a purple elastic ruffle. She drank some Coke, blotted her lips, then reached for her husband's head. She leaned toward him, kissed him on the cheek, and resumed eating. Glenda never did anything like that, Reed thought. The man chomped a large hunk from his sandwich. The kids bounced in their seats, flailing as if they were listening to built-in CD players.

The way the wife kissed her husband touched Reed, that she would put up with the guy in spite of his ill temper and his need to assert his power over his family. She was trying to calm him down so he would be less of a jerk.

Reed finished his calzone and threw the trash into a bin. The calzone hit his stomach hard. He wondered if colonic irrigation would help him. Burl swore by it—not that Burl had tried it, but he knew a guy who had tried it after a consultant told him he was going to die from dirty entrails. The guy felt like a new person, Burl reported. Here at the mall, Reed always felt he needed a cleansing.

Where was Julia? She had said one o'clock, but she was not here.

He was going to see Julia. The fact hadn't quite registered. He had wolfed his lunch mechanically, in a daze. She had finally called and agreed to see him, but she had a biology class and offered to pick him up at the mall so they could go for a drive in her new car. He didn't follow her elaborate reasoning for meeting him at the mall. He wondered if she meant to avoid his house—with his receptive, springy beauty-sleep mattress waiting—because she was afraid to get involved with him again.

He waited for a few minutes, and then he heard his name being paged on the P.A. system. His intestines flipped and twisted as he searched for the customer-service kiosk, where he received her message on a note. "Julia will meet you at the west entrance at 1:15."

Relieved, he sat on a bench by the fountain. Teenaged girls—with melanomic suntans already—promenaded past in skimpy dresses and shorts, and boys with skinny, sunken frames slouched along with them. When he was a teenager, kids didn't go shopping on dates. But now boys took their girlfriends to the mall—to show them off; the girls wanted to try on clothes to see how their boyfriends would like them. When he was a boy he liked to stomp around outdoors. He wanted a motorcycle. And he wanted girls to stick on the bike behind him.

At one-ten he went out the door into a spirited rain and dashed down the sidewalk to the west entrance. Under the canopy that extended alongside the building, he waited, shaking the rain from his thin shirt and watching for Julia to pull up in her car. She hadn't told him what kind of car she had bought, and he found it odd that she wanted him to see it.

At the Live Bait machine beside him, an auburn-haired woman in shiny black pants was trying to feed a five-dollar bill into the machine, but it kept rejecting the money. Her car was idling at the curb.

"It gets wet and keeps coming back," she said with a frown.

Reed said, "In this rain, I bet you could find some worms in your backyard."

"I don't have time to dig worms," she said. "I have to host a

turtle-burger party tonight, so I wanted to get the bait now and be
ready to go fishing when the sun comes up."

Reed and the redhead, who was obliquely attractive, stood in the
rain, yakking about bait. He was so glad about Julia that he was rip-
pling with anxious, friendly feeling. He was about to jump out of his
skin. Turtle burger? He'd have to think about that one. The woman
tried inserting the bill again. The machine had a sign: "Our live bait
is guaranteed to catch fish or die trying." The machine offered wax
worms, premium night crawlers, crappie minnows, and red minnows.

Julia honked, and he dashed dripping to her car, a chartreuse
Beetle. She gave him an enigmatic smile—part allure, part reserve.
Her hair was tousled, a bit frizzed from the rain. She wore a gray
sweatshirt jacket and jeans. On the passenger seat, her bag squatted
open-mouthed, displaying tissues, a slim wallet, some papers, and a
bandanna. She shoved the bag into her lap, making room for him.

"What do you think about colonic irrigation?" he asked as she
shifted into first. The downpour was beginning in earnest. "Burl
says death gets started in the colon."

Julia let out such a loud whoop of laughter that he felt a bit em-
barrassed.

"One of Burl's pearls," he said. "He knows a guy who did it and
is trying to get Burl to try it, and so he's preaching to me that I need
to have my entrails flushed."

She laughed again, thrilling him.

He said, "Maybe they could get out all that uranium and technetium and who knows what else I've got in me."

She didn't laugh. She was concentrating on a turn out of the
parking lot.

"I'm joking," he said. He felt shy and awkward with her, not sure
what to say.

Reed had always loved rain. He found it nourishing, as if it made
the mind grow the way it made plants grow. The air in the car was

humid, the windows misted. Julia switched on her defroster, which made a rush of pleasant sound. At a traffic light in the heavy rain, with the red light swaying and casting blurry reflections on the windshield, he realized that she was playing a tape of Tchaikovsky. She knew he liked Tchaikovsky.

"Like my new car?"

"Cute as a bug," he said. "But it's not your color."

"She's used, two years old, and I got her for thirteen thousand plus trade-in. Of course they stole the trade-in."

"That's probably as good as you can expect."

"She's got thirty-five thousand miles on her."

"Her? What's her name?"

"I haven't decided."

"You sure picked a color," he said, but she seemed a bit offended. He hadn't meant to be critical. It was just his way.

The light changed and she splashed through the intersection.

"I went to see your mom three or four times, but you weren't there."

"You did? She never told me. Damn, I'm sorry I missed you."

Reed brought her up to date on his mother's condition, while Julia drove cautiously through the downpour. In her new car and some clothing he didn't recognize, she seemed overhauled, except for her familiar worn leather clogs with the loose straps across the instep.

They were floating down a main thoroughfare in a driving rain. Her wipers were flying, and the traffic was heavy.

"I had wanted to go for a ride to show you my car," she said. "But this rain is ridiculous." Her manner was nervously apologetic, as if she had brought the rain.

"It's O.K.," he said, touching her arm lightly. "I'd go on a hayride in a hurricane with you."

"I'm going to stop here at the drugstore parking lot till it lets up," she said, gliding into the entrance.

She parked in an empty row and shut off the engine. The rain slammed the windshield. Reaching for her book satchel behind Reed's seat, she began telling him about the summer class she was taking in molecular biology. She plopped a book in his lap and spoke with animated enthusiasm, her breath steaming up the windows, as Reed flipped through her textbook, which had the heft of a crate of beer.

"It's so amazing what they're finding out these days," she said. "I've got this terrific teacher who's encouraging me to go to grad school. He's doing research on salamanders."

"I haven't seen a salamander in years," Reed said.

"He's studying the DNA of a pair of sister species to investigate the evolutionary divergence. And listen to this, Reed, some salamanders have this poison that oozes out of their skins—you know how some tropical frogs have?"

"Until they're kissed by a beautiful woman? I'm probably oozing toxic waste."

She laughed but didn't take the hint. "This stuff attacks rapidly dividing cells selectively—voilà! maybe a cancer treatment can come out of it! It's so exciting! Who knows what might be out there just waiting to be discovered."

Later that afternoon, as he sat with his mother in the hospital, Reed kept replaying in his mind the brief ride with Julia, always with the thick downpour and the blurred red stoplight swinging above the street in the rush of rain. In the parking lot as they waited for the rain to abate, and steam clouded the windows, he had joked, "I'm as snug as a rug in a Bug."

He was overwhelmed by his feeling for her. Their awkwardness seemed to disappear now as he recalled the strange little ride. All argument and tension seemed irrelevant. He would agree with anything she said, he thought now, even though he knew he had a way of sabotaging himself, saying the wrong thing, not thinking things through. It was true that she intimidated him in certain ways, but that seemed to be the quality he couldn't resist. He was glad she hadn't quizzed him on superstring theory, because he couldn't re-member the slightest thing about p-branes.

After some hesitation, she had agreed to go out for dinner with him that evening, but he was not sure why. He thought she had been disappointed in him, once she got him inside her new car that after-noon.

At a seafood place downtown, he listened to her rhapsodic rap about the biology courses she had taken the spring semester. Her hands flying, she described swarms of starlings—an example of pop-ulation biology. He stared at her, observing the delicate way she broke king-crab legs and let the naked, red-dappled flesh slither onto her tongue. She had a slim face, high cheekbones, narrow fore-head, arched eyebrows, a little freckle on the tip of her petite nose, a complexion the soft, smooth texture of a mushroom.

She said, "My plan is to get a master's in molecular biology so I can go into research. That's the most exciting field for diseases."

"Are you going to study salamanders?" Reed asked.

She laughed. "I don't know, but the university is a hot spot for salamanderology right now."

He said, "The idea is if I get cancer, then I can take poison oil from a salamander's back and treat it?"

"Something like that. Or maybe you'll grow a new leg." She laughed. "But I'm serious."

"I know you're serious. But this sounds like something witches might cook in a stew."

"Witches use eye of newt."

"I knew it sounded familiar."

"Dessert?" asked the waiter when he came to clear away their crab carcasses.

"No, thanks." She was applying her lip gloss, in that way she had of slicking it on without a mirror.

"Why did the menu say 'Cell phones cause seafood spoilage'?" Reed asked the waiter. "What does that mean?"

"Didn't you know that?" the man asked, his eyebrows following the tray of dishes that he lifted high with one hand.

Julia laughed, as though Reed had missed the joke.

"You must have a new cell phone," he said. "How did you leave that message for me at the mall?"

"It's just for emergencies. I never turn it on."

"And you never answer your messages."

"I know. But I always check them." She sipped her water. "Do you remember that movie *Silkwood*?"

"No. I saw it a long time ago. Forgot it by now."

"It's about a whistle blower at a nuclear-fuel plant."

It had occurred to Reed that if his life were a movie, he would be a whistle blower, rallying the workers, stirring up trouble. That was the nature of movies, and the situation demanded a whistle-blower hero. So it wouldn't be a movie about his life. It would be a movie about an image of his life.

"What's going on here is not a movie," he said to Julia.

"No, it's not," she agreed. Her face brightened slightly. "Did you ever notice how in movies the hero will often eat a Twinkie before going into battle—saving someone in a skyscraper fire, or rescuing a hostage or something?"

"A Twinkie?"

"The Twinkie, judging by its size and shape, is a source of strength and energy." She was teasing him.

He played along. "The Twinkie people probably pay the movies a fortune to play up their cream-filled goobers."

"Could be. But a hero usually has to eat something magic before a battle."

"I'll have to try that."

"Just don't eat any technetium," she said, lowering her eyes as if she had uttered a forbidden word.

"I never *touch* rutabagas," he said. "I have my standards."

"Oh, Reed," she said with sudden intensity. "I'm just sick about all that. How can they *do* that to their workers?" She splayed both hands on the table, her slender fingers forming angles.

Her outburst unnerved him. "You know it's not the people running it now. It's stuff from the past." He was tired of the phrase *legacy waste*. With his water glass, he made spiral galaxies on the tablecloth.

"How did technetium get into the gardens? Where did it come from?"

"It's odd, isn't it?" He scooted his glass across the tablecloth, making ripples.

"Aren't people afraid to work out there?"

"Maybe they are. I don't know. I'm not afraid."

"But how can you be so sure it's so safe if all those scrap piles are lying around?"

"In the old days they weren't so careful, but we have strict safety standards now. They didn't know any better."

"That sounds like an excuse."

"Come on, honey. We've been through all this before." His hand touched hers across the table. "It's not going to get us. There's a big cleanup underway."

"The whole thing is a disaster."

The waiter brought the bill and Reed laid his hand on it, pulling it toward him. When the waiter left, Reed said, "Back then everybody was in a hurry to beat the Russians. Nobody had time to recycle the garbage. They just piled it up or tossed it over the fence. It wasn't important then. It really wasn't a priority."

"I know. Better dead than Red."

Her sarcasm was unfair, he thought. He busied himself with the check, hoping to drop the subject. She suddenly sneezed. Finding a tissue in her bag, she blew her nose, quietly and softly. She dabbed her eyes with her napkin and sniffled. Her face was flushed, and she seemed to be shedding a few tears, but he wasn't sure. He was surprised that her concern had grown. Reaching across the table, he tried to calm her.

As a child, Julia had assigned gender to numbers, and she thought that a six was a she and a seven was a he. When, some time later, she heard the phrase *at sixes and sevens*, she thought it meant having sex. She had told this to Reed once.

"I'm at sixes and sevens," Reed said to her now, with a glimmer of a grin. "Speaking of Twinkies."

She smiled and sipped some water. Her face was still red.

"I've missed you," he said.

She looked away.

"Are you still mad at me?" he asked.

"Let's call it exasperation."

"I didn't mean to hurt you. You know that."

"You didn't hurt me."

"I'm sorry about that day at Fort Wolf."

"I was mad at you for taking me out there," she said. "It seemed like reckless disregard."

"We had a good time, didn't we?"

"Of course. But it was spoiled after all the news came out. And you knew about the chemicals out at that place."

"Didn't you trust me?"

"Actually I did."

"And now?"

She paused. "Maybe I was unfair, and you've been through a lot now, with your mom." She drank some water and rolled her stiff napkin into a ball. It sprang open and she bunched it up again.

"I wish you'd come over to my house," he said, his feelers going out, testing her mood. "But I guess you don't want to be in the presence of any of my guns, in case I might go insane and go after you with one of them."

He meant to be teasing, but she replied sharply, "I think I know you better than that. All I ever said about your cache of artillery was that you can draw a straight, uninterrupted line through history from a caveman with a rock to a megalomaniac with an atomic bomb."

"Me and my big mouth. I said the wrong thing again."

"My mouth is as big as yours sometimes."

It was still raining lightly, and they dashed from the door of the restaurant to his car. He hadn't realized how he had frightened her. He didn't know how to apologize, or make it up to her, but when she said "reckless disregard," perhaps she meant a character flaw that he couldn't tame. He often misspoke, although he thought he was just being naturally expressive.

He approached the stoplight on Constitution Avenue. To the left was his house, and hers was in the opposite direction.

"Left or right?"

"I need to get up early tomorrow, so you'd better take me home."

She was going to spend the day with her daughter Lisa, who was a freshman at the university. It was Parents' Day. They were going to meet teachers at a luncheon, and go to a science fair, a track meet, and a production of *Fiddler on the Roof.*

Julia's house was across town on a leafy street of old houses. The street seemed deserted except for the gathering of cars at the far end of the block—someone having a party. Under the streetlights, the rain glistened on the asphalt. Reed turned into the driveway and drove to the rear of the somewhat rundown old Victorian house, where she lived in a garden apartment. Julia owned the house and rented out apartments. Her Beetle squatted in a carport, like a large frog.

"You say you worry about me?" he said as he walked her to her door. "Well, I worry about you too—living alone in that apartment."

"The tenants watch out for me." She touched his shoulder, her keys in her hand. She ran her fingers through his hair. "I think about you, Reed." The key chain wiggled against his scalp. "I've missed you."

She slipped away from him before he could grasp her. He watched her go inside the house. The streetlights did not reach the depths of the bushy yard outside her glass-paned door. He waited until he saw her lights come on.

*H*e was annoyed with himself for his remark about the guns he kept at home. His mind was so twisted, he thought. He slammed his horn in frustration. A battle-scarred tiger cat sped lickety-split across the street, avoiding puddles.

Although Reed no longer hunted, he still loved shooting. The sublime satisfaction of nailing something you aimed at was the same as that little hit of serotonin some people felt when they penciled in a word in a crossword puzzle or when their team scored a point. He usually went out to Fort Wolf about once a week to camp or just to shoot at targets, but while his mother remained in the hospital, he had stopped going. Now, after seeing Julia, he wondered if their minds would ever meet on the subject of weapons.

"What do you mean, you're antiviolent?" he'd asked her once, last fall, as they were driving downstate to a Triple A minor-league ballgame. "Turn the other cheek?"

"I don't like killing."

"There's always been war," he said. "Sometimes you have to fight back, plain and simple."

"There are other ways."

"I bet you wouldn't step on a bug."

"No, I wouldn't."

"I bet you'd let powder-post beetles eat up your house."

"I wouldn't kill a bug unnecessarily," she said. "Why should I?"

"So you agree that some killing is necessary."

"That's not the way I'd put it."

"But what if a hornet was dive-bombing a child? Would you swat it?"

"Well, of course, but . . ."

"Some creatures you can kill and some you can't, depending on the circumstances?"

"You're going in circles."

"Which would you give priority to—a staghorn beetle or a sow bug?"

"I don't know! Stop it!"

Reed didn't hunt deer. Spotlights and high-powered rifles with scopes were not fair to the deer. He didn't want to kill a deer. It would be like shooting a ballet dancer. But he could kill a rat or a groundhog. He would kill chickens to eat if it were convenient and he weren't allergic to feathers. He was lucky, he told Julia, that he could work off his violent urges in ways that did not get him into trouble. He didn't want to oversimplify, but wasn't that the nature of competitive sports?

"Baseball," she replied simply. "Nonviolent."

"You're still aiming and hitting," he said. "It's fundamental."

She put her head in her hands in a gesture of submission. "I won't fight you," she said.

At the baseball game that day, a hometown hitter was struck by a pitch—an obvious beanball. The benches cleared and a fight erupted. Reed noticed Julia's alarmed face fixed on the player, who was doubled in pain on the ground.

He felt bad now, remembering the way he had bullied her. But she hadn't understood that he could actually kill someone in order to protect her, just as his dog would do the same for him. He had trained his dog when to attack, when to go for the throat. "My God," Burl had said to him. "You name a killer attack dog Clarence? I can't imagine anybody named Clarence being a bloodthirsty killer." Burl himself didn't hunt, or practice self-defense, or own a dog. He just flopped through life with little regard for the outcome.

"I was going to name him Copernicus," Reed said. "But he didn't like it."

15

Reed felt like hopping on his bike and heading for the Florida Everglades, but his mother was waiting at the hospital for him to take her back to Sunnybank. An aide had gathered her toiletries and clothing into large transparent plastic bags with locking handles. Some of her lacy underwear was visible. The aide carried the bags, and Reed pushed the wheelchair. The aide told him to back the chair into the elevator, so that his mother faced forward. His mother sat quietly, as if she were being ushered to her doom.

At the business office, the blond social worker gave him forms to sign. As he was signing the releases, she said, "I met a guy in Middletown with the same last name as yours, but he pronounced it Fu-*trell*."

"The Fu-*trells* went uptown," Reed said with a grin. "My bunch, the *Few*-trulls, stayed home. I guess they thought it was futile to be a Futrell."

"What kind of name is it?"

"It's French, I think. Search me. It could be Kurdish for all I know."

"My mother researches family history and she knows all about names."

"My cousin does genealogy, and you'd think she was a monk preserving the books in a monastery in the Dark Ages," Reed said. "It's deadly serious stuff."

She laughed and smoothed her hair. "I know what you mean. My mom is hooked."

Why was Miss Clipboard acting like a normal person now? Reed wondered. Was she flirting with him?

Reed's mother, sitting by the door in the wheelchair, grunted, then said, "Let's get out of this cow palace."

A couple of weeks went by, with summer coming on like a blowtorch. Reed changed his air-conditioning filters. He staked his tomatoes, which had shot out crazy arms in the recent rain. He couldn't get through a summer without fresh tomatoes. If he had extras he liked to give them away, and if they rotted, he loved to throw them against the fence and watch their sad-sack faces disintegrate as they flew through the sieve of the chain link. He hadn't seen Julia again, but they spoke twice on the telephone—friendly enough, but she was still reserved. He apologized for his snide remark about guns, and she dismissed it. He longed to see her, but she put him off; her studies consumed her free time now. She said she hadn't had time to plant any tomatoes. "I'll give you tomatoes," he promised.

Burl had gone with an organized group to the Smoky Mountains for a bear hunt. He went along for the ride; he didn't shoot, but he wanted to see the Smokies. Reed reviewed his gun collection. Now and then he would remove a gun from the safe and polish it, admiring the artistry and maybe reading up on its history. Old gun stocks were beautifully crafted, especially the wooden ones with ivory inlay. Most of his weapons were World War II era and would seem undistinguished unless you knew the history. His oldest was a Civil War pistol that he had bought for ten dollars at a flea market. It had been repaired with a modern bolt, which made the gun less valuable, but still it was a great addition to his collection. His funniest was a blunderbuss. The fastest was a Winchester repeating rifle. The strangest was the pepperbox revolving pistol he had assembled from a kit. As he thumbed through his books on the history of weapons, he couldn't help dwelling on how the Colt .45 was called the Peacemaker and the ICBM was called a Peacekeeper. He could turn Julia's argument completely around—a line of peace from the caveman to Eisenhower's Atoms for Peace to Star Wars. His collection was appropriate and logical, he thought. Weren't war and peace as intimately related as man and woman, yin and yang?

A woman in a pink hat was playing raucous, full-chorded hymns on the piano at Sunnybank. On a table was a large globular glass vase of green plants, the roots dangling visibly in the water. Reed was startled to see a blue-fringed ichthyoid creature trapped in the globe of the vase, swimming helplessly in circles among the roots. The fish, flicking its tail, paused and stared at him, bug eyed. The hymn emanating from the piano was "Nearer, My God, to Thee." Reed considered that it might be something of a theme song for the aged.

"Did you feed the cats?" his mother asked.

"What cats?"

"At home. I couldn't feed them all. They're starving."

Since returning to Sunnybank, she seemed to live half in dreams. She had told Reed about an orgy in the bathroom—a bearded man who leered and a nun with her skirt wadded around her waist. And she reported that camels and elephants marched past her window. Little creatures played under the bed—not mice, just gentle furry things who hid. The cats couldn't reach them. The cats were starving. She too was starving. They never fed her anything. No snacks. No marshmallows. No cordon bleu.

A bloated woman clutching a flyswatter was propelling herself backwards in her wheelchair.

"Watch out, she'll run over you," Reed's mother said. "She ran over my toes several times."

"There's a lot of traffic here," Reed said. He wished Julia would suddenly be there, playing the piano. He said, "Mom, you look terrific. I need a woman who looks as good as you. That hairdo is a knockout."

She laughed and brought her hand to her hair, as if to verify it. "You need a girlfriend," she said. Reed thought she was testing a memory of herself as a young, flirtatious girl. She said, "Did you know Bud Futrell died?"

"I saw that in the paper. Is he the cousin with the crazy wife?"

"No." She considered the question, searching her memory. She said, "He was the one with the crazy wife. Let me think." She rolled a small hand-weight from exercise class in her lap. She said, "He had a crazy, detached wife."

"What do you mean?"

She selected her words slowly. "He had a crazy, detached wife."

"O.K., Mom."

"He had a crazy wife," she said. "She was . . . detached."

"Oh. Don't worry, Mom." He couldn't bear to watch her searching for words.

At five o'clock, he accompanied her—struggling along with the walker—to the dining room table, which she shared with three frail women. A retired preacher, a craggy man in a golf-green blazer, was saying grace at a nearby table. Irreverently, Reed glanced around at the bowed heads. "He goes on and on forever," his mother commented a bit loudly.

"And heavenly father, we thank you for giving us your only begotten son who died for our sins," said the preacher. "Thy son Jesus

took up the cross and lugged it up the hill and died. We gather together on this special day to ask thy blessing." He paused, then
added emphatically, "And forgive us for our lustful sins and passions."

Reed's mother emitted a little hoot.

Divorce! Reed thought suddenly. A detached wife.

At the supermarket Reed located a can of oyster stew and some
oyster crackers. His mother loved oysters in any form—fried,
stewed, raw, or Rockefeller—and he wanted to surprise her. Maybe
there was some kind of shock therapy to shake up her cognitive fac-
ulties. Oysters might do it. He searched out his staples—popcorn,
fruit, dairy, dog food—and threw in a twelve-pack of toilet paper
(soft, in case Julia came to visit). After paying for his groceries, he
slung several plastic bags into his hands instead of wheeling the cart
out. In the parking lot, he spotted Burl getting into his truck.

"Hey, Burl, how many bears did you catch?" Reed said, tapping
on the window.

He set his groceries on the asphalt. The glass bottles clinked.
Burl scrambled out of the truck. He was wearing a garish souvenir
T-shirt that said NO SMOKING IN THE SMOKIES, green letters against
orange flames. He gave Reed an expansive hug.

"That's my bear hug, Reed," Burl cried. "You won't believe the
wild bear chase I've been on. It was a bear hunt and a game feast and
an opera, all rolled into one."

"Opera?"

"I'll get to that. Listen. These people put on a wild-game barbecue for about five hundred people. But first they take you out in
S.U.V.s, with dogs and bear rifles, and now and then they let the
dogs out to look for bear. Then they come back and you ride some
more over the mountain service roads. We never saw a bear—but it's
illegal to shoot one anyway."

"Sounds more like a hayride than a bear hunt," said Reed.

"It was all pretend. Denny Jones and his wife Tippy were along.

She's pregnant, and she had to have her cervix hole sewed up; they lost one baby because her cervix wasn't strong enough to hold it. I didn't think she ought to be out riding in an S.U.V. in the mountains."

"That sounds nuts," Reed said.

Burl, ducking into his front seat, swigged from a pint of bourbon that was concealed in a paper bag.

"That's not all," he said, replacing the package in his truck. "When we got back from the bear hunt we were at this fancy hunting lodge—deer heads on the wall? A woman was playing the piano, and another woman was in there yelling like she was being torn to pieces by coyotes, and you could hear coyotes wailing out in the woods. It was opera! She was singing opera."

"Opera does sound like coyotes, in parts," Reed said, to be agreeable. Burl wasn't staggering drunk yet, but he clearly intended to be. Quickly, Reed updated him on his mother and her delusions.

"Doesn't that sound like she's on drugs, Burl? That doesn't sound like stroke damage to me."

"What's she taking?"

"They kept her stoked up on Xanax in the hospital, but they took her off of that, and now they have her on a couple of new pills that I'm not sure about. Maybe she's not even getting her right medicine. The aides can remind them to take their pills, but they can't give them their pills. It's against the law for the aides to touch the pills."

"What if your mom drops one and can't stoop down to pick it up?"

"Hell, I don't know. Those old folks are on their own there."

"You better look up those pills. And look up the side effects."

"I'll have to. There's no telling what she's taking—or how much."

"Sometimes the side effect cancels out the effect," Burl said.

Reed laughed. "Does that sound like the story of my life?"

"I heard spinach soaks up radiation." Burl took another drink of bourbon. He screwed the top back on and twisted the paper around the neck of the bottle. "Or was it rutabagas? I can't remember."

"How's the old Prayer Warrior?" Reed asked. "Seen any major action lately?"

"I haven't slept in two days. I've got a prayer vigil going, not just for you but for everybody out there at the plant that might be in trouble. You never know what they might have done to you twenty-five years ago! And then it comes up later. It's like syphilis! I had a great-uncle that had that a long time ago. It crept up on him; it was living there all along and then one day it hatched like a maggot in a dead dog's eye."

"Is that a parable? You sound like a preacher, Burl."

"I'm telling you, Reed, it might get you. Not syphilis. Radiation."

"If I got it, I got it," Reed said. "And you sure are making me feel good, Burl. You sure know how to make a fellow feel good."

"*I've* got a headache and the scours," Burl said. "And the red-eye. And if I don't get out of here and go fix Mrs. Patterson's sump pump, she'll stop speaking to me."

"Take care, Burl." He paused. "By the way, the silverfish ate Eisenhower."

"Oh, no!"

"There were just toenails left. I was off for three days and they had a Roman orgy."

"Silverfish can eat a library in a weekend, I've heard."

"I took care of that bird like it was my own baby." Reed kicked at the pavement. "Silverfish! What kind of creature thrives in the Cascade?"

"You do. Or you think you do. Hey, you've got oyster crackers!" Burl pounced on the package and felt it. "I haven't seen any of those in a Jack Russell terrier's age. And what ever happened to oysters? We used to get oysters at that fish joint down on the river. They came in little goldfish cartons."

"It's just another one of those things," said Reed. "Probably overdosed on technetium."

"Oysters don't grow here anyway," Burl said. "You're joking."

"Well, wherever they grow, there's probably technetium or something worse in their breeding ground—their oyster beds?"

"Pyridoxine hydrochloride?" said Burl, reading from the ingredients list on the oyster-cracker package. "Disodium guanylate?"

"That sounds like bat shit," said Reed.

16

The next afternoon, after five hours of sleep, Reed padded barefoot outside for the morning newspaper, slung in its plastic duvet into the grass, which was wet from a light shower. At the bottom of the front page, a two-line heading stretched across a three-column story:

BLUE FLAMES AT PLANT MAY BE
SIGN OF NUCLEAR REACTION

Reed emitted an involuntary low whistle. Standing in the moist grass, he skimmed the story. It was about the blue fire on the scrap heap at the edge of the wildlife refuge. A couple of scientists from Boston claimed that the flames were from an underground criticality—a nuclear chain reaction. Goose pimples on Reed's legs began a chain reaction of their own and rippled to the back of his neck. He read on. Possibly the fire was Cerenkov radiation—charged radioactive particles from a nuclear reaction could give off a blue glow in water.

"Cerenkov radiation, my foot," Reed said to Clarence, who was waiting impatiently for Reed to join him in a game of knuckle-bone toss.

One of the scientists wanted to fence off the scrap heap and take core samples. Taking a core sample of a criticality-in-progress was a novel idea, Reed thought. Enrico Fermi didn't think of that one. The newspaper reported the blue flames as if they were as rare as the aurora borealis. But Reed himself had seen them probably a dozen times. He felt almost possessive toward the phenomenon.

When Reed arrived for his shift that night, he learned that a federal team had been there earlier and had left without comment.

"Blue fire when it rains?" Jim said with a laugh. "Well, now, that must be a nuclear bomb! Or else special effects from Hollywood!"

"It's aluminum shavings," a balding machinist nameless to Reed volunteered. "Or maybe uranium shavings. They'll bust out burning when they hit air."

"I'm sure uranium shavings are out there," Jim said.

"You can have hydrogen come out of a chemical reaction when water is there," Reed offered. "Or methane. Anything like that will cause a blue glow. Beryllium will catch fire if it hits the air." He added loudly, "Not that anybody would admit we have a beryllium problem."

"Don't ask me," said Jim, twisting his shoulders in an exaggerated shrug. "But if it was a chain reaction, wouldn't it have blown the whole place up by now?"

"I haven't seen it glow blue in months," a big guy known as Beau said. He had recently transferred from the tails station, where the depleted uranium was withdrawn from the Cascade.

The blue flames appeared just after Reed dreamed of the dead woman. The dream had visually faded, but she still lingered in his mind, the way the strontium-90 in global fallout settled in children's bones. He was grateful that he had not shared the blue flames with Julia.

He clocked in, a buzz of voices surrounding him. He checked his work package; he would be replacing a valve on the recirculating water system that cooled the Cascade. He wouldn't need the moon suit for that. After changing into his snot-green scrubs, he grabbed the man lift and shot upward.

Reed towed his toolbox down the painted lane to the job site and stopped at a stairway to a catwalk. Eisenhower was a ghost, just a smear of white on the toolbox lid.

"Farewell, Eisenhower!" Reed shouted to the cavernous space above him. "You were a good soldier—for a bird."

From a supply wagon, he selected a drive-impact wrench, about seventy-five feet of air hose, and a couple of chain come-alongs to pull piping. He carried them up to a section of catwalk above the cell rows, then returned for his oxyacetylene rig. It was hotter up there on the catwalk. Gazing up at the skeletal steel structure of the building, he imagined himself working lights at an arena concert, as his son, Dalton, had done one summer. While he manipulated his burning rig, his mind seemed to clear, along with the eyepieces in his goggles, as if he were peering through a retro crystal ball. The radioactive waste products from bomb-fuel processing had been left to accumulate and idle like abandoned old farm machinery. And now they were leaching into the ground and the water. Workers used to climb inside the large drums and cylinders to scrub them out with deadly cleaning chemicals like trichlorethylene, TCE, that got flushed into the soil. His father had done such jobs before him— without a respirator, without a TLD, without the anti-C suit and other precautions Reed took for granted. If his father hadn't died in a chemical accident, would he now be suffering from leukemia or liver cancer? At the plant there were plenty of cases right now, stark emblems of a hidden past, although the doctors would not draw that conclusion because they hadn't done the proper studies. His father and his coworkers had sacrificed their personal safety for the safety of the country. It was always put that way. Reed felt a spasm of grief, a longing for his father.

Of course the plant had hot spots, but he believed them to be contained. The plant was like a resort for wildlife. Raccoons and foxes played under the lights at night, and pigeons roosted on the steel stairways on the exterior walls of the Cascade. Just the other day, Reed saw a skunk scurrying beneath a piece of corrugated metal flashing. The old feed plant, where the UF_6 had been concocted, served as a storage shed for old equipment that was too hot to de-con. He thought of his mother at Sunnybank, stored among the use-less and decrepit, warehoused. The idea that his mother would die in the relatively near future still struck him as idiotic, a notion he couldn't bear. But from time to time another emotion suffused him: he might be glad when it was all over.

He remembered Nurse Linda saying, "Now don't let's have a pity party, Miss Kitty." He reminded himself that he would ride his hog off a cliff before he would have a pity party for himself in one of those final-home joints. The thought lifted his mood. He accidentally dropped a bolt through the steel grating of the catwalk and cursed.

Minimizing his motions, he finished the welding, repacked his tools, and carefully descended from the catwalk.

"I'm sorry to hear about your bird, Reed," said Kerwin later.

Reed nodded. "Eisenhower was a magnificent bird."

"He was great. I'm going to miss him!"

"He was no trouble at all. He was always waiting for me. Never complained."

"If the stuff we've collected here is so powerful, why hasn't some-body been building dirty bombs with it?" said one of the guys who had gathered to smoke. They were facing the cylinder yard, where hundreds of fourteen-ton cylinders of depleted uranium hexafluo-ride waited. Reed was gulping a can of orange soda and wondering whether intelligent life in other solar systems would take string the-ory seriously. The cylinders gleamed in the hard mercury lights.

"A lot of people love trying to churn up trouble, but we're talking jobs," said Ron. "I've got two babies to support."

"Hell, they could shut the plant down if this kind of thing keeps up," another of the younger guys said. "You know how these investigations go. And they could take the centrifuge somewhere else."

Jim, bearing a backpack, had appeared on his ten-speed personal transport.

"Nobody's going to shut the plant down," he said. "Corporate wouldn't do that—we're making too much money. It would take a federal investigation and an act of Congress to shut it down."

"Is that official?"

"They can talk about that blue fire on the scrap pile till they're blue in the face, but there's nothing new going on, really," Jim said. "It's what we've been dealing with all along—legacy waste. We didn't make that mess." He departed on his bicycle, its reflectors washed out under the vapor lights.

Reed was standing by the small grassy patch beneath a low exhaust vent. A clover plant was in bloom, big purple heads nodding in the flow of moist air from the vent. In winter the green spot turned to moss.

At home after work, Reed ate a head of lettuce over the sink and a can of beef stew—cold from the can. He felt like a slob, but nobody would know. He was dead tired. He took a long, hot bath, while studying illustrations in the Hawking book. A proton has two up quarks and one down quark, and a neutron has two down quarks and one up quark.

That day he slept soundly, heavy drapes darkening his windows. He dreamed that Albert Einstein was learning the fandango. The dream was long, with many practice sessions. Einstein seemed on the verge of getting the knack of the fandango, but then he would mess up. Then Reed dreamed that Enrico Fermi was eating an intact peach with a knife and fork. No one tried to stop him.

17

The next afternoon, when Reed arrived at Sunnybank, the director, a fashionably dressed but overweight woman with flawless makeup, informed Reed that his mother had eaten a good lunch, played miniature golf, and participated in a game of oral history.

"Oral history is a game?" Reed said, then slapped himself inwardly. Why was he always mocking people? He didn't mean to. He tended to forget that for most people irony existed only on the simplest level—jokey prattle about quotidian trivia.

In the hall he greeted a man, bald from chemotherapy, who was wearing pantyhose on his head; the legs had been cut off at mid-thigh and tied in a topknot. Although Reed recoiled, the thought of his own head in the crotch and belly of a woman's garment sent a wave of warmth over him, and then when he saw his mother, he had a distinct visual image of being born, descending from her belly, his bald head emerging from her like the tender tip of a penis. Did men spend their lives seeking that reconnection? Was that why women sometimes said that men think with their penises? He wondered if his brain was merely twirling on elementary Freud. He didn't really want to get into this with Julia.

When he entered his mother's apartment, she was standing by the window watching a bird feeder outside.

"Shhh!" she said.

There was no bird that he could see. Her bird clock, across the room, was silent. After a few moments, using the walker that she still had not mastered, she crossed the room awkwardly and sat down in her chair. He sat on the sofa—the old sofa she'd had for years.

"Gee, Ma, this is just like home. I hit that same spring on this cushion every time."

She smiled. He thought she still appeared drugged, even though the doctor had lowered the dosage of one of her pills. She sighed.

"No place like home," she said.

"Mom, I need you to talk to me about Dad," he said gently. "Can you think back and tell me what you remember about him?"

"What must I say?"

"Just tell me about when you met him, and what you did together, and were you happy? It's been a long time since he's come up in conversation."

She stared at the floor, and he was afraid he had provoked sad memories.

"Bones," she said. "No, never mind."

"Bones? Broken bones?"

"Bones and trouble. No, that's not what I mean." She paused, groping for words. "We had some trouble at the beginning. He'd start in the minute he got home, wouldn't have a drop all day, then he'd go through half a bottle of vodka. It looked like water in the glass."

Reed was surprised. "Did he get drunk?" he asked.

"Who?"

"Dad."

"No, he never got drunk. He didn't drink."

Reed realized she had been talking about Mort, her second husband, whose poisoned, corroded liver had killed him. She never acknowledged his drinking problem. She called it a touch of lumbago.

"Mom, get Mort out of your mind."

"He comes around here, just daring me to throw a pie plate at him. He had a woman with him. She laughed at me and said, 'I'm his sugar bun now.' What does he want from me?"

"Maybe he just wants to be waited on again. But you don't have to put up with him, Ma! Throw them both out."

"Hit the road, Jack," she said with a smile.

"That's right. You don't need him. He caused you enough trouble."

"Maybe Danny Daly will come back. I wouldn't mind seeing him."

"Oh, not Danny Boy! Haven't you met some fellow here who could entertain you? Isn't there anybody here you could strut around with?"

"These old men can't hop and bounce." She giggled. "There's one who always has his hand in his pocket, playing with himself! Shoot! Life's too short to mess around with these fools."

Reed kept probing—ruthlessly, he thought with regret later. She just wanted him there; she didn't want to rehash the bitter past. When an aide came around with a snack cart, his mother selected hot tea and macaroons.

"We're having afternoon tea, like the English," she said, as she fumbled with the plastic packet of cookies. She smiled. "Mort won't catch me now."

"The return of Mort," Reed said to Shirley on the telephone later that day. "Mom said he came back just to annoy her. He's been sneaking around. And he's got another woman. He's telling lies about Mom, blaming her for not taking care of him as well as this new woman does."

"I thought you talked to the doctor about her medicine," Shirley said.

"He's trying to calibrate it. But a nurse told me that this behavior is to be expected. Transition fantasy or something."

"Actually, that sounds just like Mom—only more so."

"She mentioned his drinking. She never did that before."

"She couldn't have taken care of him all those years if she thought he was an alcoholic."

"Well, I know she can't be happy with Mort around," Reed said. "And I sure don't want to run into him myself."

"Oh, Reed. Can't you ever be serious?"

He berated himself for waiting until too late to talk with his mother about the early days of the plant and her memories of his father. She probably knew little of the actual secrets, but she would know about the atmosphere of secrecy. He suspected that there was something crouching in the background that was larger than just the sieving process of isolating uranium isotopes. He didn't want to call Uncle Ed, who was a useless source, loyal to the core and given to platitudes. Reed wondered if he could find some answers in the library. Everything in his life seemed compartmentalized, like classifications in the Dewey decimal system. But at the library, instead of researching the history of atomic energy, he checked out a couple of books on molecular biology, so that he could have a conversation with Julia about her field—if the subject ever came up, and if he ever saw her again. She had told him on the telephone she was busy studying. He wasn't sure if she wanted to see him again.

Both nuclear physics and molecular biology were about secrets, he thought, mystery worlds within worlds. The books lay around on his coffee table, and every time he opened one, colorful diagrams of abstruse cellular processes jumped out at him like bouquets hidden in a jack-in-the-box.

One remarkable photograph grabbed him: the front parts of an unidentified insect magnified hideously forty times. It was a science-fiction monster with long, curved eyelashes and a hairy mouth and pincers and a shapeless shiny hard sheathing. *The Creature That Ate the Earth*, he thought.

The microscopic had a frightening character, not large and grand and soothing like the design of galaxies and nebulae. And Julia had insisted that he go right on down through the subatomic to the vibrating little strings. What was beyond or beneath the strings? Was it infinite? Wouldn't it be the same as Einstein imagined space-time—looping back on itself, seeming to be infinite but because of curvature finite without boundary? He thought of the doormat his ex-wife had once woven out of recycled flip-flops. He was plodding along by guesswork.

18

"Julia's into something a lot scarier than what I do at the plant," he told Burl one afternoon as they were driving to the lake with their fishing tackle. Clarence was riding between them, alert, polite, watching the road intently. Reed was at the wheel of his truck.

He tried to describe the library books for Burl. "Molecular biology is like trying to get a swarm of bees under a microscope so you can look for lice."

"Isn't that angels dancing on the head of a pin?" Burl said.

Reed laughed. "I haven't got past p-branes and quantum chickens, but now Julia's probably into genetic mutation. If I could get cloned, maybe she'd pay more attention to me."

"I thought that's what she was afraid of," said Burl. "You and all those chemicals."

"Let's catch some fish."

"Hey, good buddy, you're talking my language."

The outing to the lake, to a certain inlet that Burl was fond of, was restful. Clarence explored the woodsy shore, then settled down nearby while Reed and Burl fished, using the old cane poles they had had for years. Now and then they tossed Clarence a stick. The day was pleasant and not very humid. Out on the lake some motor-boats seemed to be racing, their occasional roar tearing the day. Late in the day a pair of F-15s from the nearby military base screamed down the lake, low and so fast they were almost hallucinatory.

"Cruising," said Burl. "Looking for girls."

The crappie and catfish had gone to deep water, and it was too hot to go out in a boat. Using a packet of crickets from a bait store, Reed and Burl fished from late afternoon till nearly dusk. They caught enough small-mouth bream to be satisfied, and they roasted a few of them over charcoals in a little throwaway foil kit someone had given Burl. After they had finished eating, he toasted some marshmallows over the dying coals. They tasted like fish. He had a six-pack, not enough to get drunk on. He wasn't in the notion, he said. His drinking followed its own internal rules. Reed had learned not to discuss the topic with him.

Leaning against some boat cushions in the truck bed, Reed and Burl watched the stars, old friends popping out like pixels as the dark deepened. It was peaceful here, away from Sunnybank and the plant. Clarence scrambled into the truck bed and lay on his side, his hot breath fanning Reed's legs. Mars was hanging in the sky, as brilliant and orange as the fat, bejeweled abdomen of an orb weaver.

"Man, Mars sure is a sight," said Burl, when Reed pointed it out.

Reed finished his beer and crumpled the can. He said, "Sometimes seeing the stars stops me in my tracks and makes me wonder who the hell I think I am."

"You should have studied astronomy. Then you wouldn't have been poisoning your guts."

"I don't have the patience for the math. But maybe I should study astronomy to keep my mind sharp—so I won't get Alzheimer's." They laughed. Reed said, "It's bigger than me. I know that. I look out there, and it seems like nothing much here matters."

"No, it's the other way around," Burl said, twisting away from Clarence's heavy breath. "I look out there, and I see that *this* is all that matters, right here and now."

"But that's where we get in trouble."

When they located Orion's belt, Reed said, "Did you ever hear about Project Orion?"

"C.I.A. or FBI?"

"NASA. Or whatever NASA was before it was NASA. Project Orion was a spaceship powered by atomic bombs."

"No shit. You're making that up."

"No. The idea was that one spaceship would carry a couple of thousand bombs to power it. One would go off every few seconds and shoot the ship out into space."

"That's the wildest idea I ever heard," Burl said. He actually guffawed. Reed was not sure he had ever heard a genuine guffaw before. Burl said, "It sounds like a rough ride."

"Might be. But if you've got them going off in a regular rhythm, then it would be like a putt-putt boat. Nuclear putt-putt."

"What if it exploded on the launch pad?"

"They'd launch it from orbit. This spaceship could accelerate to three percent of the speed of light! You could go to Mars for the summer."

"Did they do a test model in the lab with firecrackers?"

"Probably."

"How come they never built it?"

"The nuclear test-ban treaty."

"Right."

Reed had always been fond of doomed Project Orion. It was the prototype for his Reedmobile, one of the warp-speed breakthroughs that would allow him to whiz throughout the universe. As a kid, he liked to fantasize that the plans for the spaceship would be resurrected by the time he was grown, so that he could launch out to see the moon and the planets and the stars. He learned about Project Orion when the astronauts landed on the moon, and the thrill of space travel absorbed him throughout his adolescence. He always drew pictures of rockets in his school notebooks, and girls thought he was drawing penises.

"The Orion spaceship was shaped like a bullet," Reed said. "It had a huge plate on the tail, with shock absorbers, and the bombs would blast out the back in a big spray of fire and mushroom clouds."

"Man, Reed, you expect me to believe all that? You don't know Uranus from your elbow."

"Did you know there were rings around Uranus?"

"Like hell there are." Burl guffawed again. "Hey, see Orion's belt. Three stars? You know how he got his belt?"

"No idea. Karate?"

Burl said, "Orion put his belt on, but found he had gained weight and it wouldn't quite fit. So he asked Cassiopeia to let him borrow one of hers. She was a tad chunky herself. She flung him the belt, but its jewels were loose and they scattered across the sky: Venus, Mars, Saturn, Jupiter. Those are the big babies we notice. But there are many more, all over the heavens. At least that's the story I told my little niece."

Reed's imagination ranged beyond the planets. He tried to picture himself outside the Milky Way, in the large Magellanic Cloud, watching as Cassiopeia flung her baubles across the universe. Pinwheels of flashing colors whirled before his eyes.

19

*R*eed had been off for four days. Lately his schedule was four on, three off, three on, four off. He arrived at work at seven p.m. for his shift. He had slept all day with his ringer off and hadn't listened to the radio. When he reached the plant, he thought it was odd to see official state cars there so late. His first suspicion was a security breach, but the plant was well guarded. What could terrorists do, hijack a million-dollar cylinder of enriched uranium and drive it up the Interstate? Or perhaps they would go after a fourteen-ton cylinder of depleted uranium, but they would need a crane to get it out of the cylinder yard. Either way, they would need centrifuges to concentrate the radioactive isotopes. As for making a dirty bomb, he doubted if a terrorist could scrounge up enough fixings here among the piles of scrap.

He flashed his I.D. badge and was waved on through. "What's

up?" he asked the first person he saw in the parking lot, a lanky woman from the machine shop who was coming off shift. He couldn't remember her name.

"Haven't you heard?"

"Guess not."

"Some reporter is saying we've got plutonium leaking out. I don't believe it's true, though. We don't even use plutonium here. The media's so full of shit they don't know which end to sit on."

"Plutonium? Heaven and earth! I didn't even see the paper," Reed said. Because he was late, he had left it in the yard, under a bush, where the paper boy had tossed it.

"It wasn't in our paper; it was on the front page of the Chicago paper. How come they've heard of it and we haven't?"

In the process building several of Reed's coworkers were clocking in.

"Here I am, the innocent babe," Reed said as he punched his time card. "Fill me in. I overslept."

"Hell, Reed, it's all over television," said Teddy. "If you don't get your TV fixed, you're never going to know anything that's going on."

"Did I know anything when my TV worked?" Reed picked up the messages from his mail hole. "So what's this about plutonium?"

"They don't know how it got here, but those news snoops found it all over the place. Inside the fence and out." Teddy, still fearing beryllium disease, spat with projectile force into a waste can. He had been threatening to join the class-action suit, and he had filed a medical claim.

"Is this what the blue fire is all about?" Reed asked. He knew that plutonium could ignite spontaneously in the air, a thought too dreadful to voice aloud.

Several guys gathered by the tool shop, reluctant to speed to their jobs.

"Fucking unbelievable."

"What are they doing to us here?"

"How am I going to explain this to my wife?"

"I wasn't really shook up before, but what the fuck is going on?"

Jim rode up on his bicycle. "Hey, boys. I guess you know they're looking for plutonium now. I swear, this whole thing's turning into a treasure hunt."

"If it's plutonium, what keeps it from going critical?" Teddy demanded.

"Oh, it wouldn't," Jim said reassuringly. "There couldn't be enough in one spot. I doubt if it amounts to much of anything."

"You've been repeating yourself a lot lately, Jim," Reed said.

"I'm just doing my job, Reed. We don't want a panic now, do we?"

"Always the mother hen," Reed said. He was kidding, and he thought Jim knew that.

Jim said, "This is the solid truth, Reed. If I knew we were really in danger, I'd be the first to let you know."

"I bet the PR office is working overtime," Teddy said.

Reed wondered if the plutonium could be involved somehow in the manufacture of bomb triggers. Could that have been some of the plant's secret work in the fifties? He suspected that this latest report was true. When he had his worst exposure more than fifteen years before, he had tested positive for neptunium, a transuranic element, like plutonium. The transuranics, heavier than uranium, were fission by-products, part of the indiscriminate spray that occurred when atoms were fractured. He wouldn't ask then where the neptunium had come from. Plutonium had not been mentioned.

A couple of instrument mechanics bound for their shop lingered, caught up in the talk. One of them was wearing a purple-print do-rag and the other had a bucket of bolts in his hand.

"Where is this stuff coming from anyway?" asked the bolt guy. "Does anybody know?"

"I bet it's the scrap in the waste dump," said the other. "They must have found it there when they were cleaning it up. What do you know, Reed?"

"Hell, we've got all kinds of shit here," Reed said. He was sipping coffee. "We've had neptunium all along. And americium. They're all transuranics. You know there's a transuranics office on the second floor of Health Physics."

"That's next to where you go piss in a cup to see what you're picking up," one of the guys said.

"That's just for uranium."

A cell rat called Hot Nuts spoke up. "I've had neptunium on my body scan," he said. "They never said anything about it. It was no big deal."

The guys went on talking, but Reed grew quiet. The coffee tasted bitter and bad, as though it had been recycled.

One of the younger guys, an electrician named Mike, said, "I know about that transuranics office. They wouldn't just come out and say 'plutonium.' But it'll be all right. I know we're trying to clean it up. That must be what all the new ventilation systems are about."

"We're getting a royal house-cleaning."

"I wonder if the plutonium is in the underground plume that goes to the river," the big guy known as Beau said. "With the technetium."

"Isn't plutonium real heavy?" asked Mike. "Wouldn't it be slow?"

"The Transuranics, a heavy-metal group," Reed said. He thought he was joking, but his tone was flat.

"It's just a big scare to get the D.O.E. to shell out the money for cleanup. They've been promising that incinerator for years."

"Plutonium's not supposed to be here. What's it doing here anyway?"

"That's what everybody's wondering."

"It's just rumors. Hey, let's wait and see."

Jim had been parked there, straddling his bicycle, listening. "Hey, guys, let's calm down," he said. "This kind of thing gets blown up like a hot-air balloon. It's just some kind of accidental contamination. We'll straighten it out. Hell, this ain't Rocky Flats."

In the cramped, windowless break room of the maintenance division, Reed found a printout of the story from the Chicago newspaper. It said that four hundred picocuries of plutonium per kilogram had been found in soil samples outside the fence.

He whistled. "Those must be some *hot* hot spots!"

"Wonder what would happen if you stepped on a hot spot?" an instrument mechanic called Woolly asked, reading over Reed's shoulder.

"You wouldn't know it," said Reed. "Not like you'd know if you stepped in a puddle of puke."

"Reed's the big expert on exposures," Woolly said to a couple of guys hanging around the break room.

"I've been hotter than Reed has," said Beau. "When I worked at product withdrawal. Doesn't it stand to reason that would be the hottest place? You've got the assay up to five-and-a-half percent. That's as hot as you get here."

"U-235's chicken shit compared to plutonium," said Woolly.

"If one of these hot spots glowed, you could probably see it from the moon," Reed said, kidding along.

But inside he was raging. A Vesuvius of memory and awakening bitterness caused his guts to churn. He remembered the blaring siren, the rush to the de-con room, the sudden car-wash sensations from the force of the hot spigots trained on his body. The rawness of his skin, the scrubbing, the grittiness in his mouth. His skin felt as though he were being spray-painted with a high-pressure nozzle. And then it was over. He was naked, his hot scrubs sealed in a yellow rad bag. Someone handed him an old sweat suit to wear home.

The Chicago story offered little explanation for the plutonium, so he discarded it and picked up the local newspaper. Scanning headlines, he noticed a small story on page three that said a federal team had dismissed the blue-flame scare; there had been no criticality. I knew that, Reed said to himself. The federal team still was not sure what the blue flames were. He flung the newspaper onto the cabinet where he had found it. It seemed that everything nowadays was a pattern of hype and then deflation. It wearied him.

Reed's first job that evening was unclogging a section of barrier sieve with chlorine trifluoride, which, until he heard of the plutonium, he would have said was the most dangerous substance at the plant. He worked with a new gingerliness, handling the cylinder of CLF_3 with unusual precision and care. On the break, when half a dozen guys cornered off to smoke, he didn't join them. He stood outside the building alone and observed the sky, illuminated by strings of floodlights. The plumes of steam from the cooling towers flowed like gauze-veiled dancers through the lights. Plutonium was first named ultimium, he recalled, because it was thought to be the ultimate element. The symbol, Pu, was a joke. It should have been Pl. Reed appreciated the sense of humor, even though plutonium was not amusing. He was bothered by the thought that the transuranics might have been present when his father worked at this place. They could have been part of the atomic secrets so carefully guarded, and if they had been around so long, they could have permeated the place.

In the cafeteria at one a.m., Reed selected roasted chicken, lima beans, mashed potatoes, and salad. He ate perfunctorily, Atomic Man stoking himself with fuel. The chicken seemed undercooked, and the gravy on the potatoes tasted like paste. The chatter around was quieter than usual, threaded through with murmurs of disbelief. Later, he joined a bunch of guys gathered around a bicycle on the operations floor. It was slowly turning a circle on its kickstand, motivated by the vibrations of the Cascade.

At the end of his shift, he paused by his truck to watch the early light. He glanced toward the largest classified burial mound, the grassy rise where a mystery mix of toxic waste was buried. It was yellow-taped, off limits. An anthropologist studying the ancient Mound Builders might regard that mound as a likely target for study—a molded bank of dirt with a rich, intricate history, layers of houses and bones and garbage and pottery. One wouldn't expect it to hold a hidden curse, like something in a horror movie.

20

Another shock: Julia was waiting for him when he arrived home from his shift, soon after seven. After he quieted Clarence, she emerged from her chartreuse Beetle dressed for work and appearing fresh scrubbed, her hair still a bit damp.

"Plutonium!" she cried. "What's all this I'm hearing about plutonium?" Her face was pinched and anxious.

"Somebody forgot to mention it," he said, giving her a quick hello kiss. He noticed yesterday's paper and today's lying together, an intimate couple, under a weigela bush.

"Is there a lot?"

He stooped for the papers. "No, no. We would have known. It would have registered on our TLDs."

She reached for him and pulled him close. "I hate this," she said. "I'm afraid you're not safe."

"Don't worry, honey." Fumbling with the papers, he tried to embrace her.

Suddenly she loved him, he thought. Clarence was barking, as he always did whenever he saw Reed with his arms around a woman.

Julia said, "You know, we're going to pull the lid off of something one day and the whole world is going to collapse into it. What do you know about this plutonium?"

"It's made in a nuclear reactor," he said, opening the side door for her. "Hush, Clarence."

"Well, I know that! And I know the plant doesn't have one." She stood in the open door, forgetting to go through. Clarence entered before her. Reed guided Julia in, lightly touching her trim, firm behind.

In the kitchen, while he worked on coffee, he tried to soothe her fears. Had she lost a little weight? Her eyebrow pencil had been applied unevenly, making her left eyebrow seem fashioned with a T-square. Clarence stayed beneath the kitchen table, near Julia.

"How much plutonium do you think is out there?" she asked.

"It can't be much. Just a smidgen." He grinned. "About as much as you could get in your pocket."

"I wouldn't put any in my pocket!" She laughed. Again, she held on to him, her head on his chest. He hugged her tight. "I'm so worried," she said.

"I don't think it will amount to much. Anyway, it's not gamma rays. You can be in the same room with it and not get dosed."

"But I still wouldn't want to be around it."

He stroked her hair and tried to utter assurances. "There's fifty million gallons of all kinds of radioactive waste at that plant in Hanford, Washington. And what about Rocky Flats? They had Dumpsters overflowing with it. But they cleaned it up, and we will too. This is nothing compared to all that. It *can't* be that bad."

He broke away from her to pour water into the coffeepot.

"There's no safe level," she said.

He measured the coffee grounds slowly, precisely, as if he were still working with dangerous chemicals. "It can't have been much, or we'd all be dead by now," he said.

"Damn, Reed, I'm outraged! Why aren't you?"

"What good would that do?"

"I hope you haven't been in contact with it," she said.

"You know I'm always careful. I shower and scrub at work like I was trying to get cat piss out of upholstery."

He turned on the coffeepot, then held her shoulders and gazed directly into her eyes. "I don't like it—and sure, I'm a little rattled."

"What are they saying at the plant?"

"Oh, they're downplaying it. PR's working overtime." He selected two clean coffee mugs from the dishwasher. "To tell you the truth, I'm not sure everybody there knows much about plutonium. Anyhow, they're not going to get their jockstraps tied in a knot over it. It might cut off circulation." He grinned. "They don't know what to think."

She had hung her shoulder bag on one of the ladder-back chairs. She lifted it and began rummaging in it, as if she had brought along some cancer statistics. He stared out the kitchen window and thought about his love for her. It was as though he were meditating, holding a single thought, to steady himself. *We're in this together,* he thought. But he would never tell her about his exposures. He didn't want her to feel sorry for him, and he didn't want to scare her off. She zipped her bag and hung it on the chair.

"Did you want the blue mug with flowers on it or this tall, skinny one?" he asked when the coffee was ready.

"The blue one's fine. Thank you."

"You pick up a couple of hundred millirem a year just for living, you know," he said, pouring coffee. "Hell, there's americium in smoke alarms. Americium, the patriotic transuranic." He grinned.

"You still don't have a smoke alarm," she pointed out, glancing at the kitchen ceiling.

"So you want me to invite more carcinogens into my home?"

She smiled, acknowledging the contradiction in her thinking.

She sat at the table, sipping her coffee. In her lab coat and Dutch clogs, she seemed surprisingly fragile. Her concern for him made him feel elated; his fear that she didn't want to be around him because she might get contaminated took a twist.

He sat down in the chair nearest her and touched her forehead lightly. "I don't like to see your pretty face all scrunched up with worry."

She sipped more coffee. "How's your mom?"

"She's better, but she just sits in her apartment."

"Is she able to go out to lunch?"

"I guess so. We haven't tried it."

"I'm disappointed in you, Reed! You should take your mother out to eat or for a drive, if she's doing so well. And you have to keep her mind active."

"Hmm. I hadn't thought of that."

"Do you feel all right?"

"I never have anything wrong with me but my usual minor maladies. Or Merry Melodies."

"You mean Porky Pig? Or Bugs Bunny?" She smiled, warming to him.

"Bugs was my guy."

"I think Clarence loves me," she said distractedly, pushing the dog's nose from her lap.

"Let him sniff your hand. There. Good Clarence. Good boy. Julia's sweet." Julia gave the dog her hand, then moved it to Reed's leg. He said to Clarence, "She's so good I'm going to take her in my bedroom and love on her and leave you outside. You'll just have to be jealous!"

He was embracing Julia, and she was responding, her hands caressing his face. He was glad he had showered at work, and again he reassured her about that. She had come back to him. He relaxed, and they let some kind of mutual grief flow between them.

"I've missed your lip gloss so much I was tempted to go buy myself a tube of it."

"You can borrow mine," she said, as he was kissing her.

"I want you," he mumbled.

"I have to go to work," she murmured.

"This won't take long," he said.

She laughed. "Hey, not *that* fast!"

A memory of a cartoon, Pluto the Dog, flashed through his mind. He felt like Pluto, feeling a bit dumb and simple at the moment, overcome with stupid desire. Hastily, he shooed Clarence into the backyard, promising him his breakfast soon. When Reed returned and saw her standing by the door of his bedroom, he thought too late of his dirty sheets.

"Do you want to see a movie this weekend?" he asked, trying to slow down his approach.

"No, I've seen enough movies for a lifetime."

"Friday night let me take you to that fancy place where you dab your bread in a puddle of olive oil."

"I want their lobster penne," she murmured, as she began removing her lab coat.

"You got it."

On Friday, after his shift ended, he didn't sleep. Jacked up on coffee, he whirred through his house, cleaning it for Julia. He laundered the sheets, scoured the tub. He mowed the yard, trimmed the hedge, washed his truck. Sex on Tuesday morning had been so spontaneous that they both gasped at its pleasure.

"What a swell idea," she had said.

Mr. Como's was a white-tablecloth restaurant known as a combo-bistro. Historical photographs of the town covered the walls—old street scenes with department stores, even a series of construction scenes from the plant. Reed and Julia sat next to some 1930s photographs of factory workers.

Mr. Como was not serving lobster penne that night. The seafood special was grilled salmon drenched with lemon aioli sauce and rosemary orzo studded with yellow-pepper-and-portobello tidbits.

"I think I had a date once with Rosemary Orzo," Reed said as the waiter recited the specials.

"She was my roommate," Julia said, flirting with Reed.

The salmon was good. The breakfast-hour sex in the dirty sheets earlier that week had been exceptional. If he were writing a review, Reed would say it was delectable, with the pièce de résistance coming last. The restaurant was noisy, blaring like heavy-metal music, but he didn't mind.

"You're beautiful," he said.

He could not hear her reply. She was savoring her rosemary orzo.

"What a neat picture," Julia said, touching an old photograph on the wall beside her. Workers posed at a pants factory—mostly women in thin floral dresses. "All these women with their eager country faces. This would be during the Depression? And see that man up there at the top, with his arms folded and his elbows sticking out? I guess he's the paterfamilias."

"The pot of what?"

"Paterfamilias."

"Oh," he said. "I thought you said 'pot of camellias.' "

"It's noisy in here," she said, laughing.

"I'm deaf," he said.

The background music was drowned out by the loud chatter in the crowded room. He stopped trying to speak. He wondered whether she had thought he didn't know the word *paterfamilias* and so was covering for his ignorance. He concentrated on his salmon and braved the mound of tricolored, julienned roots. He smiled at Julia. She smiled back and mouthed something. He couldn't hear her words. He felt anxious, as if something were closing in on him, filling up his ears with cotton. The place was so loud. He began to sing. He sang "Chattanooga Choo-Choo." She kept smiling at him, kept eating. He chugged through a couple of the verses, feeling that he was boarding the train. The pants makers in the photograph seemed to shoot glances at him. He launched into his next selection,

"Wake Up Little Susie." No one in the restaurant—not the waiters, nor the patrons, nor the bartenders—noticed that he was singing. Everyone was busy—jawing, guffawing, gossiping, gulping, guzzling. Julia was smiling at him as though she loved every note. But no one else seemed to hear. He switched to "The White Cliffs of Dover," an unexpected challenge. He was sweating, and little caffeine-powered butterflies fluttered around his heart. When he finished, Julia applauded, and the waiter came and cleared away the dishes.

He listened to his messages while Julia was in the bathroom. His answering machine held a message from Burl. "Hey, Reed, I've just got one call, and I didn't have a lawyer, but they picked me up and I'm in the city jail. I did a naughty—D.U.I. Can you bail me out, good buddy?"

"Why don't I just say a prayer for you?" Reed said aloud to the machine.

Julia appeared, tucking her toothbrush into her purse. "I brushed my teeth," she said.

"Burl's in jail," he said. "And he expects me to bail him out."

"What happened?"

"It's not the first time. Burl goes to the liquor store, buys some whiskey, and starts drinking in the parking lot. The cops have learned to wait for him to open his pint and pull out into the road."

"What are you going to do?" Julia asked. Frowning, she slid out of her clogs.

"He can wait till morning," Reed said. "It's his chance to practice yoga. And a jail cell would make a great meditation space." His voice didn't hide his disappointment in Burl.

"Go ahead and get him," Julia said. "I need to go home and get some sleep anyway." She entered her clogs again.

"No, you don't," Reed said, grasping her waist.

"Maybe I won't go right away," she said, easing into his arms.

Reed telephoned the jail and told the turnkey, who sounded like a teenager, that he would fetch Burl in the morning, like a dog boarded at a kennel. "I want to be with you," he said to Julia.

In bed, he felt like a little boy, snuggling up to her. "I missed you," he said.

"I missed you too. You're so good to be with."

"We're good together, aren't we?"

"It feels right. Your arms are so hard and smooth."

"You have a nice feel, too, your sweet cheeks and your shiny nose."

She giggled. "Remember this?" She touched him with her long, angular fingers.

He spent a long time caressing her, shushing her, smoothing her hair, smooching. He wanted to make it last, to allay her fears and move her close to a hypnotic state. Being with Julia was like being in a luxurious spa. She was warm, liquid, steamy. He thought about being in a hot-tub with her and wished he had one. He decided to price hot tubs as soon as he got a chance.

They lay curled together, the stereo playing *100 Piano Masterpieces*. In his mind, she was playing the piano. He didn't know what would ever become of him, but he wanted this moment to last. After a while, when they were sitting up, talking, he told her about the dream of the woman shooting herself. Although the vividness of it had faded, he couldn't forget her children's pictures taped to the dashboard. The woman might have rearranged and caressed and considered those photographs for hours before she pulled the trigger, he said.

"That's awful! Why would you dream that?"

"My dreams don't have anything to do with me," he told her. "It's like I'm going to the movies and watching someone else's story. I didn't tell Burl about that dream, because he would say it's a premonition."

"Ha! Not that a hundred women didn't shoot themselves somewhere just today." Julia punched the pillow, her breasts moving against the sheet like a gentle surf. She said, "I could predict right now that a woman is going to get in her car with a gun and go shoot herself. I don't know who or where, but you can be sure it will happen." She shuddered. "Those psychics you hear about—they're just playing on something like that. A premonition of the probable."

Reed was aware of Clarence barking at traffic, but he didn't want to interrupt this train of thought with Julia.

He said, "So in my dreams I see some scene about somebody else, somebody I don't know and have no involvement with. Detached dreaming."

"You're standing outside your life?"

"Yes. And sometimes I'm not even asleep. Or the dream keeps haunting me when I'm awake, like it was something real that happened. Now what kind of sense is that?"

"Well . . ." She shifted against the pillow, as though she were going to summon an encyclopedic knowledge. She stared across the room at the dresser mirror.

He put two fingers on her mouth. "No, don't explain it."

He suddenly feared that she knew him very well. She cared enough to have figured him out. He was afraid to hear what she knew.

"Maybe it's a substitute for television," she said, joking. Giggling, she ripped the sheet off the bed, exposing their naked bodies. "Let's do it again," she said, her eyes dancing.

21

On the way to the jail the next morning, Reed was slowed by school buses. Children scooted across Constitution Avenue as if they were pushed by wind. As he waited, in a little fog of happiness, he thought about the evening with Julia. They had avoided talking about his job. For once, she didn't criticize or scold. She seemed to make a deliberate effort to make him feel warm and protected. They had rolled in his bed for more than an hour, and she had acted as if she had all the time in the world and as if her only goal was to give him pleasure. But then she left before midnight, saying she had to go to the university early the next morning to do lab experiments. Sex with her was urgent and timeless, and simultaneously it seemed like a great joke. Their kisses and caresses were punctuated by little jokes and giggles. But there was still something about her he couldn't reach. It was as if, unlike most of his women, she didn't need a commitment from a man. She could take care of her own needs. She seemed so levelheaded that she couldn't be hurt or disoriented. Yet that couldn't be true. He realized how careful they were with each other. He tried hard to avoid saying foolish or inappropriate things. She politely tiptoed around sensitive subjects. They didn't seem to trust each other fully. There was something he didn't know about her. Or was he the problem? Was she standing back from him, afraid he might have a core of heavy metal where his heart was? Still, she had come to him, and he was on fire, with or without a major transuranic in his system. She had remarked upon the clean sheets.

The jail was a nondescript aluminum-sided annex tacked onto an elegant nineteenth-century brick courthouse. When the annex was built a few years before, people complained that the jail spoiled the beauty of the courthouse. But, Reed asked himself, why should a jail be tastefully designed? Did Frank Lloyd Wright ever design a jail?

Reed waited for paperwork. Burl had no family he could call upon, except his sister, Sally, who was pious and relentlessly suburban. His brother—a CPA with pretensions—lived in Detroit, and his grandmother, who depended on him to mow her grass and fetch her groceries and prescriptions, couldn't do anything for him.

Burl appeared, glaring at Reed. "You sure took your time getting here," he said.

"Isn't your motto 'Happy to be anywhere'? I thought I'd let you catch up on your sleep."

"They stripped my license this time, Reed. Six months."

"No kidding."

"They impounded my truck and now I have to get somebody to pick it up."

"Oh, shit," Reed groaned. He headed out of the Customer Parking area behind the jail. Burl was a good customer, he thought.

Burl said, "I'll have to drive anyway, though. I have to do another job for Mrs. Patterson, and I have to get Grandma her groceries. And I've got a job starting next week where they're building that new pizza place—another goddamn eyesore the world needs like it needs another strip mine."

"You need a chauffeur."

"I need some ham and eggs," Burl said.

"Didn't they feed you?"

"Leather-and-onions. And wallpaper-paste gravy. That was last night. This morning it was coffee they had left over from their Christmas party. And they had square rubber eggs. Jail cuisine leaves something to be desired."

Burl drummed his fingers on the dash. He was jittery. He needed coffee. He bounced in his seat. He jerked to inaudible music. Reed drove to Dinah's Cafe, where they nodded at the regulars and settled into a wooden booth. The waitress who took their orders eyed Burl's dirty T-shirt and naturally distressed denim. He tipped his greasy cap to her, a thin high-school girl with braces. She was clumsy with the coffeepot, sloshing the liquid over the rim of his mug.

"The way I look at it is this," said Burl after she left. "We're going to need more than colonic irrigation to deal with this plutonium thing. We're going to have to call in the big guns. It's going to take more than a prayer breakfast, buddy. You're going to need Jesus to descend from his throne with a Geiger counter and something like a heavenly minesweeper."

"I'm sure he'll know what to do, Burl," Reed said.

"I don't know transuranics from Transylvania. But Reed, you know as well as I do that a lot of guys out there are getting cancer. There it is, the bottom line."

Reed was genuinely touched. Apparently Burl had been thinking all night on the problem. Even though Reed had never gone into detail with Burl about his particular exposures, Burl had always claimed that Reed had routinely absorbed too much radiation on the job.

Reed gazed out the window at the parking lot for a moment.

"Did I tell you I'm seeing Julia?"

Burl's jaw dropped—a proverbial jaw-drop, Reed thought. "No shit," Burl said quietly. "Hey."

The food came, and Burl assailed his sausage and pancakes.

"She going to take you back?"

"She's after my body." Reed grinned.

"*That* body?"

"Thanks, buddy." With deliberation, Reed peppered his eggs. Then he said, "She's flipped out over the plutonium."

"Wasn't all the stuff coming out of the plant the reason she left you before?"

"I guess. But now it hit her harder. She says it's more real somehow." He stirred his coffee and sipped it. "The jailhouse coffee couldn't have been worse than this," he said.

"Believe what I say, Reed," said Burl. "I may not know much, but I know coffee. So is it more real?"

"Depends on what that means. What's real? What if we learn that transuranics were bubbling through the Cascade all these years and we didn't know it—wasn't it as real then as it would be now? If we knew it was real, somehow that seems unreal to me."

"You're jawing in circles."

"It's Schrödinger's cat all over again! We can't get away from that darn tomcat. It's both there and not there. Like you in your jail cell." Reed lifted his coffee mug. "Julia's wondering how you're coming along reconciling Christianity and relativity."

"Oh, I'm working on it. Tell her I'm working on it."

Reed dropped Burl at his house, one of those hastily built little frame dwellings that popped up in the fifties during the plant construction boom. Burl had bought it at auction and with his carpentry skills he had repaired its sagging structure, so that now it was sturdy if not attractive.

"Call me when you need a ride," Reed said.

"I'll get Rita to drive me around."

Rita was a woman Burl went out with from time to time. She could outdrink him, and Burl said she had an "incredible butt."

"Wasn't she mad at you?"

"Yeah, but she's been in a good mood lately. I bet she'll go with me out to the fairgrounds tonight. It's Christian night, and they're having Christian rappers and rockers. Want to go?"

"What *isn't* the church into these days?" Reed said. "Wrestling matches? Do they have a gift shop? Do they have ATMs at church?"

"Have your fun," said Burl. "But one fine day you'll stand in the heavenly dock."

"That might be any day now, at the rate I'm going."

*R*eed greeted Clarence and filled his water bucket. Clarence had dug a new dirt bowl under the umbrella of the mimosa. The fenced yard was virtually bare, owing to Clarence's warlike depredations. Feeling a small surge of freedom, Reed romped with him around the oak tree in the center of the dog's domain. Reed was released, momentarily. Free. To be a skunk, if he wanted to. To rat out, monkey around, stomp on bugs.

"Hey, Clarence. Catch." He tossed a worn-out leather glove. "Kill it, boy!" Clarence grabbed the glove and shook it deftly. Reed growled to get Clarence going, and Clarence, the glove falling from his mouth, began cutting didoes in the backyard, huge figure eights around the oak trees. He was unstoppable, a master dog, a killer dog, the only being Reed felt he could truly rely on. Clarence loved him without question, and Clarence would kill for him if he had to. Reed envied him. He'd like to be Julia's killer dog.

He was catching his breath between disasters. He didn't want to visit his mother at Sunnybank or take her out driving or try to get her into a restaurant with her walker, as Julia had suggested. The energy fueling his fear for his mother had flipped him onto another level—flat and gray and stoic. He wanted to think she was all right for now. After the doctor made further adjustments to her medicine, she hadn't mentioned Mort again. Reed would wait to be surprised by the next episode threatening her life. Meanwhile, he needed a respite from her, which he intended to fill with Julia. That was natural enough, he thought—unbuckle himself from the umbilical, go for Julia hard and fast, wrap himself with her, their limbs intertwining and flailing and knotting into a throbbing ball.

"Clarence! Bring me the glove! Get it!"

Clarence bounded and dove, brought the glove like a retriever, then gazed at Reed with the collie-love look, that show-dog quality that could be a ruse and a pose. Or it could be genuine love, Reed thought.

*J*ulia actually telephoned him on Sunday, suggesting that they take his mother to lunch. After months of being unreachable, Julia was right there now. Reed was driving. His mother was fastened into the front seat, and Julia was in the back with his mother's folded-up walker.

"I would have driven you in my new car, Mrs. Daly," Julia said, leaning forward. "But it's one of those little cars. It might hold a dozen clowns at the circus, but it's so low to the ground I was afraid it would be uncomfortable for you."

"Aren't you glad we're not in my truck?" Reed said. Their destination was only a few blocks away.

"I haven't been out riding around in a year," his mother said.

"Hasn't Reed taken you anywhere?" Julia said. "He should take you out on the river gambling boat."

Reed's mother laughed. "I may have lost my marbles, but I don't want to lose my money too."

"You're doing great, Mrs. Daly," Julia said. "For someone who has had a stroke, you're doing incredibly well."

"Reed would do well to settle down."

"I *am* settled down, Mom."

"Reed never knows what he wants," his mother said.

"Oh, I *do*. She's sitting in the back seat." He glanced in the rearview mirror but didn't catch Julia's eye.

Captain Mack's swarmed with the Sunday after-church crowd. It took about ten minutes to get his mother inside. While waiting for a table to be cleared, she clutched Julia's arm and leaned against the walker. Julia wore black pants and a blue silk shirt. His mother had on a bright floral blouse with a ruffled throat. Together they seemed chummy and elegant, Reed thought.

When their table was ready, Julia helped her sit down, and Reed folded the walker and placed it against the wall behind him.

"I want liver-and-onions," his mother said, before the menus were dispensed.

Reed nudged Julia. "It's lip-smacking good," he said.

"Liver has more cholesterol than eggs," she said, making a face.

"Julia's afraid of cholesterol. She was traumatized in childhood by a giant egg," Reed explained to his mother.

"He's teasing," Julia said, touching his mother's arm. "It was a Halloween costume my sister wore."

Reed's mother made an effort to read the menu, but she was awkward with her reading glasses. Reed read the printed insert of specials to her. Julia wanted sparkling water, which Captain Mack's didn't have. So she asked for plain water. Reed's mother ordered the liver-and-onions, with mashed potatoes and broccoli, and Reed ordered a strip steak and French fries. Julia chose baked flounder. Waiting for the food, Reed sat back in his chair and regarded the two women, who were laughing together, the way women did in that easy intimacy they fell into within two minutes of meeting. Their laughter made him feel good, even though it excluded him. His mom was definitely better, he thought. The doctor had calibrated her medicine, and she seemed much less dopey. Reed knew she wished she could be playing poker.

He turned to Julia. "I bet you didn't know that my mom was on the stage when she was younger."

"Oh, wow," said Julia, holding her water glass paused halfway to her mouth.

"How would you know that?" his mother asked him.

"She was in the Atomic Players back in the fifties," Reed said to Julia. "She was in *The Glass Menagerie*."

"I'm impressed," Julia said. "I'd love to have seen you on the stage, Mrs. Daly. A leading lady."

"Reed needs a woman around," his mother said.

"Julia's too busy for me," Reed said. "She's always studying."

"I'm studying for exams and I work at the lab all week," Julia said.

"Julia studies salamanders," Reed said to his mother.

"Is that on the menu?"

When Reed and Julia burst out laughing, Reed's mother laughed too, insisting that she was just joking. "I'm not that addled," she said.

For several minutes, Julia trotted through an enthusiastic description of the genome project, which didn't register with Reed's mother. Reed had to admit that genetics didn't inspire him—it was too much like genealogy—but he loved to watch Julia bubbling her information. The food arrived then.

During the meal, Reed's mom said to Julia, "You eat like a woodpecker."

Julia choked on her food. A dot of flounder flew from her lips.

"That's not what I meant."

"Oh, I'm sorry," Julia said. "I wasn't laughing at you."

"You've been listening to your bird clock, Mom," Reed said. "But you may be right about Julia. You should see the holes in my siding."

Now his mother laughed. She tried to do the Woody Woodpecker call, and her face turned red. Julia cracked up.

"Bring us all some pie," Reed said to the waiter.

22

All over the city plutonium continued to be the topic of rumor and gossip, like a celebrity awash in the aftermath of a fresh transgression. The official word was minimal. "We're looking into it." "It's not part of any present function of the plant." "It's of no danger to employees or the community." The Department of Energy was sending a representative. According to a press release, the plutonium that had entered the plant was "an insignificant amount."

Reed swam through the theories and the official statements, the terse assurances of the well-oiled managers.

"They're saying it came in the fucking feed stock—back in the fifties," Teddy said. "It's been here all along, I heard."

"They brought in reactor tails," Jeremy J. offered. He was leaving the day shift, and he ambled out the door indifferently.

Reed pieced together a version of the story from the guys coming and going. It was part rumor, part speculation, part memories of men who remembered the tales from older, now retired workers. They claimed the plutonium had arrived over a period of twenty years in secret shipments of reactor tails—spent uranium fuel rods that had been used in nuclear reactors to make plutonium for atomic bombs. The plant recycled the fuel by retrieving the last remaining traces of valuable uranium. But plutonium—and other bomb-making by-products—had contaminated the material. When the stuff sped through gaseous diffusion, the contaminants lingered behind, clinging to the lining of the pipes in the Cascade.

"The plutonium got into the nickel lining," a chemical engineer with an office job explained to a group of process workers from Reed's division. "You can't get nickel really clean and purified. So my guess is there's a residue of plutonium in the system—but that would be totally insignificant."

"So that accounts for the technetium too," Reed said. And neptunium, he thought.

"What about the warheads? Didn't some of it come in on the warheads?" an older man in the gathering asked. His name was Bert, and he was an old-timer Cascade operator.

"What were warheads doing here?" Reed demanded. "Warheads? What the fuck?"

"Not my bailiwick," the chemical engineer said.

As the engineer bustled away with his clipboard and his advanced degree, Bert turned to Reed. He was gray haired, probably in his early sixties.

"I know who knows all of that, Reed," he said. "Wes Thornhill. You know him. He used to work with your daddy."

Reed nodded. He hadn't seen Thornhill in years.

"He probably knows all about it," Bert said. "They were both here when those reactor tails came in. And the warheads. I heard a lot about the warheads."

"Thanks, Bert. I'll look him up." Reed disappeared into the break-room kitchen and found a bag of pretzels and a ginger ale.

In full C-zone dress, he squeezed through narrow niches inside a dusty cell on the cell floor, where the UF_6 gas rushed through the pipes in dizzying monotony, washing through the barrier sieves again and again until the uranium-235 isotopes were isolated. Tonight, the process seemed different. If transuranics had somehow gotten into the Cascade, the atoms would have become embedded in the walls of the pipes, jostling loose here and there and sloshing finally into the wastewater that poured through drainage ditches through the wildlife refuge and out to the river. Some of the atoms might be in the aqua cylinders near the parking lot. Plutonium, slower than a tortoise wearing lead boots, was so very heavy that it probably had not traveled very far. When Reed wriggled inchmeal from the cramped space, he imagined he could feel hot wind blowing through fissures in his moon suit.

23

It was nearly two weeks before his schedule meshed with Julia's again, but they had talked on the telephone twice late at night. He supposed it was a version of phone sex. She had described, her voice sensuous and breathy, the replication of some bacteriophages she was studying.

He scoured the toilet and changed the sheets, even though they weren't really dirty. When she arrived, he was waiting for her outside in the blazing late-afternoon sun. Her dusty chartreuse Beetle needed hosing down, he noticed. She had on a clashing color, a skinny red tank top, with faded jeans and her usual worn brown clogs with the loose straps.

Reed pointed out Clarence's dust bowl beneath the mimosa. "The heat wave's getting to him, but he's so macho he won't admit he's about to faint."

Reed curved his arm around Julia, feeling her warmth radiate through him, as though the freckles on her arms were sparks. He sang the syllables of her name.

"I brought you some fennel toothpaste," she said, taking the tube from her purse. "It's natural stuff, with no carcinogens."

"Good. I'll use it to clean the plutonium out of my tooth sockets."

In the kitchen she hooked her shoulder bag on a ladder-back chair and set her satchel of books and papers on the table. She frowned at a speck on her arm.

"Find a microscopic toxic-waste dump there?" he asked, touching her arm. He was going to kiss it, but she pulled away.

"Why did you say that about your tooth sockets?"

"Just joking. Hey, why so uptight?"

"Plutonium collects in the bones, doesn't it?"

"Maybe. I was just making a joke."

"Do you think there's any plutonium out there at that place where you had me *frolicking* around so innocently?" she asked.

"I told you there's just old TNT chemicals out there."

While reminding her that those chemicals at the munitions works predated the atomic plant, he was aware of the flexing of her nostrils.

"Don't worry, honey," he said. "It's thinned out by now. And that stuff's not radioactive anyway."

"But someone told me yesterday that the plant dumped tons of radioactive slag in those bunkers out there."

"Oh, slag is everywhere. I doubt if it would cause a Geiger counter to panic."

"I'm not so sure about that."

Some of the administrative personnel had desk doodads fashioned from gray slag—helpless-looking elephants and dinosaurs. Slag was merely a by-product of conversion, turning used UF_6 into D.U. metal and greensalt. Reed was used to seeing piles of it around.

"So what are they saying at work about all this now?" she asked.

"There's a lot of buzz. Nobody really knows anything."

"Or wants to know?"

"We've been over all of this before, Julia."

"I know. But I can't get it out of my mind."

"This may be just a big scare that's going to blow over, you know." They were leaning against the kitchen counter. He touched her shoulder tentatively. "How do we know those guys with their Geiger counters were right about how many picocuries they found?"

"Well, I myself wouldn't want to work at a place that had any picocuries, whatever excuses anybody could think up." She stiffened her spine, as if she had just remembered the rules of good posture.

"It's not much plutonium," Reed said in a tone like hollow boasting. "Management said it couldn't have been more than half a pound altogether."

He filled a measuring cup with water from the tap. "It couldn't have been more than this," he said. "Eight ounces."

"Fifteen ounces, I heard. This morning the TV said fifteen. If I remember my chem classes, that's a lot of plutonium."

"Depends on how it's distributed," he said, pouring the water down the drain. He imagined the atoms of a pound of plutonium scattered through the spent fuel, like a pinch of salt mixed throughout the dark load of a coal barge.

She said, "And the news guy on TV said nobody really knows how much got in. It could have been a lot more. A *ton*."

"A ton. You really believe that?"

He gave her a bottle of beer and she rejected a glass. He opened a beer for himself. After they were settled down on the back porch, where there was a breeze, he said, "At Rocky Flats they had eighty-nine tons of it. They tried to mix it in big slabs of concrete and float them in water, to stabilize the stuff, but the concrete wouldn't set up and it turned into jelly. They call it plutonium pudding." He laughed.

She said, "You told me once that working with uranium was hilarious, but I guess plutonium is just a real laugh riot. Those buggers could make a comedy duo. They could juggle isotopes."

"Buggers. Nobody around here says that. That must be a Chicago thing."

"You're changing the subject. That means I'm too wound up."

She made the gesture of zipping her mouth shut. Learning made her excitable. He always loved the way she spewed out new information. But now he saw how distraught she was.

"Let's get this straight," he said. "Don't worry about one day out in the woods. There can't be any plutonium out there at Fort Wolf; it's so heavy it would take years to get out there. It's all inside the fence, or close by."

"But it's *you* I'm worried about. Working at that place."

"Well, thank you, but I think it's been blown out of proportion." He noticed his leg was jiggling, as though the vibrations in the Cascade had hijacked his nervous system.

She was stroking the long neck of her beer bottle in an unconsciously suggestive way, Reed thought. It didn't mean anything.

She said, "I don't understand your loyalty."

He rose from his deck chair to adjust the awning against the western sun, so that she wouldn't be sitting with her face in the sun. He stared over the porch rail at the neighbor's grass, which was being smothered by a growth of broadleaf weeds. He tried to think.

Facing her, he said, "Working there is a sort of destiny."

"Destiny?" She laughed. "Go on. Tell me about karma. And predestination!"

"I've told you—my uncle and my dad worked there. It's what I was brought up to do."

"I know, but . . ."

"What I'm saying is I have a responsibility. The safety of the plant depends on guys like me. We're responsible for keeping the Cascade going, and that's important. If you do a good job and keep the thing humming, then you *do* develop a little pride and loyalty.

It's just in the atmosphere of the place. I mean the Cold War and national defense—"

"Better dead than Red—isn't that a little outdated?"

He ignored that. "Maybe I don't mean destiny. It's a legacy."

"That sounds like legacy waste."

"It boils down to this: the place is safe now. And if I picked up some bad stuff in the past, then I can't undo that. It's safe now, because of guys like me. Give me a little credit, Julia."

She didn't reply. She was watching the sunset. He had bullied her again. He didn't know why he was compelled to do that. He turned her toward him.

Quietly, he said, "You know I'd do anything in the world to keep you safe. That's my job. It's the one thing I'm good at."

"That's not all you're good at," she said, with a hint of a smile.

"Let's relax," he said, touching her forehead lightly.

"I'm sorry. I get wound up and I just go like a yo-yo."

"Come here. Let's yo-yo together." He nodded toward the bedroom.

She squeezed his arm and nudged him with her shoulder like a cat rubbing on someone's leg.

A rampant red honeysuckle shaded the west side of his back porch, and later they sat there with a bottle of zinfandel. Julia approved of his choice. She admired his garden. Most of the tomato vines were drying up, but the beefsteak tomatoes were fat and heavy. He placed some marinated chicken breasts on the grill, although he had vowed to stop eating chicken because of all the poultry that fell off the trucks that carried them to be murdered. He washed a choice tomato for their meal and shucked the corn he had bought that afternoon. Earlier Julia had spent some time with her books, and now, while he manipulated the grill, she filed her nails and did some arm exercises, as if she couldn't waste a minute. They had dropped the touchy subject of plutonium, but he was disturbed that he might have driven her into silence.

The heat of the day made the sky shimmery and their skin glisten. As they ate, twilight disappeared into night. The fireflies were winking their frantic courtships. The stars were coming out, faintly, and Mars was setting.

"What was the Greek name for Mars?" Reed asked. "Do you remember?"

"No. Why?"

"Just wondering about Greek gods."

She laughed. "Wondering if you're one?"

"I like to imagine myself out there, in the heavens, tooling around with Mars and Orion and all those guys."

"Parading around like a Greek god, huh? Were you in a fraternity in school?"

"No. They wouldn't have me."

She said, "When I look at the stars I think about the world coming to an end. I feel there's so little time. I feel like everything is urgent." She stared at her lap.

"Relax, honey." He scooted his chair nearer to hers and reached for her hand.

She tuned up an octave or so. "You know very well that the pit facility I keep hearing about is just nuke-speak for bomb factory. I wouldn't be surprised—I have no doubt—this country is already building a whole new generation of bombs. Didn't you say the D.O.E. never tells what it's up to?"

"That's the nature of the beast," he said.

She crossed her legs and then uncrossed them. "I read up on this, on the Internet. They're talking about a 'plutonium pit facility' as a way of 'refurbishing the arsenal.' Did you ever hear such language? Refurbish the arsenal! It sounds like redecorating. But what they mean is they can go ahead and make little bombs without violating the nuclear freeze. Or seeming to. The whole nuclear show will be on then, and sooner or later—"

"Honey, the mind can't hold a thought like that." He tried to caress her face, but she jerked away from him. "O.K.," he said. "Turnabout is fair play. What good would it do to find a cure for Puumala or Ebola if you think the world is going to end soon anyway?"

"Am I *that* paranoid?"

"Shhh." He drew her close to him, and she softened. "Look. Right now I've got you, and the stars are out. What could be better? And nothing should stop us from just enjoying the hell out of a good bottle of wine on a fine Friday night. We have to go about our business, no matter what might happen."

"Well, then, I have a question," she said, touching his cheek. "What time does the Jiffy Lube open in the morning?"

She gathered their plates, deftly arranging their stripped corncobs on top, and headed for the kitchen. "Don't move," she said. "I'll do this." Through the window he saw her set the dishes on the counter and disappear into the bathroom. Reed stood and leaned against the porch rail to get a better view of the sky. Only a few stars were visible. Although the city lights obscured it, the Milky Way was spread out somewhere overhead, a blanket of vapor as insubstantial as morning fog. Julia's pessimism wasn't really like her, he thought. He threw a scrap of chicken skin over the porch rail to Clarence.

Julia returned, the kitchen light flashing through the porch door into the darkness. She stood with her back to the rail, blotting out a section of stars. The evening was still sweltering, and he suggested they go for a drive by the river. He let the car's air-conditioning run for a few minutes before they got inside. The bank marquee said 86 degrees. At the downtown riverfront, bunches of people were strolling. A piebald dog dashed by. Reed parked, and they walked along the riverfront, in the shadow of the concrete-and-steel sports stadium.

"Have you been to any of the games here this summer?" he asked her.

"No, I don't have time to go to games."

"Gotta hurry up and cure the plague, I know."

She didn't reply. Reed kicked himself. Where did he get this put-down style of his—from his father? He had no idea if his father ever cracked a joke. Across the river the lights of the chemical plant burnished the sky. Flames shot from a tower. On the river, a barge was gliding past, and in the distance one of the foghorns blasted. Sheet lightning flashed on the horizon, as if responding to the sound.

Reed stared into the dark, swift water. He said, "I say all the wrong things, and I don't know why. I don't mean to do that." He laid his arm around her shoulders. "But I don't know what's going on with us."

She was thinking for a while before she answered. "I'm under a lot of pressure," she said. "I have to finish this lab experiment tomorrow on T-4 bacteriophages and—"

He groaned. "I should have known it would be bacteriophages."

"My exam is Tuesday night. And I'm thinking about going to Chicago in a couple of weeks. My sister's got something going on— I don't know what it is, but I'm worried. I don't know if she's sick or depressed or just doesn't want to tell the family some embarrassing secret, or what. I haven't heard from her in two months, and I've called several times."

Reed grasped Julia's small, damp hand. "Is this the sister with all the kids?"

"Yes. Diana. She had her first baby when she was seventeen—and she's got four kids now and she's only thirty. She had two bad husbands, and she hasn't been very happy."

"When are you thinking of going?"

"I've got two weeks' vacation coming, but I really do need to see Diana, and maybe I'll just go for a weekend. I want to help, but she's so independent."

"What could you do?"

"Well, I don't know. I just have to go see. She needs to know she's loved."

"I could take you up there."

"No, that's all right. I need to handle this myself."

"I wish you had told me about this."

They reached the center of the plaza outside the stadium, where a postmodern fountain flung river water to the sky, while a spotlight paraded over it, colors shifting. Around the perimeter of the fountain, jets spurted water into the air at a specific velocity so that it fell down in a straight line of perfectly spherical drops, like hail. The little water bombs rained precisely, and their rush and plop created a semblance of music.

"I love this," Julia said, standing so that the drops bounced on her. She squealed. "They sting! Come on, stand right here and let the drops hit you." She maneuvered him around. "There!"

They laughed, standing side by side, holding hands, letting the large drops of water pummel them until they were soaked and felt they had had expensive massages.

On the way home, they drove by Burl's house, but he wasn't home. His vehicles were there, but only his porch light was on.

"He must be out with Rita," Reed said. "She's been giving him rides since he lost his license."

"Is he serious about her?"

"Is Burl ever serious?"

"Am I too serious?"

"No, you're just right—Goldilocks."

He got her to laugh. The bank marquee had gone down to 82.

Reed wanted Julia to lean on him. He wanted to go along with her to Chicago. He had plenty of time to make the trip next weekend, since he was working three on, four off during the coming week. But she didn't bring up the subject again, and he didn't push it. She spent the night in his bed—a hot, unexpected bundle, her little whistly breaths like faint music.

In the morning, she was ready to leave his house without any breakfast. Once again she was a woman with a mission, a hundred things on her mind—school, daughters, telephone calls, errands, the Jiffy Lube. Her red tank top had grease stains on it from the chicken they had eaten the night before. Her hair had frizzed in a peculiar way, from all the heat and action in bed, he thought. She scooped her panties—a little silky black heap—from the floor and stuffed them into her shoulder bag.

Barefoot, and carrying her book satchel, he followed her out the door. He set her bag in the passenger seat as she slid behind the wheel.

"I meant to hose off your car," he said.

"That's all right."

He walked around the car to her window.

"Can I see you again next weekend?"

"I'm sorry, Reed. I love to be with you, but I go nuts sometimes over this crazy business you're in."

"You know I love it."

"I don't want to insult you, Reed, but you don't work in national defense. You work for a corporation out for profit. What do they care about *you*?"

She turned the key. The car purred.

"Don't you think maybe you're being a little dishonest with me?" she said. "I always feel you're holding something back. I'm like somebody in those dreams you were describing. What did you call them? Detached dreams. That's how you look at me sometime."

"Let me take you to Chicago then," he said. "We'll find your sister."

She shook her head. "No, I need to do that myself. Don't worry."

"I wish you'd let me help."

"Bye-bye," Julia said, waving from her car.

"You forgot to take some tomatoes!" he called, but she didn't hear him.

He watched her car turn at the end of the block and head toward the boulevard. He was angry with himself, but he was a little angry with her, too, although he could see her point of view. If she knew about his exposures, perhaps she would be sympathetic, but he was afraid she would retreat. Why would she take a chance on him if she knew?

Reed picked up the newspaper from the grass and flipped through it as he walked back into the house. The radio was playing *Saturday Classics*. He poured a second cup of coffee and nursed it while he skimmed through the news.

Every day there had been lively letters to the editor about the plant. Today a civic leader had written an op-ed column with the headline, GIVE PLUTONIUM A CHANCE: SURPRISE HEALTH BENEFITS. Reed read a breezy account of the healthful qualities of plutonium and radiation in general, not only in nuclear medicine—where would we be without the old-faithful cobalt treatments?—but in life-giving traits. The essay traveled from normal background radiation to X-rays to irradiated foods. The civic leader had personally been cured of lung cancer with cobalt. And countless prostates had been treated with implanted radioactive seeds that zapped cancer cells. The writer concluded, "The flap over plutonium is just one more example of how our society is trying to test and examine everything to death. The human race cannot survive this kind of willful tizzy."

Reed sat in his kitchen and laughed, the first good laugh he had had in a while. He wanted to say to Julia, "You're in a willful tizzy."

24

When Reed got Burl on the telephone, Burl said, "Rita and I drove past Atomic World yesterday. That place was crawling with all kinds of official cars! I thought there must be a grand opening with free giveaways."

"They've been there all week."

"I wish they'd find that plutonium and get it out of there," Burl said.

"Yeah. Julia's giving me a hard time."

"I don't blame her."

"Burl, tell me what you think I ought to do, and I don't mean colonic irrigation."

"I don't know, good buddy. I guess you need to get checked out. Just keep on trying to find out what's going on, like you've been doing."

"I guess so. Thanks."

"Man, if anything happens to you because of this, I don't know what I'll do. Somebody'll have to pay. I'll take it to the Supreme Court."

"Thanks, Burl."

"I mean it."

"Do you need a ride to your job site next week?"

"No, that's all right. I've already got my Bobcat out there. The boss came and got it. I'm O.K. I'll bike over."

"See you later."

Reed tried to nap, so he would be alert for work that night, but he was wide awake, his thoughts whirling. If Julia really cared, she would let him go to Chicago with her. Maybe he should tell her what he knew about his exposures, but he couldn't bear for her to regard him as some scarred victim. It would send her into a tizzy of another kind. What did she want him to do? It was as though she had shown him one of her more mysterious experiments with T-4 viruses and said, "Look. You just don't want to understand this."

He rose from his nap and searched for T-4 bacteriophages in the index of one of the molecular biology books from the library. He found a photograph, magnified 275,000 times. The thing resembled a nuclear-powered spaceship. Project Orion! Its head was the bulbous crew compartment, its body was the long cargo/fuel bay, and the pod end carried the nuclear shield. The monster was covered with fuzz and had button eyes. It was the virus Julia was spending her time with. Here it was. An ugly bastard.

While browsing through the book, he noticed a section on radioisotopes. Julia had not mentioned working with radioactivity. He realized, of course, that in nuclear medicine, radiography used tracers like technetium and hydrogen isotopes. But they were low level. It would be very safe, he told himself. Not worth mentioning.

With a bit of time to spare before he clocked in, Reed stopped at the crossroads near the plant. A flea market had sprung up in a parking lot on Saturdays. In the fifties, a scrap dealer had built an underground fallout shelter there. It was a private bomb shelter, stocked with *Playboy* magazines and cans of soup and a foot X-ray machine from his brother's shoe store. The man had parties there for years, until nuclear fears eased and he retired to Arizona.

Today an emaciated guy with long, dark hair was selling ammunition packing cases—ammunition for cannon projectiles—for three dollars apiece.

"Hey, these wooden boxes would be nice for tools," Reed said.

"Tools, or anything you want to put in them," the guy said, with minimal movement of facial muscles. "Old tarps, shoes, buckets."

"They're not big enough for buckets," Reed said. "You could put tackle in them. Or ammunition. There's an idea."

"You can plant petunias in 'em for all I care."

Reed bought two. He was surprised when the man whipped out a laptop computer from his truck and began entering his sales.

"You've got to keep up with technology or go set on the porch," the guy said.

Reed bought a watermelon from another trader, a friendly counterpart to the sinister ammunition-box peddler. "That watermelon patch in Georgia looked like a field of jewels," the man said with a watermelon smile.

Reed loaded his purchases into his car. The watermelon made him recall the dummy A-bomb that once sat on a post here at the old scrap yard. It occurred to Reed that the place had collected its scrap metal from the plant—barrels, drums, siding, tons of it—and that it was probably contaminated. Reed had bought some scrap pieces himself, pipes for plumbing repairs and assorted metal rings. That was another house, another life. It was the house his children grew up in. And for all he knew, it was as hot as sunshine. Little readjustments like this were coming hard and fast, reconsiderations of his whole life.

The entrance to the plant was a pleasant parkway with a median of geraniums. It opened out into the military-gray expanse of structures, like a cluster of forbidding fungi popping out of a fertile ground. Its deadening familiarity seemed to shift now, like a hologram.

Reed had been coming here for more than twenty years. He could see that the place was getting old. Its grayness seemed a feature of its age, although it had always been gray. With a career in skilled maintenance, Reed knew the structure, the innards, the joints and seams of this place. Sometimes he faced difficult jobs that seemed impossible to solve. He had to be innovative then, and the more complicated the problem, the more he came out shining.

Tonight he moved through his work with the usual surge of energy he demanded of himself. He had to be charged up when he was on the job, even if the place had kicked him in the balls. First he worked on the operating floor resetting the pitch on some fan blades that were drawing too many amps, and then he went upstairs to work on the Freon systems. Even such small tasks indirectly helped keep the Cascade flowing, the stream running like blood. It wasn't brain surgery, but it was delicate, demanding work, and he loved it.

At midshift, some of the men were laughing about the newspaper column on radiation. But Strom, who wore a little pigtail at the nape of his neck, said, "That guy was dead-on. He really told it straight."

"Oh, come on, Strombo, you know they crapped it up from the start here," said Teddy, who still held a grudge against beryllium.

"But we'll clean it up. It hasn't hurt anything," said Strom. He laughed. "Hey, Teddy, how are you coming with your medical claim?"

"It's a fucking pile of paperwork, but I'll go ahead with it. Somebody's got to start the ball rolling."

"You haven't been here long enough to get beryllium disease, Teddy Bear," said Strom. "And you don't work in processing. We do *real* work here, not that pussy stuff you do in shop."

Teddy sauntered over to Strom and said, "The guy in the paper was talking about plutonium-238, not -239. But he didn't come out and say so. There's a world of difference."

"Radiation is good for you—right, Stromboli?" Reed saw himself making fun again. He stopped. People always believed what they wanted to believe, he thought.

The talk echoed in Reed's mind as he continued his work that night. There had been a time when he might have agreed about the healthful qualities of radiation. He had always thought that idle allegations got exaggerated and twisted into myth. But he knew that hundreds of tons of depleted uranium were lying around in cylinders like aliens waiting to burst from their pods. He knew of half a dozen guys who had come back from the first Gulf War with vague symptoms of illness. He knew that tons of D.U. had been dropped in Iraq in warheads. D.U. metal was used in tank-killer artillery and in armor plating on tanks because of its impenetrability. He didn't know what all that added up to. He knew that a former frontline manager for the Cascade had liver cancer. And one of the industrial chemists had died of a rare sarcoma last year. Guys in their fifties.

He wondered what images of the future ran through Madame Curie's mind as she worked through her eight-ton pile of dark-chocolate pitchblende searching for the golden needle of radium. He had always thought of Marie Curie as an iridescent, undulating French babe, a cure-all earth mother beaming out of the darkness. But now he felt a sort of radiation sickness of the spirit.

25

*R*eed rearranged the planets. He was coming home from the stars and checking in with the neighbors, in the one solar system familiar to humankind. For several hours on Sunday, in the loneliness of his computer, he played with these planets as if they were marbles. He created a new slide show, scanning in photographs of the planets from his astronomy books and pulling in Hubble images from cyberspace. He flipped painfully scarred Mercury on his side. He beheld a spectacular view of russet-green-and-blue Venus, her clouds dissolved by the magic of infrared. He tossed in the white-swirled whole blue Earth and her acned moon; cinnamon Mars; and then that great hog, Jupiter, with his evil eye, followed by gently haloed Saturn in a ladies' Sunday hat. Saturn had always been his favorite through the telescope.

He paused on Uranus—and his twenty-seven playful moons,

most named for Shakespeare's women. Uranus and Neptune: giant gasbag planets, blue balloons so enthralling he forgot to breathe. Uranus, a pale blue sphere, beautiful, with delicate rings; Neptune, ethereal and deep blue, with a Great Dark Spot that had since disappeared. Neptune and Pluto, the transuranic planets.

There was no good photograph of tiny Pluto, nearly invisible from earth, a distant icy spot, a mystery at the periphery of the solar system. It tilted funny, had polar caps. Neptune's winds were off the charts; no one knew how hard the wind blew on Pluto. Jupiter and Saturn were perpetually stormy. Mercury couldn't do wind, and the winds of Venus were all up in its topmost clouds. Reed imagined he was a solar meteorologist whipping up the night's forecast.

Uranus and Neptune were hydrogen, helium, and methane. Little but frozen methane was known of lonely, frosty Pluto and his big moon Charon—the god of the underworld and his satellite shining into caves of ice.

26

*R*eed had Monday off. The humid weather was suffocating, and he was too distracted to work on any of his projects. He stayed only briefly at Sunnybank, where his mother was participating with some difficulty in a spelling bee. He told one of the aides he was going out to grapple with his midlife crisis, and she told him to be careful—as if he had said he was going rock-climbing. Overcome by the nagging awareness of a permanent fatal error in his system, Reed drove out to the plant, parked in the side lot, and marched straight into the Records Office of the Administration Building, where he asked for the records of his 1980s exposures. Young Nancy, with her name badge affixed to her dosimeter, received him. He had not seen her around before. She was wearing plaid and tiny glasses.

"I'd be delighted to help you," she said, her smile shooting across her face like a fish. "How many events are we looking for?"

"There were three incidents," he said. "Not events. An event is a point in space-time with four coordinates. Nowadays, an event is planned—like a birthday party. But an incident occurs without warning."

"You still have to fill out a separate form for each one."

"Do I have to know the exact dates?"

"We can run a search."

"Don't you have all my records in one folder?"

"Probably. But we have to have all three forms."

Talking to Nancy, with her regulation procedures, was as dull as the old-fashioned atmosphere of the office, with wall calendars and scattered piles of paper. He expected to see a mimeograph machine.

Nancy said, "The records are in the vault, and we open that only on one day a week."

"Which day?"

"I can't say."

"What if there was a medical emergency and I needed my records?"

"I have this other form that you fill out." She began hunting in a drawer for the form.

"No, no. It was a hypothetical question. I don't have a medical emergency."

"But you seem to have some kind of emergency."

"Only with my girlfriend," he said. "No, forget that. Do you have records back to 1962?" It occurred to him to ask for his father's records too.

He waited while she checked with a supervisor and returned with the news that early plant records were in the D.O.E. archives in Washington. "I can't get those," she said.

"Well, just get my records then. When can I pick them up?"

"We'll send you a notice in the mail."

He began filling out the form, then stopped. "If you mail me a notice, that means you've gotten my records out of the vault. And if they're here waiting for me, then they're no longer protected by the vault. Had you thought of that?"

"Don't worry. We secure them."

Reed wrote fast on the form. He said, "I don't remember seeing you here before. You must be new."

"I am new. One month and a day."

"Welcome to Atomic World," Reed said.

Later that afternoon, Reed dropped by the construction site to give Burl a ride home. In what was once a cornfield near the Interstate, a small plaza was in the works, and Burl had been packing dirt around the foundation with his Bobcat. The tank tread that covered the two left tires had been unhooked, and it lay flat on the ground. A young Mexican was unchinking clay mud from the tire treads.

Burl, kicking a tire, said, "I plugged that leak this morning, but this ground is so heavy it blew out again."

"That's too bad."

"This is Santos. Reed, my buddy. *Mi amigo.*"

"Glad to know you," Reed said.

Santos nodded shyly. "Nice to meet you," he said slowly.

Burl was showing Santos how to reattach the tank tread.

"I'll get in and back up and go real easy, and you roll the back tread up this way." Burl demonstrated the plan. Then he climbed into the cab and inched the tires forward. Santos lifted the metal tread in back of the rear wheel and rolled it onto the surface of the tire until it was looped over the top. Burl got out of the cab, and together they pulled the tread over the front tire. The challenge was to hook the two ends of the tread together again, but because of the slack around the tires, the ends were still far apart—about eight inches.

"Hand me the slack adjuster, Reed," said Burl. "There in the back of the truck."

Reed handed Burl the tool, a yellow canvas belt that hooked onto each end of the tread. With an iron bar shaped like a duck foot, Burl was able to cinch the treads. He worked methodically, demonstrating the procedure to his helper. Reed observed the strength it took to tighten the belt.

"Come here and give her a few turns, Reed," Burl said.

Reed seized the paddle and pulled. "Man, this is like milking bricks. You could get tennis elbow from this."

Burl explained tennis elbow to Santos, whose face lighted with recognition.

After Reed gave the slack adjuster a few cranks, Santos took a turn, and then Burl tried again. Gradually, the two ends met—just barely, like God's finger touching Adam's on the ceiling of the Sistine Chapel, Reed thought.

Santos said, "Here it is. Now." He inserted the bolt that held the two ends together.

"Tighten it like this," Burl said, showing Santos.

Watching the men work moved Reed. The job seemed so straightforward, out in the open, without secrets. The work was safe—no sinister chemicals. Reed tried to study what was happening. Was he an observer or a participant? Did either Burl or Santos feel as though he was watching a movie?

Reed found his mother in the lounge, staring at the odd fish in the vase of greenery. He helped her to her apartment and helped her lay out her oil paints. The silver-and-red balloons Shirley had sent for their mother's return from the hospital still floated limply above the TV. He hadn't talked to Shirley since, but he had kept her informed by e-mail, and she often called their mother.

Reed had once sent a T-shirt with the words BALLOONS KILL BIRDS to Shirley, who ignored his environmental gesture. He couldn't really nag her for promoting nonbiodegradable crap that was dangerous to animals, since he worked in the nuclear industry, where the half-life of the wicked leftovers lasted an eternity longer than a child's balloon.

"Balloons kill birds," he said to his mother now, indicating the sagging bunch of balloons.

"Slingshots," his mother said.

"That's sharp."

She beamed brightly and reached for him to hug her.

"You're good to me," she said.

"I try."

"The food here is worse than the hospital food," she said. "I don't know how they expect to keep their customers."

"You liked the oyster stew I brought, didn't you?" He had heated it in her microwave. She ate it with pleasure, exclaiming over the oyster crackers—"little biscuits," she called them.

"Oyster stew? I haven't had oysters in thirty years."

Reed didn't argue. He checked her air-conditioning; he thought the air blowing out was too cool for her, and he adjusted it.

"You need to do some crossword puzzles to exercise your mind," he said, patting her shoulder. "It's like a muscle—use it or lose it!"

"Am I losing my mind?"

"I wouldn't know. Have you been looking for it?"

He suddenly remembered when she was a young widow. He had only flickers of memory of his father, a man with a ruddy complexion, reddish-blond hair, angular hands. He remembered him coming down the hall and setting a carton of ice cream on the table. A pair of jumper cables hung from his neck. Or perhaps it was a jump rope. Or a fishnet. A lasso.

"Tell me about when you first got married, Ma," Reed asked. "Did he open doors for you? Did you go to double features at the drive-in? Did you ever write any letters? When he got on at the plant at first, building it, what was his job? Did you all live nearby?"

"Slow down!" she cried.

"I'm exercising your mind," he said. "Maybe you can just tell me if you remember if he worked on any recycling at the plant."

"Go ask Wes Thornbush," his mother said. "You remember him."

"Thornhill," he said.

Leaving Sunnybank, Reed shook his head to clear it. It was like sneezing. The need to clear his mind was becoming a habit. His head was like one of those snow globes. He remembered Rosalyn telling about a Jesus snow globe she got in Branson, Missouri. But Reed, instead of hearing her say "Jesus," heard "Cheez-Its." For a while, he saw a startling image of little orange crackers falling through the globe instead of snow.

27

Weston Thornhill lived a few miles beyond the city limits, near a large apple orchard. When Reed was growing up, Thornhill and his wife used to drop by the house, sometimes bringing fruit from the orchard. Reed hadn't seen his father's friend in years.

Thornhill was bent over in his garden—stooping at the feet of hollyhocks and sunflowers. He straightened, holding on to his hoe as an anchor, when Reed turned in the driveway. He stared questioningly as Reed emerged from his truck. A clump of weeds fell from his hand.

"Reed Futrell, it's about time you showed up here," Wes Thornhill said in a thunderously welcoming voice. "Where in the world have you been all these years?" He pointed his hoe at Reed.

"Your garden's looking good, Mr. Thornhill. Your tomatoes are ripe and your beans could be Jack's beanstalks."

Thornhill examined Reed. "You look more like Robert Futrell than he did himself!" he said as if he had just retrieved a quiz answer long stored in memory.

"I'm Robert Futrell's, all right," Reed said, pleased.

"Your daddy was a good one. Everybody liked him."

They sat down on two stumps under a canopy of oak trees behind the modest white dwelling. The tatterdemalion back porch over-flowed with junk, and a makeshift awning sheltered more. Thornhill wiped his face with a wadded handkerchief he plucked from his shirt pocket. Reed noticed some small white splotches on the man's cheeks. For a while, they caught up on general news. Thornhill had not heard about Reed's mother's stroke, but in the way of older peo-ple he seemed to take news of illness and decline in stride.

"I'd offer you a beer if I had one," Thornhill said. He was still clutching his hoe. "But I can't drink fizzy drinks anymore."

"That's O.K., Mr. Thornhill."

"How many hot spots do you have to step on to get through the parking lot nowadays? Are they getting that mess cleaned up?"

"We don't throw anything away," Reed said with a grin. "It's like people in Alaska. They just pile up their broken old snowmobiles and pretend it's sculptures." He was facing a rusty riding mower piled with plastic crates beneath the tilted awning.

"That plant's a poison pit," the older man declared. "We breathed a lot of black dust."

"My uncle Ed always said that didn't bother him."

"They said you could eat the stuff! But they also thought the work was dangerous enough to keep it top secret. Does that make sense?" He steadied himself with his hoe handle. "Back at the start, people didn't know any better. Do you drink tap water?"

"Well, I've been known to," said Reed, thinking he was being of-fered a drink of water; there was a hose lying on the ground.

"It'll kill you," Thornhill said. "It's full of TCE—that's as bad as anything. We used to crawl inside those big cylinders and wash them out with TCE. Tons of it drained into the groundwater."

"I know," said Reed. "They were sloppy in the way they handled it."

"That stuff's built up in the groundwater and killed the fish and all."

Reed poked at the bark on the stump, which was pressing his testicles. "Now we wash out the pipes with Formula 409 and Kool-Aid." He laughed.

"That TCE will kill you," Thornhill repeated.

"Mr. Thornhill, tell me, when you were there did you know about the transuranics?"

He paused to think. "It's funny. We were sworn to secrecy, but what the hell did we know? They said if word had leaked out, the Russians could have used the information. We weren't smart enough to figure it out for ourselves, but the Russians would know. We were afraid to say anything, in case it might be something the Russians could use. Hell, do you think if I heard somebody telling a secret in Russian that I'd know what to do with it?" His laughter was bitter.

"But did you know you were working with reactor tails?" Reed asked.

"Oh, yeah. We did that. The shipments came in on the railroad cars, and we processed it. But we didn't know how hot it really was. It was spent fuel rods, all ground up into black oxide." He laughed. "We called the stuff 'rat tails.' "

"And what about warheads?"

He nodded. "I remember those too. I remember when the bombs came in. They rolled them out on a huge cart, on tandem wheels." He grinned. "The tandem wheels were nifty. I'd make toolboxes out of them. All the electric circuitry in the bombs was gold plated. The bomb had a parachute inside made out of mesh, and I made a hammock out of one."

Reed laughed with him. "I would have done the same thing." He stretched out his right calf, pulling his toes toward him. His muscles were tight as fence wire. "Mr. Thornhill, you don't really mean bombs, complete and ready to roll, do you?"

"No. They'd been broken apart before they were shipped."

"They were old bombs that had been dismantled."

"Right. The shipments would come in the dead of night, and we'd unload them off of a conveyer belt and put them in a storage shed. It was all hush-hush. Then later on we'd strip down the gold and the nickel and the aluminum and some other stuff. We'd toss it all in the smelter."

"That must be where the nickel scrap came from that was going to be made into barbecue grills," Reed said.

"We didn't know about anything radioactive in there; we weren't told everything, just what they said we needed to know. But that's where the beryllium came from, you know. The nose cones. Nobody said anything about plutonium though. The trigger had been taken out—"

"The plutonium pit?"

"Yeah. A hole was there. I don't know what they did with all the triggers."

"The hole where they were must have had traces of plutonium," Reed said. "That must be where the plutonium contamination came from."

"That's what I figure," said Thornhill, nodding.

"They're cranking up some old plants, like the one out in New Mexico, to fix up the worn-out triggers."

"Oh, yeah. I know all about that. I figure it's just an excuse for making more bombs."

Thornhill repositioned himself on his stump seat. The hoe he had been holding fell to the ground, and he turned its blade downward. In his mind, Reed conjured up the stricken expression on Julia's face if she heard this conversation.

Hesitantly, he said, "The thing is—management has been good to us. But somebody along the line should have told us the truth."

"Hell, they were good to us then," said Thornhill. "I don't think they knew. Back then nobody really understood radiation."

Except moviemakers, Reed thought. *Them. Godzilla.* The Japanese knew.

Thornhill said, "I knew back when your daddy died that it wasn't good to work with that stuff. I stayed because I didn't have much choice. I had three little ones and a wife who wanted too much. But I'd come home green and they'd all laugh. We had to get the kids not to tell that I was green at the supper table—but how could you expect a kid not to blab that? Of all things in the world, that's what they'd want to tell. We told them if the Communists found out, they'd come and take away all their playthings. Oh, it was ridiculous." He laughed. "I had the kids scared to say boo."

At Reed's urging, Thornhill began to reminisce about the days when the plant was built and the atomic cloud was a popular symbol, appearing on everything from license plates to souvenir trinkets.

"Oh, it was like Christmas and the circus all at once," he said. "People were coming in from everywhere to build the plant. Apartment buildings were shooting up. People whipped out shacks in their backyards and rented them to workers. They rented out lean-tos and even chicken coops. It was a few years after the war and people here were still hurting pretty bad. When the plant opened, the President came and rode in a parade downtown. It was crowded with people from miles around."

"My mother used to tell about all that," said Reed. "She said it was like Hollywood had come and taken over the place."

"You have to remember we hadn't seen anything like it," he said, his eyes gleaming. "We'd never seen tall apartment houses, and we'd never seen so much money and so many promises. And the President!" Thornhill stopped and shook his head. Flexing his age-spotted hands, he said, "I had skin cancer—in three places. But I reckon I'll be all right."

"I'm sorry to hear about that, Mr. Thornhill."

"My wife died from breast cancer. My grandbaby was born still-dead. Had no idea. But you know, I carry on! Look at them hollyhocks. Did you ever see such a sight? I reckon I'll keep on going, even if it's for nothing more than a fucking hollyhock."

"Those are good-looking hollyhocks," Reed said. The spikes of bright faces reminded him of a chorus line.

"My wife loved them, so I carry on with them."

"I'm sorry about your wife," Reed said. "I remember her."

Reed again inquired about his father. "Tell me what working there was like for him, Mr. Thornhill."

"We worked with liquid fluorine," Thornhill said. "We knew that was dangerous. You could cut diamonds with it—if you had some diamonds."

"I've been burned by hydrofluoric acid," said Reed, showing the puckered little hole on his wrist. "Boy, fluorine smokes."

"Well, then, you can imagine how bad your daddy's accident was." Thornhill paused to scrape something from his shoe. "I wasn't there when it happened, but I know when the fluorine leaked he was working in a real tight place, and he couldn't get out fast enough. Those fumes took him down. I believe he caught his foot on something."

"Stubbed his toe in the dark," Reed said. "Damn."

Thornhill nodded. "You couldn't see in that feed plant for the dust—except once in a while when a ball of fire rolled across the ceiling." His face brightened. "The hydrogen collected up there and a spark would set it off. It would just roll right out the door and we'd go back to work. It might singe your hair a little."

Reed stretched his leg slowly, choosing words. "My mother always told me my dad was a hero of the Cold War," he said. "She said he died in the service of his country."

Thornhill grunted. "And my boy died in Vietnam. He died in the service of his country. But nobody ever said he was a hero—except his mama and me."

A little breeze was making the hollyhocks tremble. Reed felt the hairs on his arms move in unison with them.

28

At the end of the week, Reed picked up the exposure records he had requested. The manila envelope lay on the passenger seat of his car unopened while he stopped for gas, lingering to chat with a couple of contractors Burl sometimes worked for. Rosalyn wasn't there. Then he drove to a market for dog food and eggs. He came home, stowed the food, romped around the vacant lot with Clarence, drank a ginger ale.

Testing was routine. Once a month he gave a urine sample, and at least twice a year during the eighties he lay on a table in the dark trailer of a mobile health-physics testing lab while a body counter, in the manner of space aliens examining abductees, trundled slowly over his flesh.

He had seen these reports back then, but he had filed them away, and they had disappeared during his divorce. Now, at his kitchen table, he calmly considered the numbers under his bioassay analysis and his in vivo monitoring. His numbers were usually less than twenty-five percent of the radiation protection standards. He was "within range." But in 1982, 1986, and 1987 the numbers had shot up. In later years, with the safety uprating, he hadn't worried. He figured the numbers would average out.

He remembered this one—1982. His urinalysis revealed twice the "safe" level of uranium. But the next year he was normal.

He flipped to 1986, the year of the worst incident. Yellow dust and sirens. The body-counter numbers for uranium and technetium were approximately what he recalled—within limits. But 0.15 nanocuries of neptunium had slipped into his body. Then he saw the word *plutonium*.

An air sample taken on-site contained an unusually high concentration of plutonium-239 and an equal concentration of neptunium-237.

This was new. He had not been told about plutonium on his tests before. Or had he misremembered?

The paper in hand, Reed stood up, as if he were levitating above his body like a patient who would later claim to have died briefly. He read on.

Mr. Futrell was protected from airborne radionuclides by the full-face respirator with canister. His in vivo results are acceptable.

Maybe he had stashed all this in the back of his mind, knowing his safety suit had protected him. Now he realized that the body counter couldn't register plutonium, but if neptunium was in his body, then an equal amount of plutonium was there too, like a shadowy twin. The 0.15 nanocuries of neptunium from this incident was matched by the same amount of plutonium. He thought of fund-raisers on the radio seeking matching contributions. Airborne radionuclides, like radio waves.

But a flyspeck of plutonium packed a bigger wallop than a flyspeck of neptunium, he realized. The numbers wouldn't match at all.

He set the papers on the table. Under the ceiling fan, the top sheet fluttered almost imperceptibly. The numbers might not fore-shadow anything at all. Nobody really knew. His trusty moon suit had shielded his lungs—maybe—from a large airburst of transuran-ics. No problem. He took a deep breath.

It really wasn't much, he thought. It was far short of the permis-sible body burden for rad workers. But Julia had insisted that there was no safe level.

Sure, he thought of saying to Julia. *I smoked plutonium a time or two. But I didn't inhale.*

In an oblique way, he had been informed long ago that pluto-nium was present, and he had chosen not to ask questions. His own life was a reflection of his father's. In incremental bits he had tres-passed upon his father's fate. He felt closer to his father, seeing the parallel. They were both willing participants.

*R*eed sorted the planets, edited and cropped them, made a new arrangement of the nine—two gorgeous goddesses and seven action-hero gods. He thought about what it would be like to see Neptune from the surface of its largest moon, Triton: how Neptune would be a huge blue breast rising from the horizon, filling half the sky. He made a special pop-up feature on Uranus and the transuran-ics, Neptune and Pluto, stranded out on the edge of the solar sys-tem. He had internalized them. Gazing at them made him feel as if he had vaulted out of earthly gravity into warped space-time. He had a modicum of power. He sped the planets through their orbits. He really was Atomic Man.

*W*hen Reed returned the overdue books to the public library, he or-dered from interlibrary loan a book on plutonium and one about Rocky Flats, the nuclear-bomb plant that produced most of Amer-ica's arsenal and was then condemned, with a shit-load of plutonium in its backyard.

At the library, he decided to look up his father's obituary; he didn't remember ever seeing it. An attractive librarian in high heels helped him find the microfilm from 1962 and set up the reel on the reading machine. He chatted with her for a while, noticing the curve of her breasts when she bent to insert the microfilm.

"Do you have anything about the history of the atomic plant?" he asked her.

"I bet we do. I'll check."

Whipping through the pages of microfilm, Reed quickly located his father's obituary. Robert Futrell, age thirty-six, worked at Main Atomic, as it was known then, and he left a wife, Margaret ("Peggy"), and son, Reed, six, and daughter, Shirley, two. Reed had forgotten that his father was a member of the National Rifle Association, and that he attended the Baptist church on Grand Avenue. It was a brief story. It said his father died shortly after an accident at work.

Turning the knob back, Reed searched for a story about the accident. The swift, jerky motion of the microfilm was unsettling. He found nothing. But he treasured the small facts he had found in the obituary. He remembered his father walking through the front door, hanging his hat on a peg, walking down the polished hardwood floor of the hallway, then making a sharp L-turn and sitting down to play the piano. Would he have gone directly to the piano? Didn't he want to play with Reed, his little son, age six, first? Did he embrace Reed's mom? Hoist baby Shirley to his shoulders? Reed tried to remember what his father played on the piano. Something fast and loud. And his mother danced. That was how his parents said hello to each other at the end of the day—in a burst of joy. She skipped down the hardwood hall, scooped Reed up in her arms, and presented him to the piano-playing pop, like a prize at the end of the number. And then they had supper.

His memories of his father, and the bits and pieces people had told him, had long ago combined into an image, the way George Washington or Abraham Lincoln is summed up by a single visual image. His father was simply his father: guy who worked at plant, played piano, died in accident. Reed had long ago ceased to ask questions about the pleasant face in photos. When Reed turned thirty-six, he was acutely aware that his father had died at that age. At that time, Reed rolled over the memories and images in his mind quite frequently, but he and Glenda were raising kids then, and he didn't pursue his questions. Now Reed wished he knew the textures of his father's working life—the feel of black oxide and greensalt, the heat and noise in a darker, more reckless time.

The librarian was at his side, with a folder. "I found this in Special Collections. I thought it might interest you."

"Thanks."

"I wasn't supposed to take it out of the room. So be careful you don't tear anything, and if you take notes, use a pencil."

"Thanks. I'll be careful."

The folder contained a newspaper feature about the plant, printed as a special section of the paper in 1955. The principal features of the gaseous-diffusion process of enriching uranium were unexpectedly detailed, with photographs of the compressors, the cylinders, the pipes, the drums, the skilled-maintenance department, the railroad cars.

The story covered several pages, with splashy photographs of the building interiors. He stared at a bank of fluorine generators in the old feed plant, where his father had been burned. He could see the copper buss work connecting them above. The fluorine cells— like coffins on legs—were set on spring shock absorbers attached to a metal frame. He saw how his father could have tripped over the network of framing on the floor. Although the picture was bright, Reed knew the area was dim, like the lighting in a movie theater. Atomic energy dawdled in the dark ages. Gaseous diffusion was to a centrifuge what a hot-air balloon was to the Wright flyer. The technology was crude; the machinery sported sharp corners and ungainly protrusions. It would be precarious moving around the old feed plant, which kept up a steady tremor while the fluorine cells jiggled on their shock absorbers. Even though it had advanced somewhat since his father's time, the enrichment process struck

Reed as absurd. Making atomic fuel was a witches' brew; it was like Dr. Frankenstein rigging up his crazy-quilt monster with baling wire and eyeballs from an organ depository and screwed-in limbs and mismatched feet.

The newspaper section was presented as a civic promotion, a celebration of the city's good fortune. The lead article said, "We're not revealing any secrets. Some procedures and materials remain highly classified."

"The KGB wouldn't give a shit how many welding rods I use," Reed said aloud, startling readers at the other microfilm machines.

29

At home he found a message on his answering machine from Julia: "Hi, sweetie, I'm taking off for Chicago right now. The girls are going to meet me up there for a couple of weeks. I'll call you when I get back. Don't worry."

Reed cursed himself for missing her call. He had hoped to see her again this weekend. He wanted to gaze into her sharp eyes and touch her smooth skin and study her freckles. He felt hollow with longing, wishing he hadn't gone to the library. It was odd that she left so abruptly, and he wondered if she had been summoned by some emergency.

After trying unsuccessfully to reach her on the telephone, he drove to her house, but her Beetle wasn't there, and no one answered the door of her garden apartment. He peered through the glass panes and saw only a corridor, with a peg rack and a row of worn shoes. He walked around to the tenants' entrance at the front of the house and entered the vestibule. The second door was locked. Through the glass he could see a corridor, with two closed doors, and at the end of the corridor was a small table with a yellow bowl on it. He heard a radio playing upstairs, up a white stairway.

Back at home he called the cytopathology lab and learned that Julia had left work two hours before. He called her home number again and left a message on her answering machine. "You're turning me into a radionuclide, Julia—my heart is breaking at the rate of thirty-seven billion disintegrations per second. Or thereabouts." Later, he regretted saying that. He kicked around his place aimlessly. On the kitchen counter, two aging tomatoes had leaked rot. He threw them out against the fence. Clarence cast him a critical glance.

He contemplated the planets floating across his computer screen. Then he found himself playing with his photo files, tossing the planets around, ejecting them from the solar system, aiming them at black holes. Then he made a greeting card, with blue, glossy Neptune on the front. Beneath Neptune, he wrote, *I'm coming to you from Outer Space.* Beneath the silver marble of Pluto, he wrote, *I'm just a frozen gas-ball. I'm getting lonely waiting here in my Fortress of Solitude. Yours forever, Captain Plutonium.* He decided not to print it.

That evening he brought pizza to Burl's, and they watched two violent movies Burl had rented. Reed had the satisfaction of watching people and buildings blow up without having to feel anything personal about them. Burl, cozy with his pint of bourbon, seemed wrapped up in the fate of the characters. He watched with the purity of a child, Reed thought. Burl's facial expressions ricocheted between terror and pity. Now and then he laughed when something exploded. Reed didn't want to bring Burl down, so he didn't mention his numbers. He didn't mention Julia. Since his divorce, Reed thought he had come to know himself more keenly. He saw a pattern in his past mistakes; he thought about the way he did things; he recognized his blind spots. And all that had happened to him recently—Julia, his mother's stroke, the atmosphere of uncertainty at work—catapulted him along the stages of self-examination. He could see himself in parallax, jumping back and forth, depending on which eye was watching. The Great Red Spot of Jupiter, remarkably like a whale's eye, was watching.

Reed slept fitfully, the familiar body-clenches and moans punctuating the night. The next day, Saturday, he swabbed his truck, paid bills, mowed his neighbor's yard. She was an elderly widow who didn't trust boys with machines, so he helped her out with her yard work. His weed trimmer had quit, and he suspected a terminal was loose. He found mud-dauber nests in the recessed circles around the screw heads. The mud patches were neatly formed, as if the insects had spackled bullet holes in a wall that was to be painted. As he jammed his electric screwdriver into the holes, dirt flew out. He discovered nothing wrong with the terminals, so he investigated the trimmer head. As he probed that, he realized the whole head was stripped. The thing was junk. Methodically, he joined the parts back together.

He was restless. He didn't know where to find Julia in Chicago. He didn't have the number of her cell phone, the one she used only for emergencies. All his women were like the dead woman in the dream: his ex-wife had gone, exited into some alternate universe in Iowa; Rosalyn was too nice for her own good. Jennifer's mother, whose name he still couldn't remember, was long gone. All the other women were casual acquaintances, no one to keep up with. He had stopped reading the e-mail responses to his ad, which were still trickling in even though he had canceled the ad weeks ago. He had written a few enigmatic notes to Hot Mama. The last time he checked, she was ranting about the poetry of connection. When people most wanted connection, they screwed it up somehow, he thought. It was like damaging the terminals.

30

In the Sunnybank lounge, Reed looked for the fish among the roots in the globe of greenery on the piano and was startled to see it hanging motionless and apparently shriveled down to bones and skin. The fish hung against the roots in a pose of horror, like someone locked in a closet who screams until he starves to death. Probably no one had noticed that the fish was in distress.

Reed's mother waved to a woman who was steering a rolling walker, which she scooted along too far ahead of her, as if she were pushing a grocery cart. The woman was dressed in a floral wrapper, with pale aqua scuffs on her tiny feet.

His mother called, "Come here, Mrs. Valley, tell my son what you did!" Reed waited what seemed like five minutes for the woman to reach them. He felt suspended, like the fish.

"Tell that story again," Reed's mom urged her.

Laboriously, Mrs. Valley sat down. "I was just a little squirt," she said, puffing from her exertion.

"Listen, Reed. A—what were they called—aeronauts? Aviators? An aviator landed in her father's field, and . . . Mrs. Valley—" Reed's mother prompted. She was clear headed, in good spirits, Reed thought, while he was empty and fuzzy.

"He landed in my pappy's pasture," the woman said. She cleared her throat. "He had a copilot with him. And the neighbors all gathered around, and the airmen went and got some gasoline. And the pilot said he'd take us up for rides, and there was a little neighbor girl that wanted to go too, so my daddy said yes and he went up with me and the other little girl. . . ." Mrs. Valley paused to recall the other child's name. "Rose. Rose Barn? And he took us up. Oh, the noise that thing made! And the wind whipped our cheeks. And we saw the river and all the trees—my, it was trees as far as you could see. And he found his way back to the same field and set us down right where he picked us up!"

"Get on to the main part, Mrs. Valley."

"Well, it was two years later, when Charles Lindbergh's picture was in the paper, for flying across the ocean. And there he was, with the *St. Louis Spirit*! That was our pilot! And our plane! Lord, we never could have imagined."

"And you saw it again, Mrs. Valley," Reed's mother said.

"Yes—in the Smithsonian." Mrs. Valley looked straight up at Reed, who was still standing. She said, "My daughter took me there in 1990. And there it was. The very airplane."

"That's a great story, Mrs. Valley," Reed said.

"I have such a delightful son," said his mother, turning her attention to him as an aide came to accompany Mrs. Valley to her manicure.

"That wasn't the *Spirit of St. Louis*," he said to his mother. "The *Spirit of St. Louis* didn't even have a copilot's seat."

She squeezed his hand. "But it might have been Lindbergh. He went barnstorming around the country after he flew to Paris."

"But wasn't this episode before that?"

"Well, he must have flown around before, to get practice." She shrugged. "You never know what might be true."

31

*P*lutonium had been found in the body of a deer at Fort
Wolf. It was a weighty piece of news, heavy like the heav-
ier-than-uranium, transuranic, stupefyingly titanic heavy metals.
Plutonium-fed deer. The news flew around the plant, like the joke
of the day. Q. "How do you know if there's plutonium in your veni-
son?" A. "If you can jump-start your truck with it."

Reed floundered in perplexity. He didn't know if this was an im-
mediate crisis or just another toxic-modern doomsday theme to
carry around in the same pocket with global warming and the per-
forated ozone layer. What kind of assurance could he offer Julia
now? He did not know how much plutonium you could ingest and
survive. Evidently the deer had thrived, until the wildlife biologists
shot it to find out if it harbored anything life threatening.

"How do you imagine plutonium got into that deer?" Burl asked when Reed arrived at Burl's early on a Friday evening. "Is it in the water or on the trees or what?"

"That's not what killed the deer," Reed said.

Burl tossed Reed the keys to his truck. Reed was driving. Exactly three weeks ago, he had been shucking corn on his porch with Julia. He had had no word from her, and he was becoming anxious.

"A dirty bomb," said Burl, slamming the passenger door. "A hot deer! Just hurl a deer through a plate-glass window into a mob of shoppers."

"It wouldn't work that way," Reed said. "Alpha rays don't go very far."

The truck's flank scraped some overgrown bushes as he backed out of Burl's driveway.

"The hunters won't care if the deer have plutonium or kryptonite or turnip greens in their bones," Burl said. "They just want to shoot something."

"Maybe they hunt because supermarket food is tainted," Reed said. "Maybe they're hunting for something pure."

"Maybe if I ate plutonium I'd turn into Superman." Burl laughed.

Reed shrugged. Burl beat a rhythm on the dashboard.

"I'm telling you, Reed, that place is going to eat you alive. Wonder if that deer felt funny, or glowed? Could it still have Bambis—or would they have two heads and fins? I mean, do they know any of this stuff, Reed? Do they really know what kind of danger we're dealing with?"

"Maybe they do. Or there wouldn't have been so many secrets."

"Maybe so."

"I give a urine sample every month and every month they tell me I'm safe. And lately we're getting *negative* numbers on uranium."

"What kind of sense is that?"

"They seem to be saying that I get less uranium at the plant than my mother does at Sunnybank."

Burl laughed. "They want you to feel good about yourself, Reed."

"Oh, sure. I feel really positive about my negatives."

The sun had set, and Reed switched on the lights. Thick lines of cars were headed toward the malls, and parking lots at the chain restaurants were jammed. Instead of his own more reliable vehicle, Reed drove Burl's hapless, multicolored truck because Burl loved it so. Burl talked in a stream. Sometimes with him, Reed felt as if they had gone off on a tangent, like a space probe that went too fast, escaped gravity, and went speeding out into space.

Burl's truck was a throwaway vehicle, like the cars in Clawber's Dead Car Museum, which they were passing now just outside of town. Clawber still had every vehicle he had ever owned—and many others—displayed in his yard. There were about twenty old hulks, their lives spent, their engines dead, their fenders rusted, their tires piled into an old-tire graveyard beside his house. Each beloved old car was deposited at its final roosting place like a spectacular new model in a show window.

Burl was eating peanuts and talking. "Man, Clawber's place sure is neat! He's keeping it mowed pretty good, and he weed-eats around the cars. He ought to make a place for dancing, and a bandstand." Burl raced along on that topic for a mile, then switched abruptly to methods of brewing coffee, followed by nanotechnology, Merrill Lynch, and the French Revolution. His jumpiness was accelerated today, making Reed feel uneasy.

They were driving out into the country to see Burl's cousin Beloit, a childhood pal from Michigan. He was a man who didn't mingle and who returned to Lansing for months at a time. He had been arrested a few times for petty thefts, and last year he had been charged with cooking methamphetamine, but the charge was later dropped.

Reed said, "Burl, I swear you're going to end up in the penitentiary if you keep fooling with Beloit."

"Oh, he learned his lesson."

Apparently Burl's cousin had siphoned several gallons of anhydrous ammonia from a farmer's tank in a remote cornfield. It was corn-planting time, and the farmer had rolled the tank out to his freshly plowed field, intending to apply the fertilizer to the soil. In the dead of night, Beloit had attached a hose and siphoned off about three gallons of it. Suddenly a searchlight turned on and Beloit skedaddled.

Reed said, "Anhydrous ammonia will soak right through you. It'll burn the hide off of you."

"Can't be worse than plutonium now, can it?"

"Touché. You need to get your cousin to go to church with you and straighten him out," said Reed. "Which one is your sister dragging you to now?"

"Pilgrims' Rest. It's a new church, with a big new brick building and a rec hall." Burl laughed. "The preacher gets his sermons off the Internet."

"Those new religions scare the pudding out of me," Reed said.

"They're going to have a pageant," Burl said. "They wanted me to play one of Christ's disciples." He laughed. "But I told Sally I didn't think I could give that role my all."

Reed said, "On second thought, Burl, if you join some cult that's going to blow up something or meet flying saucers or commit mass suicide, then I'll feel obliged to step in and become a cult-buster."

"I'm not that stupid," said Burl, wadding his peanut package into his shirt pocket.

"I didn't mean that." Reed glanced at Burl's face, still faintly pockmarked from teen acne.

"But if I get drunk and join up with some TV evangelist, I'm counting on you to come and bail me out."

"What else am I good for?" Reed asked. "Just call on me. I'll be there."

"You know I'm not a fool. I'm not taken in by these things," Burl said, swigging whiskey from the bottle in his paper bag. "But if your sister's out dancing with the holy spirit, you can't just make fun of her dancing. Sally's so purely ordinary that she broadens my mind in some strange way. And I'm always learning something useful when I'm around her, something that makes me feel holy."

"That would do it."

In a way, Reed thought, Burl was the holiest person he knew. Burl seemed to know that the world's complications were far greater than his understanding, and he had his life worked out in some obscure, irrational linkages of myths, dreams, adages, angels, prayer rituals, rosary beads, Guatemalan worry dolls, hexes—a moral juggling act balanced against the indifference of everyday facts. Reed often thought that Burl, in his diffuse enthusiasms, made more sense than the average person who lived by the simple tenets of commerce and acquisition and clockwork regularity. Reed had read that 15 percent of Americans comprehended the scientific process, and 60 percent believed in psychics. Burl could interweave psychics and physics and still sleep soundly.

Burl was taking a shopping bag of supplies to his cousin. Reed couldn't see what was in the bag because Burl kept the top folded over. When it popped open, he held it closed with his foot.

As Reed turned onto a blacktopped country road, Burl asked about Julia. Reed, jolted by the question, found himself swerving to avoid a Rhode Island Red rooster that was scooting across the road.

"Julia's still in Chicago," Reed said, his heart quickening. "I haven't heard a word. Her sister was in some kind of trouble."

"Hold it," Burl interrupted. "Was that a rooster? What's a rooster doing out after dark?"

"I don't know. I was wondering that myself. Furthermore, why was he crossing the road? Anyway," Reed said, hitting the high beams, "I wanted to take her up there to Chicago myself. She's treating me like Schrödinger's cat. She puts me in a box and just leaves me there. She doesn't know if I'm alive or dead."

"Did you hear about Dan Forgy's cat?"

"No. That cat he's so crazy about?"

Dan Forgy, an old friend, ran Forgy's Hardware. Burl told about

Dan's hyperthyroid cat, Boone, who had been isolated in a cage at a veterinary hospital for ten days after being injected with radioactive iodide.

"The cat had no toys, no music, no voices, not even a tuffet to sit on!" Burl said.

"They nuked his thyroid," said Reed.

After the cat came home, Dan had to isolate Boone, in his yellow collar that said RADIOACTIVE, for ten more days, Burl explained.

"Boone was so glad to see Dan he just danced with joy. Dan wasn't supposed to touch him—no snuggling, they said! And this cat was just wild to get ahold of him, climb up in his lap, and purr in his ear. He leaped up on Dan's shoulder, and Dan was afraid his thyroid would be zapped."

"They probably didn't give the cat more than a few millicuries of radioiodide," said Reed. "The cat didn't need to be in a deprivation chamber at home. They're just covering their ass." Reed slowed down, for he was driving down an unfamiliar road that seemed to have no shoulders. "How's Dan's pussy now?"

"Calm as a footstool. That cat was always scared and jumpy, but I guess he had time to think things over when he was in solitary. That's what it's like in the pokey. Yep, you get a lot of quality mental time when you're doing time."

"They didn't have to keep that cat shut up that long," Reed said. "That's cruel. If those rules applied at an atomic plant, we'd all be in an isolation booth half the time."

Reed listened in a trance as he drove, as Burl continued speculating and humming alternately. Burl was going on now about mind over matter, wondering if it applied to cats.

Their destination, a house on the outskirts of a village across the county line, was a crumbling premodern relic, with weathered gray siding and a patchwork roof. The porch, covered with a shredding outdoor carpet, sagged. The house had a visible concrete cistern, fed by a downspout from the roof gutter.

"Drive around back," Burl said.

As he got out of the truck, Burl disclosed the contents of the bag of supplies he had brought for his elusive cousin—oranges and bananas, garbage bags, cans of vegetables and soup, and a large bargain box of chocolate Easter bunnies. Reed didn't offer any judgment; the discount-eclectic assortment seemed innocent enough. He waited in the truck while Burl entered the back door with the bag of goods. Reed had read newspaper reports of cops finding meth labs in bathtubs or in motel rooms, or even in vans rushing down the highway. If Beloit was cooking meth, it was easy enough to accumulate the ingredients from various drugstores—plastic tubing, lithium batteries, ether, ephedrine pills. If this place got raided, it would be by a Haz-Mat crew in moon suits, Reed thought. He felt like the secretary of defense touring bombed-out neighborhoods. The landscape of his life was reduced to assorted toxic-waste dumps.

Chemicals had always been Reed's friends, because he treated them with respect. But they had turned on him. He held the truck door ajar for air, forcing himself to concentrate on the moment at hand. Here he was, sitting behind a ramshackle house where a man might have messed with liquid fire. Reed wondered what he was supposed to do. He didn't believe Burl was involved with meth. But Burl embraced life to such an extent that he was pulled in many directions and too often made excuses for others' failings.

Burl emerged from the dark house and slipped into the truck. In the dim interior light, he appeared older. He had a small cut on his finger, from a metal snag on the screen door. He opened his wallet to locate a bandage strip he carried amongst his condoms. In the layers of bills, Reed saw fifties. The worn, off-brand condom packages appeared almost antique.

Reed saw himself moving from one fantasy island to another. His workplace was science fiction; this seedy house was like an old juke joint without the music; Reed's own house, neglected and cluttered, was like a rundown hotel; the hospital where his mother had been was like the government of a small dictatorship; and Sunnybank was a madcap Utopia, like first grade without a future.

32

After leaving Burl at his house and retrieving his car, Reed bought gas at the mini-mart. Tonight, Rosalyn's blond hair was swung into a casual knot on her crown, and she wore slim jeans and a tight red T-shirt with a V-neck. He loved to hang around her because she was always cheerful. He needed that now.

"Hey, Rosalyn, did you ever know anybody who did meth?" he asked. They were chatting by the motor-oil rack.

"Why? What's the trouble? You don't want any of that, do you? You look beat." She touched his brow.

"Hell, no. I just wondered about it, there's so much of it around." Spotting lithium batteries, he pointed to them. "A chief ingredient," he said.

Rosalyn nodded. "I sell a lot of those." She straightened a stack of pipe cleaners. "I know some of the truckers that come through are on meth," she said. "It makes them a little crazy; they act like they're ready to pick me up and carry me off." She laughed, touching her hair confidently.

"One look at you, Rosalyn, and anybody would want to grab you and carry you off." He liked Rosalyn, who had always been warm and maternal toward him. He said, "A couple of guys at work take it. They come in wired and go out wired. They may as well hook in directly to the power lines out there at the plant."

She laughed, but she was worried. "I heard there might be layoffs, Reed," said Rosalyn.

"I haven't heard that. They won't lay off unless they cancel the new plant."

"It won't affect you, will it?"

"Nah. I've got too much seniority."

"I hate to see anybody get laid off."

"Me too. Those young guys just starting out, just married—first they get laid and then they get laid off. But don't worry. It won't happen. When the centrifuge goes online, we'll have plenty of jobs. We could even make bomb fuel again if we had to."

"Well, I could do without that." She shuddered. "There's so much going on in the world—I'm just going to enjoy myself."

"Sounds like a good plan."

"I'm taking my break," she said to the young Korean behind the counter.

Reed sat with her on the bench in front of the mini-mart, where the neon and vapor lights shone eerily on her face. She lit a cigarette. Reed hadn't smoked in years, but Rosalyn enjoyed smoking and refused to quit. They watched a frowsy woman pump her gas, then leave her kid in the car while she went inside to pay.

"I'm getting a hysterectomy," Rosalyn told Reed.

"Oh, no! Cancer?"

"No, just what they call fibroids. They make me so miserable I can't sit. They could take them out, but it's easier to yank out the whole bag than to try to cut them out individually." She laughed loudly and went on explaining in more clinical detail than he could focus on. "The risk of having them cut out is bleeding to death, so I'll just let them take the whole shebang." She laughed again and drew on her cigarette. "What do I need with a uterus anyway?"

Rosalyn naturally laughed all the time, regardless of the subject. She said, "I'm going to ask if I can take my uterus home. I want to bury it in the backyard."

"Dogs might dig it up," Reed said, catching a lock of hair that was falling across her cheek.

"Maybe I should give it to your dog."

"Clarence would love it."

Rosalyn laughed until she had to catch the pain in her side.

33

The marijuana crop was coming in. Reed knew, because he saw a pair of choppers flying low in the early morning sky, black against the sunrise; they were heading toward the cropland and the forest preserves along the river. A team called the Flying Ferrets cruised with their infrared, searching for patches. When they located one, they landed and set up a stakeout. On the choppers, they carried canoes, all-terrain vehicles, assorted weapons, anything they might need for their weed war. Reed liked watching helicopters, although he always imagined that one day he would see one spiral out of the sky, its spinning beanie gone berserk. He was sleepless, not a winged ferret, but a bear in need of a cave. Ursa very major.

———

*R*eed had pushed his mother from his mind. As she grew stronger, her resentment of her surroundings grew more particular. She complained of having to listen to Guy Lombardo music, of having no one to play poker with, and of having to tolerate the decrepitude and dementia of the Sunnybank inmates.

"This place is full of old people," she said with a sigh.

He had just left work. He was exhausted. During the first half of his shift he had repaired a sprinkling system, changed a fan belt on a large ventilation fan, and aligned a motor; and after eating he had returned to the Venusian greenhouse atmosphere of the Cascade with Darrell and Kerwin to start changing a joint seal on a compressor. He had drunk three orange sodas and about a gallon of water during the night. The window of his hood had a scratch on it that bisected his view like a split screen.

His mother had already been to breakfast, but she was still wearing her nightgown and robe. Reed, although realizing that he patronized her, told his mother how lovely she looked, how good she sounded, no longer slipping on any of her words. The newest drug seemed to have cleared out her mind like a bush hog, he thought. She joked about the daily devotional program. Yesterday it was Jesus and the miracle of the loaves and the fishes. She said, "They're praying for a miracle here. They don't have enough good food to go around, so they pad it with generic helper."

"I'll order you some loaves and fishes, Mom," Reed said, touching her hair. The soft, dark hair of her younger days was now gray and bristly, like the brush he used to clean greasy tubing at work.

"I have a song in my head and I can't get it out," she said. "I don't know what song it is. I hear one line, over and over. I'm sure I know the song but I can't catch it. Am I losing my memory?"

"No, we're all like that," Reed assured her. "That's the story of my life, a song I can't identify."

"Well, I doubt that," she said.

34

$\mathcal{P}$lutonium was a crazy element that crawled and burrowed. It melted at room temperature. It was different colors—silvery or purple. Someone said it felt like a newborn kitten in your hand. It was elusive, a shape-shifter, a trickster. The word *plutonium* was evocative—a faithful dog with a big wet mouth and floppy ears, or a distant planet that was cold as leftover biscuits. Pluto, the Greek god of the underworld, wore a helmet that made him invisible. For all Reed knew, Julia was on a distant planet, or perhaps somewhere on the outer rings of Saturn.

He cruised the Internet, seeking plutonium. After wading through some cursory histories of the Manhattan Project, he got bogged down in several conspiracy-theory websites. He went off on a tangent to the Aurora Project, a hypothetical hypersonic spy plane. He bypassed several familiar lunatic claims that radiation was a healthful rejuvenator. Reed stared at the screen until the Hubble pictures of the planets appeared.

His eye on Neptune, he lifted the telephone. He had hoped Julia would be back from Chicago after the weekend, but it was already early Wednesday. He had refrained from calling for a few days. After plastering her with assurances about the wildlife refuge, how would he ever explain the deer at Fort Wolf? He rang Julia's number. It was three a.m. Mars floated slowly forward. "It's me again, from outer space. Call me when you get home," he said to her machine. He thought he and Julia must be in relative motion: traveling at different speeds, each thought the other was standing still. She had called to let him know she was going to Chicago; and she had even called him sweetie. So why should she drop him again? What if she didn't get in touch at all? What if something had happened to her?

Would it make her happy if he joined a class-action suit? If he went back to school and studied astronomy? He really should shift course. He didn't want to think of himself as a whiny, has-been oldster, his spirit tamed and boxed, his lust dimmed, his mouth turned down in a frown. But he seemed to live in a different space from her, a variant dimension, his string furled like fishing line.

One of the books he had ordered through interlibrary loan had arrived. After exercising with Clarence and feasting on catfish and black beans, he settled down on the back porch with the book about plutonium. He intended to refresh his understanding of how science arrived at radiation protection standards. And he wanted to find out how much plutonium the body could bear. The book documented the secret government plutonium experiments in the decade following Hiroshima and Nagasaki. The topic sounded familiar, something he had shut out of his mind. Now, as he flipped through the book, the memory erupted like a malignant pustule hidden in a brain fold. In medical experiments, the essential substance of nuclear weaponry had been shot into the bloodstream of human beings who were told only that it was good for them.

"Holy Venus and Mars!" Reed said aloud.

He read on. Besides trying to figure out tolerance doses of radioactivity, researchers used plutonium and other radioactive substances as an experimental cancer treatment. Most people lived only a short time, but a few lived for years with plutonium locked inside them.

Why not put it in breakfast cereal, in case it proved healthful? Reed wondered. Why not sell it as a miracle cure for obesity? What might it do to cholesterol? He remembered that the plutonium experiments had come to light during the nineties, and the D.O.E. had apologized. Some reparations had been paid and then the subject was forgotten. Reed couldn't remember what he was doing then. Had Glenda left? He must have been off on one of his desperate motorcycle escapes. Little was said at work, just renewed vows of safety. It was past history.

He read on, skipping parts, reading ahead, doubling back. Radioactive substances *had* been tried in breakfast cereal—boys at a correctional school had been fed radioactive iron and calcium in their oatmeal. He read about a radioactive iron experiment on pregnant women—a nutrition study that backfired. He read about huge black tumors in the mouth, grapefruit-sized growths on thighs. Some doctors thought plutonium might jazz up spermatocytes.

On the atomic level, plutonium was a little bomb in itself when it entered the body, Reed thought. It initiated something like a chain reaction among the body's cells—a kind of mutation that could turn into cancer. Reed wondered if a chromosomal change could then eventually pervade the human race. He remembered that Julia had told him that in biological terms cancer cells were immortal. Like something obsessed, they couldn't stop replicating.

It was growing too dark to see. He went inside, cleaned up his dishes, then continued reading in his recliner. Clarence was barking outside, but Reed paid little attention as he read on, skimming parts, flipping to the index, studying pictures of forlorn victims.

Some of these experiments led to workplace safety practices that he was accustomed to. He didn't know whether to puke or be thankful that humans had been used like rats so that he could be a cell rat. Even though researchers figured that a microgram of plutonium might cause cancer, they injected people with many times that amount. One horror after another leaped from the page. The testes of prisoners. Plutonium mixed into vaginal jelly. Whole-body irradiation. The book said all baby boomers carry around a trace of plutonium in their bones, from fallout. One venturesome scientist accidentally created a criticality—in his hands—while demonstrating the daring test they called "tickling the dragon's tail." The instant blue halo dosed him with eight hundred roentgens. He lived nine days.

Roentgen, rad, rem. The Three Rs. The words started to undulate in Reed's mind, and fearing his dreams, he fought sleep. But he slept all morning and awoke when he heard a siren pass by. His head had a case of water hammer.

"I'm dog-tired from sleeping so hard," he told Clarence. "Do dogs ever get headaches?"

Reed dished out Clarence's morning chow. He swallowed some pain pills and ate half a cantaloupe and some scrambled eggs with coffee. He would be off work that night, so he ran some errands, mowed the yard, patched a screen, tended to his tomatoes. The vines were shriveling, and some of the tomatoes were rotting. His headache was better, but the headache pills made him feel as if he had been in a swimming pool for ten hours. He hadn't finished reading the book, and he had lost his place, but he got the idea. It stymied him. He didn't know what to do with this knowledge.

He got chills remembering one of the nuclear accidents: a processing worker struck by more than twelve thousand rem of plutonium. The man burned, swelled up like sausages, went into shock, breathed like a frog. When doctors tried to get bone marrow samples, their syringes drew up what they called "slop" or "mush." After he died, his body was systematically dismantled for studies—like an old warhead, Reed thought. The man's body contained nineteen nanocuries. Scientists had thought the permissible body burden was twice that amount, but they learned different.

"Don't count your nanocuries before they hatch," Reed murmured. The words *slop* and *mush* kept tossing around in his mind like contaminated oatmeal.

The day was sweltering. It hadn't rained in weeks. Clarence lay beneath the mimosa in the cool dirt, motionless during the afternoon. Reed's house needed cleaning, or perhaps sandblasting, but he did not feel like mopping floors. The plutonium book sat on the table like a little bomb.

35

Late in the day, he ordered lasagna from Mr. Como's and picked it up, a hot aluminum tray with a plastic lid nestled in a sissy little fuchsia shopping bag. After a fling around the vacant lot with Clarence, Reed jammed his camping gear into the carriers on his motorcycle. The tarp was wadded, the tent in a tangle—just like his feelings, he thought. An assortment of urges was making it necessary to fly once again to the Fort Wolf Wildlife Refuge. He told himself that he needed at least to say good-bye to the blighted place he had loved all his life. One more visit couldn't hurt. It would be nice to believe that radiation was good for you. But that would be like having faith in Internet self-improvement elixirs. He knew that behind every magic solution was an abstruse circuitry of ulterior motives and flummery. And beneath that, in the infinite regress of Russian dolls nesting in coffins of themselves, the invisible strings of the universe oscillated dizzily. He felt a buzzy anxiety about what lay ahead.

Reed faced a sunset view of the plant. The cooling towers were billowing away, breathing with vigor and optimism, as if the energetic outlook at the beginning of the Cold War was caught in a time warp. It was still a marvel, Reed thought. The Cascade had never been shut down for a moment since it was activated in 1953. The gas had to keep moving or it would solidify and clog the pipes. But the pipes were possibly lined with exotic spices that lingered, clinging like shrink-wrap. In order for plutonium to be washed away, half of it had to be washed away, and then half of that. It was Zeno's paradox. If the turtle traveled from A to B by halves, it would never arrive. It was turtles all the way, Reed thought, remembering, with a pang, Julia's laugh. He knew he always got Zeno and Aesop mixed up, but he figured they were drinking buddies back in the B.C. years. Plutonium had a half-life of twenty-four thousand years. Maybe Zeno meant time, not space. Reed knew he was toying with his own mind.

Skirting the security stations, he rode past the green ponds, the glistening lagoons, the fouled ditches marked with yellow tape. There were no frogs or fish in the ponds; they had been killed to keep people from eating them. After some deformed frogs had been found a few years before, the NO FISHING signs were erected. He remembered seeing a newspaper photograph of a frog with one eye and a stunted extra leg—something like a formless pouch with toes. At the time, he simply thought deformed frogs were common. But how could he have pretended this place was anything but a malignant jungle? He trembled with sadness—this violation, a crude intrusion into a natural place that he held to be sacred.

The history of the place was swathed in fog. He would take a risk to do a good job, but if he ever suspected he was being manipulated, Reed was not an easy buddy. And he felt responsible. He had played a part in ruining this wilderness.

As he entered Fort Wolf, he stopped and removed his helmet.

With the hot breeze flying through his hair, he roared through the refuge toward the levee. Suddenly, it was as though he'd never been there before. The scenery, while familiar, took on an unfamiliar air, as if every leaf held a toxic secret. The weather had been dry, and the poison ivy vines were already turning red; river birches were shedding their leaves. The ironweed was in oblivious bloom, patches of purple against a multitude of shy faces of Queen Anne's lace folding inward as if they couldn't bear the presence of a transuranic.

The summer growth of poison ivy and greenbrier and blackberry bushes hugged the shoulders of the road, but deeper into the refuge he located a familiar grassy clearing—one of his favorite camping spots. A shot of late sun yellowed the greenery. He could see one of the ammo bunkers in the distance. Chemicals from the manufacture of TNT had seasoned the soil, and newer, hotter elements from the plant added to the stew.

One could write a history of modern war from this corner of the earth, he thought. The TNT and the chemicals used in the shells of World War II, the nuclear fuel of the Cold War, and later the D.U. metal for bullets and tanks of the high-tech, "clean" wars—clean, except for uranium oxide spraying in all directions when the bullets hit, along with a dozen other pollutants that were the subtext of the clean wars. His close proximity to an enormous history made him quaver. Reed had lived with the Cold War, like a cold serving of nameless meat on his plate. The image of his grandfather ill in a tent near here long ago flashed through his mind. His dad in a chemical bath. Reed here, on this ground, his body hastening to join them.

As he made his camp, he was aware of a quintet of deer bedding down not far away. They had probably scattered when his bike approached, but now they had returned, out of habit. He was only a boy, with his uncles, when he killed a deer, years ago, out here at the refuge. He shot the deer in the morning, at dawn, a youngish buck with a hardly creditable rack. In his eagerness, he shot the first animal he saw, not stopping to reflect. His aim was luck. That night he glimpsed several deer feeding in the light of the full moon, their tawny coats shining silver, the highlights leaping like fish. The beauty of that moment overcame him, irrationally and strangely, and he decided that it was wrong to kill any animal that fed by the light of the moon.

Now from the levee he could see the lights and stacks of the chemical company far across the water. The land on both sides of the river was flat as truck beds; the dangerous eddies near the shore kept revelers away. He counted seabirds—squatters on the levee—parked downstream at a respectful distance from him. Staring ahead at the lights and the dark water, facing a world in motion, he thought he knew his own mind.

Surely, he thought, the scientists did not think of themselves as monsters. They were thinking of the safety of the atomic workers; they wanted to know what the body and the planet could tolerate; they wanted to find peaceful uses for their deadly discoveries; they offered the gift of nuclear medicine to the future. With enough good intentions, Reed thought, you could find yourself giving atomic cocktails to poor women or irradiating the testes of prisoners; you could inject a child's leg bone with a purply, sticky, shape-shifting gel.

At the campsite, he pegged his tattered pup tent and hunkered down beside it. Minutes passed and he still posed—like *The Thinker*, he thought. His mind was virtually blank. His strength was sapped, and his surroundings seemed no longer nourishing or uplifting as in the past. He could feel his anxiety about Julia worming across the borders of his consciousness.

He had thought they were together again. But maybe it was only the sex. The strain between them had begun much earlier, long before the news about the rampant radioactivity. He always suspected that she didn't want to be involved with a cell rat. The chemicals had disturbed her, and from the beginning she had been uneasy about his gun collection, which had not made her feel protected at all. Dangerous chemicals and guns weren't the best props for courtship, he realized. They weren't wine and flowers. What did being a ro-

mantic wooer mean? In taking her out to the slag dumps and the
munitions works, he had foolishly created an impression of himself
as a reckless, maniacal, redneck suicidal gun-nut. No, that wasn't
true. He was beating himself up.

He felt small for his defensiveness, for his reliance on the plant,
even for his good-natured acceptance of the plant's culture of secrecy. Julia would say that if the government was capable of injecting
people with plutonium and not telling them it was plutonium, how
could he trust the plant—owned and regulated by the government—
to be truthful about the toxic waste? But that was too simple, he
knew. The plant had been generous to its workers, he reiterated to
himself now, as if he were arguing with her. But that was a lame
thought, like reaching in desperation for the smallest evidence of
love. Everything was more complicated, a tapestry of histories and
individuals. *You can't just wrench yourself out of your history*, he imagined telling Julia. And she shot right back at him, *Of course you can*.

But when she said he was holding something back, Julia had fired
her wad straight into his passivity, into the whole community's for-
giving myopia. *A foolish consistency is the hobgoblin of little minds*, she
remarked once, apropos of nothing he could detect. The phrase
rang a bell, as if someone important had said it. Now it caused a
heavy turmoil inside him, but he resisted, daring to visit the thought
in the hope that it could give him strength. He thought of the line
of loyalties—the labors of his grandfather who helped imagine the
plant into being, toiling right here at this river's shore, without an
inkling that he was helping to start the seeds of destruction in an
atomic hothouse. And his father had sacrificed his life. Reed had to
honor that. Didn't Julia see that? It was the same as if a father had
died in a war; the widow and mother and all around them would say:
he died for his country.

It was still light when Reed heard the rumble of a small motor. It
was an ATV. He and his son used to ride their four-wheelers out
here. He felt a twinge of regret that he and Dalton hadn't continued

to share outdoor sports after he was grown. In the space of three seconds Reed imagined a full-blown scene, Dalton riding up and making camp with him, sharing a beer with him.

Its lights sweeping the foliage, the four-wheeler stopped at Reed's camp.

"Howdy!" said a young guy in green cargo pants and military boots. His Aussie bush hat shaded his face. He cut the engine and lights on his ATV and stood in the fading daylight. "Fine night, huh?"

"Fine," Reed said.

The guy, inexplicably wearing a dagger on a studded leather belt, seemed to step out of a movie. He said, "I lost my dog and I've been looking everywhere."

"That's rough," Reed said. "I haven't seen or heard any dogs around. What kind?"

"A little beagle. I lose him about half the time."

"He probably can't keep up with you on this four-wheeler."

"Oh, I let him ride some. Them dogs is the craziest fools to get lost I've ever seen. That's the third one I've lost out here. We were out hunting. My truck's way on the other side of the channel."

"Don't you know there's a ban on hunting here now?" Reed didn't see a rifle or shotgun.

"Oh, they said that last year, but I figure this is a pretty big place."

"What's your dog's name?"

"Little-Bit. He loves beans. When we're out, he'll eat a whole can of beans and wienies."

"Well, I'll keep an eye out for him," Reed said. "If it was my dog I'd trail him to the ends of the earth."

"Let me give you my phone number, in case you find him."

The guy searched his pocket for scribbling tools. Reed found the nub of a pencil in his gearbox. The guy wrote his phone number on the back of a gasoline receipt.

"My name's Cobb," he said. "Cobb Kilgore."

"Glad to know you, Cobb," said Reed.

He did not give his own name. It annoyed him that the guy might abandon his dog. He tucked the receipt into the jumble in the gearbox. Then, seeing that Cobb Kilgore wasn't rushing off, Reed said, "What's with the dagger?"

"Do you ever go to the Renaissance Festival?"

"I saw something about it in the paper."

"It's coming up in June, over at the lake. I wear a medieval costume and play a part." Kilgore did a little whoop of self-mockery. "My character's named Lance, and I wear a costume—a half-sleeved tunic, with a hood, and tights, and Three-Musketeer boots. And I carry a leather pouch." He laughed. "My sister calls it a purse, but it's not." He touched the weapon at his side. "I've got several daggers, but they only let you carry one and you have to keep it sheathed. And I've got a chain-mail helmet. Oh, this stuff gets involved. And you have to learn this old language. You have to talk like they did in the old days in England."

"Prithee?" Reed said. "Gadzooks? Methinks?"

"Yeah! I'm not very good at it, but there's a lady that helps me. She goes to the festival in this long dress with the top bare down to the nipples. In fact, there's a whole slew of gals at this fair in low-cut gowns. They could be selling biscuits or fried pies and they'll be in these fancy dresses with their boobs hanging out."

"Sounds like those Civil War reenactments," Reed said. He expected to see a flanged mace or a spiked flail in the arsenal of this warrior.

"It's just a chance to enjoy history. We play war games. And we have a wild boar hunt with spears. It's like going to a pay ranch where you can shoot antelopes and zebras. I did that one year and got an antelope for my den. What I like best is the Highland games. I'm Scots-Irish and it's a chance to strut around with a little Celtic pride."

"Didn't the English run the Scots over to Ireland?" Reed asked.

"How come you're old England in one place and Scots-Irish in another?"

"Oh, it was so long ago. We got over it." He laughed. "Now we're one big happy family."

"We're all hooked up together in the Great Human Family Tree," Reed said, hoping that would be the last word. But Kilgore burbled on for a while about the wars of his ancestors. They knew there would always be war, Reed thought.

The light was growing dim. It was past sunset. "Well, I better go find my dog," Kilgore said at last.

Reed built a small fire, opened the still-warm lasagna, and ate, alone with the shrill, erratic sounds of the night. A line of a song from a distant radio was audible for a moment and then it faded. He studied a patch of sky above. He thought he could make out Jupiter, but Uranus, Neptune, and Pluto—that nefarious trio—were out at the boundary of the solar system, unnoticeable, like the little invisibles on his computer.

He called out "Little-Bit" a few times during the evening, before settling into his tent. He listened during the night for the beagle's yelp. He heard coyotes. The sound of the yelps of a large pack of coyotes carried high. Some military planes flew overhead—heavy transports, growling loud with their load. He missed Clarence. If he had a female dog, he'd name her Millie Rem. He tried to remember Buford, the bench-legged fice, a comical excuse for a dog. A groundhog had slit Buford's nose with its claw once, when Buford had ventured into its burrow. As Reed tried to fall asleep, he reviewed his memories of all the dogs he had buried. Buford, Happy Jack, the German shepherd Buddy, the bird dog Hans, a squirrel dog called Fabian, and the two Border collies he trained to unusual commands like "Whoop!" and "Ha-ha!" Since they didn't have sheep, he could teach them jobs irrelevant to sheep. When they played rough, he said, "Be sweet," which calmed them. Grace and Jack, the Border collies.

A tick was crawling on him, and he cast it away from him. Julia loved telling him about the rickettsia viruses, those spread by ticks. With flutters of her eyelashes against his skin, she had pretended once that she was setting ticks loose on him.

His dreams that night were surreal scenes, stretched images of birds and microwave ovens, and writhing coils of colorful tooth-paste. He dreamed that Julia was playing the piano with Artie Shaw. The clarinet dissolved into a flock of starlings. He slept sporadically, with his usual screeches and groans. He listened carefully to the in-sect music that performed in shifts, the nighttime munchings of busy nocturnal creatures, the whirring flights of owls. But the sen-sations seemed tentative, threatened, too noisy at times, too quiet at other times. He dreamed of lava flows and cauldrons of boiling witches' soup on display in a show window. The memory of the dream about the dead woman grabbed him in a brief nightmare. In the waking periods, he felt suspended, watching, waiting for the next act.

36

Reed had to zigzag through church traffic as he biked through town on his way home from the wildlife refuge. His retreat had offered no respite or renewal, not even a sound sleep. Lying awake, with the insects' wall of sound and the thrumming of the plant in the distance, he had felt angry with himself. With the heaps of corroded metals and sea-green sludge and green water, the place was spoiled and ugly. His heart had been a slag heap, his gut a rusted-out chemical storage drum. For the first time out there in his tent, he felt truly alone. Julia seemed like a will-o'-the-wisp, the sanctuary like a setup in a gangster film.

At home, Reed listened to his telephone messages while feeding Clarence in the kitchen. A chatty monologue from his daughter, who was apparently no longer concerned about workplace safety. A reminder about an ice-cream social at Sunnybank. No bad news about his mother. Nothing from Julia. She had simply disappeared, perhaps kidnapped and murdered, her body dumped into Lake Michigan. He dialed her number and got her answering machine again. He hung up without leaving a message. Then he realized that Clarence was standing on his hind legs, paws on Reed's chest. The sleek feel of the dog's fur and the pleasant weight of his paws felt good.

"Clarence! I didn't mean to ignore you, buddy."

Clarence danced in circles, barking.

Reed said, "Next time I go camping, you're going with me. We'll go to some pure place where you won't burn your tootsies on poison ground. Wherever that might be."

He thought that if Julia never came back to him, he would light out for some other territory. He would become a hermit and surround himself with dogs. He could be happy with dogs. Dogs had always offered him moral instruction. *Happy to be anywhere.* Burl's motto could have been a dog's. Dogs were storage drums of happiness, he thought.

After a short run around the dismal vacant lot with Clarence, he telephoned his mother. She sounded alert and cheerful. It struck him that she did not have an old-lady voice.

"Mom!"

"What?"

"Oh, nothing. I'm counting on you. You're my best girl."

"You're my baby," she said.

Reed felt a shard of guilt for isolating his mother in a remote cubicle of his mind, but it was a helpful arrangement at the moment. If she were occupying the back bedroom of his house, as he had earlier imagined, he might be checking himself into a psychiatric ward by now. He hung up the telephone and started for the den. A plastic jug on the kitchen floor was in his way. He stomped on it, smashed it with an angry explosion.

Canceling out the face of Venus with a quick click on his keyboard, he checked his e-mail—only one nonjunk message. One person other than his daughter had bothered to think of him all week-end. Click. Hot Mama!

She had written, "Showdown. I challenge you to meet me for coffee Sunday morning. No strings. I'll be at the Dairy Queen on Grand Avenue, and I'll be in a green 1987 Chevy. 11 a.m."

"I'll be there," Reed replied impulsively. He told her he would be wearing a red T-shirt and driving a blue truck. He was not more specific about the truck, and he didn't want to go on his easily iden-tifiable motorcycle. He showered and slapped on some musky after-shave, just in case. The red T-shirt fit smooth and tight, and he tucked the ends into his black jeans, consulting himself in the bath-room mirror. Hell, he was Atomic Man.

The Dairy Queen was next to a carpet showroom. When he ar-rived, about five minutes late, he intended to circle the place and try to get a look at the woman calling herself Hot Mama. He spotted the old green Chevy. As he paused to turn into a parking spot, he saw the green door open and a giant head appear—silvery, like a cabbage. Then slowly a woman materialized, standing and leaning against the door frame as she collected herself. She was an Amazon, with the biggest head of hair he'd ever seen. Her unruly hair was like an overgrown honeysuckle vine, its tendrils floating in all directions. She hauled a large purse—the size of a cat carrier—out of the pas-senger seat and clutched it against her. Closing the door, she stood still and gazed around. She had on jeans and a loose floral-print top. Her hair was light, not gray, and she seemed younger than he had expected.

Reed would have floor-boarded away from the Dairy Queen at the initial sight of her giant head, but he hesitated because she had gone to the trouble to come here. Her lines about Beethoven and sitting on the porch in the rain came to mind. Actually, what had in-trigued him all along was the juxtaposition of Beethoven and the personally cured country hams. Now, he thought, he was seeing hams like none on earth. He couldn't guess what all that brawn weighed. She was striding to the entrance, military fashion.

Atomic Man parked his truck. He should have a bumper sticker: I'M A WORKING MAN—ALL MY PARTS FUNCTION. He fearlessly strode to the woman's side, catching her before she reached the door.

"Hot Mama!" he said—as gallantly as one could utter "Hot Mama," he thought, then wondered how that must sound if he had guessed wrong and she was someone else.

"I was afraid you wouldn't come," she said, with a terse little giggle.

Her handshake was as firm as a man's. She was almost his height, but she wasn't as large as he thought at first, and she had a rather sweet face beneath the frightening honeysuckle bush she wore on her head.

They sat at a corner booth, Reed with coffee and Hot Mama with coffee and a pineapple sundae. He had offered to pay for hers, but she would not allow him. She sifted two sugars into her coffee and stirred noisily. She could probably lift a fifty-five-gallon drum of chemicals, he thought. She tested her coffee. Then she startled him.

"I thought I recognized you!" she said, with one muscular arm flying up as though she were about to hail a taxi. "But I never knew your name."

"No names. Didn't we agree?"

"Right. But didn't you used to run around with Sammy Blew?"

"Yeah. I still see him now and then. How do you know Sammy?"

"I used to date him, ages ago. Before he got so pitiful."

"Oh, Sammy's not pitiful! What makes you say that? But I haven't talked to him in a while. He might be worse than pitiful by now. He might be downright sorrowful." Reed squirmed in the booth. He didn't want to reveal that he knew Sammy from the plant.

Her eyes flashed fire. She said, "Well, he was snorting coke in my dinette and I told him to leave, that it was one time too many to get messed up when he's around me. I don't think he even noticed what I said. He just left, left a box of cigarettes there too and his lighter, and he never came back and got them. After that I wouldn't answer his calls. I've got my pride. Anybody that thinks he can use me to support his habit has got another think coming. How about you, Atomic Boy, you got any bad habits?"

"I'm sure I do, but they don't involve snorting, or anything criminal." Reed tried to grin. Her hairdo belonged in the *Guinness Book of World Records*, but he wasn't sure in what category. Flyaway fractals?

"You don't have to tell me who you are," she said. "But I do remember you. It was years ago. You had a couple of young kids. I used to see you at Little League. My nephew played shortstop."

"Probably." He didn't remember her.

"I've got certain rules I live by," she said, as she dipped into her sundae. "And one of them is that I treat people the way I want to be treated. That's the golden. And another one is that I don't turn anything I can't deal with into a joke—because I'll deal with it or else. No jokes. Also, some things I don't tolerate. One thing I can't stand is for somebody to say they'll do something and then not do it. Last year I hired a guy to fix my gutters, and he came out and installed scaffolding around the whole place. Then he disappeared. No show. So I finally got my nephew to come over, and he climbed up on the scaffolding, fixed the gutters, and then tore down the scaffolding and sold it for lumber at the flea market."

"Same nephew from Little League?"

She nodded and spooned the last of her ice cream.

"Did you ever hear from the guy you hired?" he added.

"No."

"Maybe he died. Or got called up by the National Guard."

"Just the same, I'm not having scaffolding around my house. It looked like a damned roller coaster." She ran her fingers through her tangle of hair. "I'm glad we decided to get together," she said. "A little Internet intrigue! I might not have gotten any replies if I'd called myself Betty—fond of classical music, self-sufficient, loves to watch the rain."

"I like big bands," Reed said. "And rain. Tell me about Beethoven."

"Deaf as a stump, but he made up melodies to die for. It was all in his head."

"He must have had a big head to hold all that," Reed said idly, then spilled his coffee. Her wild hairdo made him cringe. He saw rampant mutant space-worms writhing.

"You know what I want to do sometime?" she said, her eyes in dreamy half-moon phase.

"What?"

"Go to one of those symphonies in a big city. I like to watch those conductors on television, the way they swing their arms. I always imagine that's the way generals run a war."

She finished her sundae, which was so small Reed figured she would want another one, but she didn't. She said, "Your turn. What big wish do you have?"

Reed was thinking about the slag heaps and the green ponds. The green-clad warrior and the lost dog.

"Hello! Earth to Atomic Man. Come in, please."

"Oh. Where was I?"

"Your big wish."

He started inventing something, just winging it, wondering where he was going with it. He said, "I like to ride my motorcycle. So I ride around a lot, but I want something different. I want to take a longer trip." He had no idea where the next sentence would take him. "My dream is to take the same trip Jack Kerouac took, only I'll do it with my dog, and I'll write my own book about it, with snapshots I take, of my dog in different places, like at the Alamo. Maybe I'll write it from my dog's point of view—that's it; I won't be in it. It'll just be *Dog on the Road*." Not a bad notion, Reed thought, if Clarence would agree to it.

"Is this Jack a friend of yours?"

"No. He died years ago. He wrote a book about his trip, *On the Road*."

"I like to write down my thoughts," she said. "I do a little journaling. The trick is to do it every day, regardless. I find I always have some little something to write."

Reed was heartsick. If he made her feel good, then she'd just get disappointed. He didn't want to be rude. So he babbled on, inventing more dreams. He described his dog as a mongrel with spots and red eyes, resembling a wolf. His reckless chatter made him feel unhappy. Her manner was flat, abrupt, almost abrasive, and her mass of hair overpowered him.

She said, "I've been married, and here's how it worked out. I had to be in a hospital once for about six weeks, and when I got back home my husband had gotten rid of all my knickknacks. He didn't throw them away. He just put them out of sight. He found them annoying, I guess, because he had to do the cleaning during that time, and they were too much trouble to dust. But he had gotten rid of all my embroidered pillows, all the little boxes and frills on my dresser. He hid my silver comb and brush that belonged to my grandmother. In the kitchen all the ceramic chickens and owls were shut up in a drawer. He had trashed the bedroom. It was like some bachelor pad, dirty sheets and clothes everywhere, and not a trace of me."

Hot Mama seemed ready to cry, but she pulled herself together, and said, "I was well rid of him. He didn't have a poet's soul to begin with."

When they left the Dairy Queen, Reed felt the impulse to help her into her car but was afraid she wouldn't like that. Yet she seemed to linger, as if she expected an embrace. She flung her door open.

"I enjoyed the chitchat," she said, settling into her seat. "You never know who you might meet out here in the world."

"Glad to know you," Reed said. "Take it easy."

He tunneled home through a mental fog. *Glad to know you*. He remembered his father saying "Glad to know you" to a man who came to their house. Reed didn't remember who the man was. It didn't matter. *Glad to know you*, his father said. It was a phrase that was so genial, so old-fashioned. And not necessarily sincere.

37

At home he ate a head of lettuce over the sink, pinching out the brown parts, then opened some cheese and a box of crackers. Without a woman around, he had turned into a slob, like Hot Mama's erstwhile husband. If Julia were here, they could have something elegant and delicious at the Cavalcade, or Mr. Como's— some mesquite-grilled salmon and some complicated salad that had a choice of fifteen dressings and its own fork. *Fresh ground pepper?* from a pop-up guy with a phallic pepper mill. That would be nice, he thought—Julia twinkling across from him, self-assured and tender as asparagus tips.

In his mind, Hot Mama grinned at him, her teeth on fire, her Einstein hair like some radiation experiment gone awry. She was heavy like the gel form of plutonium. He tried to pound the image out of his head.

Later in the afternoon, after washing his car and puttering mind-
lessly around the house, Reed dropped by Burl's with a half-formed
notion of going to Chicago to find Julia. When he thumped on
Burl's screen door, Burl yelled "Entrez!"

Reed battled a caterpillar-green sheet hanging on a line across
the front room. A crude mural was painted on it. Reed ducked under
it into the kitchen, where Burl was microwaving a burrito.

"What's that? It looks like David and Goliath, with Goliath taking a crap."

"No! It's the Apostle Paul meeting Jesus. Jesus is up on high, so he
looks bigger. His halo was on crooked, and I tried to fix it and made
a mess. It was for the pageant at Sally's church. I volunteered to do it,
but she took a look at it and said, 'Burl, you are *out of* your mind.' She
wasn't even half polite about it." He laughed. "Hey, I like it."

The microwave beeped. Burl put another burrito in the microwave for Reed. Burl said, "I thought I'd get a truckload of statues
or something and set up at a flea market. The mural would make a
good display—and an awning."

"Well, it would, I guess, Burl. And when you get done, Goliath
can use it to wipe with. He reminds me of this humongous woman I
just met." He told Burl briefly about his Dairy Queen date with Hot
Mama. "She had this head of hair that looked like it could have bird
nests in it—or anything. You couldn't tell."

"Big hair to the max?"

Reed nodded. "And she was huge. Man, every woman that comes
my way is either too busy for me or too old, or too young, or uptight
like that social worker at the hospital—or too weird."

"Well, don't feel bad that you can't screw them all."

Burl twisted his fingers as if he were knitting a bonnet for a baby
mouse. "Didn't you tell me there are ten or twelve dimensions in
string theory? Maybe she was really little-bitty and she just popped
out of another dimension."

"I don't know her dimensions, but man, she was a load of
woman," Reed said. "She said she used to go with Sammy Blew."

"Sammy always liked big strong women—weight lifters."

"I didn't know that."

"Sammy's got a streak of masochism."

"This woman was *scary*! I thought I'd encountered a mutation from a radiation experiment—you know, one of those movies?"

"Aren't you living in that movie?" Burl asked, flipping the cap from a bottle of beer. "*The Uranium Follies,* or some such."

"That's not the half of it." Reed took the beer from Burl. "I've got atomic mutation on the brain."

While they ate the burritos, Reed told Burl briefly about the plutonium experiments, describing one of the cases, a four-year-old boy with a bone cancer.

"A child came all the way from Australia for a special treatment, and they injected him with plutonium-239. The boy was in pain when he left home and he was screaming when he left to go back. He didn't live long." Reed took a slug of beer. "They were trying plutonium on all kinds of ailments. They'd give them a hundred times as much as they thought might be safe just so they could find the tolerance dose. They'd try it on people with heart attacks, ulcers, anything handy."

Apparently Burl was speechless.

"Hello. Earth to Burl."

"Man, oh, man. Awful stuff."

"Maybe you can eat it, but you sure can't breathe it."

"How do they think up stuff like that?"

They finished the burritos and went to the living room.

"You know, Reed, there's no telling what the government's still up to."

"Right." Reed nodded.

Burl said, "If the government did it back then, why wouldn't they do such a thing now? It might not be plutonium. It might be something else."

He flapped his sheet mural in Reed's face. "This calls for church," he said.

The church pageant had slipped Reed's mind. Burl had wanted him to go along. "When is this bacchanalia, anyway?"

"Tonight. I reckon you could go with me."

"Hmm."

"I promised Sally I'd clean up and go."

"Why don't you get Rita to go with you?"

"Oh, she's gone to a family reunion, one of those genealogy weekends. I told her my family tree had dry rot."

Reed helped himself to another beer from Burl's refrigerator and stood at the window watching a group of children walking along in a crowded, tight bunch. They seemed to be little grade-schoolers, and they struggled along under backpacks, even though it was Sunday. When his kids were little, they traveled light; he recalled them jumping around, unencumbered. But now it seemed as though children were beasts of burden, hauling their essential material possessions, as if they had to be prepared for a quick escape from the nuclear cloud. *The hobgoblin of little minds*, he thought, visualizing the backpack as a hobgoblin that had hitched a ride.

Still watching out the window, Reed saw a little girl stumble and fall. Another girl tried to help her up, but two small boys skirted them, laughing. The child who had fallen kicked at the boys, like a bug thrown onto its back, her tiny foot drumming the air.

Reed turned to face Burl's mural. He couldn't see Jesus and the Apostle Paul in it. He scrutinized the figures, realizing he should give Burl some credit for his artistic effort. "I didn't know you could paint," he said.

"Neither did I." Burl surveyed his work. "But why not? We can do a lot more than we think we can. Maybe I'll start a website and sell sheet paintings." He laughed.

Burl's schemes were sometimes so extravagant that he was paralyzed by their very grandeur, Reed thought. But the enthusiasm of the plutonium experimenters obscured their vision, and they sprinted ahead, their perversity an energy source, like radium.

Not Einstein. He balked at the atomic bomb; he resisted quantum mechanics.

"Where does Sally's church stand on Einstein's theory of relativity?" Reed asked.

Burl laughed, spurting out some droplets of beer. He had been washing dishes but then forgot and was wandering around with a wet dish mop.

"Einstein believed in God, didn't he?" Burl said.

"Well, he looked like God anyway, with that hair."

"Like God had been traipsing through the universe like a hobo for about a hundred million years. Like he'd lost something out there in one of those galaxies and couldn't find it."

They laughed.

"Maybe that's where Jesus is," Reed said. "Maybe he took a wrong turn. He could be in imaginary time. One of those books I read said imaginary time is at a right angle to regular time—if you can believe that."

"That's no way to talk about Christ the Savior!" Burl said.

"Who bailed you out of jail, me or Jesus?"

Burl fell onto the sofa laughing. This kind of banter with Burl had long been a chief source of entertainment for both. It felt good to go at it again.

"You're full of shit, Burl."

"You're full of shit, Reed." Burl shook the dish mop at Reed. "If Jesus came back here now, he'd be in over his head. Just the cleaning alone."

"He'd need more than a dish mop," said Reed, draining his beer.

"Come with me to the pageant," Burl said. "It'll be fun. It'll cheer you up. You'll see. There'll be lots of singing—and eats."

"Why the hell not," Reed said. "If there's food, how can I go wrong?"

Before leaving, they finished the six-pack and painted for a while on Burl's mural. Now Goliath had a crown of flowers and David was standing in a soybean field. Burl still insisted they were Jesus and the Apostle Paul. Reed thought the painting resembled the work of two schizophrenic monkeys at a research lab engaging in self-expression on Art Day.

Burl showered and dressed in Sunday rigging—khaki pants and a clean short-sleeved plaid shirt. Reed was still in his red T-shirt and black jeans, which he considered might not be appropriate for church, but Burl assured him it was. "Sally says that some Sundays everybody wears overalls, or another Sunday they'll come in old-fashioned costumes. Sometimes it's Hawaiian-shirt Sunday."

The parking lot at the church was enormous, the size of the lots at the big-box stores. Burl, in a bubbly mood, introduced Reed to half a dozen people in the throng as they made their way into the church, a big box with a spire. Burl greeted people with backslaps as if he had known them for years.

"See, these are just good folks," said Burl, sending ebullient greetings all around. "They've got the spirit."

Reed felt buoyed by the beer, but unscrewed. "Holy shit," he said to Burl.

"There's my ever-loving brother!" cried a woman in a red blouse, white pants, and blue shoes. It was Sally, Burl's sister, all smiles and suntan. She had a gang of small children in tow, and they all jumped on Burl, tugging and squealing. He hugged them all and teased them. Sally acknowledged Reed and whispered "Beer on your breath" in Burl's ear—loudly enough for Reed to hear, but the children didn't notice.

Sally and her brood joined a group of children in front, and Burl and Reed found plush seats in the middle of the basketball-arena-sized auditorium, where American flags adorned the walls.

On the stage a painted scrim represented a blue sky with a scattering of cumulus clouds above a broad desert. At one end the desert became a seashore, with stark tropical trees scattered about and white seabirds hanging in the air above the greenish water.

"Sally didn't want my sheet messing up the scenery," Burl said.

"It's a pageant-in-a-box. They rent it and put it together like a piece of furniture you get from a warehouse store. It's got the costumes, the stage sets, the play, the whole works."

"Batteries included?"

"Right!"

A minister kicked off the evening with an exuberant prayer. Surveying the bowed congregation, Reed thought of the flock of praying mantises caught up in the filter rooms. He had liked those big bugs.

The crowd hushed under the abruptly dimmed lights, and the drama began. The pageant—*The First Missionary*—was about the Apostle Paul on the road to Damascus. Damascus was represented by a large tropical plant resting on a beige blanket—a palm tree in the desert. A teenager in a burnoose was walking along a winding, gray cardboard road. He was gasping with fatigue and thirst, and when he spotted the palm tree, he staggered across the stage, then knelt and drank from a bucket of water next to the tree.

Suddenly a spotlight beamed down from the ceiling, and a voice from above said, "Saul, Saul, why persecutest thou me?"

"Who art thou, Lord?" Saul jumped in fear, shielding his eyes from the bright light.

"I am Jesus whom thou persecutest: it is hard for thee to kick against the pricks."

Reed elbowed Burl.

"Lord, what wilt thou have me do?" said the man Saul.

The voice said, "Arise, and go into the city, and it shall be told thee what thou must do."

From the shadows a bearded man in a white robe, trimmed with gold glitter, appeared, gesturing kindly to the thirsty man. It was Jesus. The audience gasped. The lights played on his gold glitter.

As the play progressed, Reed began to fidget, and the seat grew less comfortable. The beer buzz wore off. He was hungry and agitated. He was stranded, perhaps like a traveler on the road to Damascus. He had placed his faith in science, and he felt it had eluded him. He had pledged his allegiance to big institutions, and they had fucked him over. His best friend was living on the edge. He missed Julia.

Saul, who had become the Apostle Paul, was being persecuted. Escaping his pursuers, he was lowered out of a high window in a large basket. A live donkey was led onto the stage to whisk Saul out of Damascus.

"I know that donkey," Burl whispered. "Pedro. Belongs to a guy I know."

At one point Reed misheard "the Apostle Paul" as "Parsifal," and his imagination inserted the Celtic warrior he had met in the refuge, or perhaps the Green Knight, waylaying Parsifal from behind a tree. Reed imagined the factory worker who packed the pageant into the box accidentally mixing up the parts from two or three different pageants. Reed considered how the pageant committee might accommodate the Green Knight in the drama. In church, Reed's mind had always wandered.

In his mind were vials of liquid stuff that could blast into fire if improperly handled. He saw heavy black rubber gloves jamming plungers into flesh. He could see Jesus on the cross, the thorns dripping poison into his eyes, the nails driven in like fuel rods. What was the fatal dose? How much could hide in your body before it made itself known?

Reed wondered if he would end up filing a medical claim. He wondered if Sammy Blew had had any bad exposures at the plant. Hot Mama had said he was pitiful. What did that mean?

It was odd to be in church. He was happier cruising the ether in his jaded Reedmobile, knowing that he didn't know shit, than he would be nestled in a silk bed of blind certainties. Religion could explain a billion angels dancing on a pinhead but reject subatomic structure as a blasphemous fantasy. The chasm inside him, the emptiness that made him cry out in the night and dream Salvador Dalí paintings, wasn't for lack of a faith.

The play ended with a crowd onstage, representing the multitudes the Apostle Paul had converted to Christianity. When they burst out singing "Onward, Christian Soldiers," the audience rose and joined in. Next was "God Bless America."

Reed sang along. He hadn't sung in church in a long while, and he felt nostalgic about the times his mother used to take him to church. He couldn't read the meaning of the rapture on Burl's face—whether Burl badly needed to belong, or whether this church reminded him somehow of going to church in Detroit when he was a kid, or even whether he was inwardly amused.

The buffet line was long and boisterous, and people were piling their plates high. Reed and Burl were chagrined to realize they hadn't contributed any food, but they were hungry. Besides meat and vegetables, there was a generous selection of processed snacks, arranged with the bags open-mouthed, like cornucopias. A whole table was laden with pies and cakes in supermarket packaging.

"I've died and gone to heaven," an older woman in front of Reed in the buffet line said with a sigh as she loaded her plate.

"I feel an urge to go ride a camel across the desert," said Reed.

"Don't rely on a donkey," Burl said.

In the parking lot after they ate, Burl sneaked a swig of whiskey from his truck. Sally sailed past, a couple of cars away. She waved and called out, "It just thrills my soul to see all these good people out here celebrating the Lord. You come back now, Reed."

"Didn't I tell you she had the holy spirit?" Burl said.

Reed waved to Sally. He leaned against the truck and observed the people streaming out of church. The parking lot was a traffic jam.

He said to Burl, "You can't see the stars out here with all these Florida-orange vapor lights."

Burl lifted his eyes skyward. "People don't worry much about the stars out here," he said.

Suddenly emotional, Burl said, "You're my best buddy, Reed."

He touched Reed's shoulder. "I don't know what I'd do without you. Look at that. I'm weeping tears. I'm sorry."

"That's all right, Burl. Nowadays men blubber and hug."

"Thanks, Reed, good buddy." Burl laughed and banged on the truck door. "Sometimes, life is just so—you know, goddammit— *whatever*, that the best thing to do is just enjoy the spectacle."

38

*R*eed reached home shortly after nine. The day had not smoothed his disquietude. He was restless and disturbed, still wondering if he should take off for Chicago. But surely Julia would be back for work the next day, Monday, after her three-week absence. Regretting that he had called her previously at three a.m., he refrained from dialing her now. If she had returned, she would be tired and busy, preparing for work the next morning. She wouldn't want to hear his mood.

He contemplated the solar system—Uranus close up with its halo askew, the thousand-faceted face of Jupiter's moon Callisto, Venus unmasked. The planets seemed so watchful, a steady presence, but as full of mystery as the human soul. As Mercury faded from the screen, he clicked on his e-mail. Hot Mama had written at two-thirteen p.m., "I checked my horoscope just now; usually I would have done it first thing in the morning. It told me to avoid Geminis today, and I have a feeling you are a Gemini. No offense, but you have this expression on your face, like you're whistling some private tune to yourself. I got the feeling that for you life is just a show, everything is for your entertainment. I was a sideshow."

Reed zipped back: "Now why would you think that? I am known as a kind and tolerant person. I gave you my time and interest. Everybody I know is fucked up. Do I need to add an opinionated loser to my list of troubles?" He paused for a moment, then wrote, "My best friend always says the best thing to do is enjoy the spectacle of life. I know he's right."

He clicked SAVE and shoved his message into the Drafts file. Don't act in haste, he said to himself. Did Jesus say that? Or Burl?

He decided to call Sammy Blew. Sammy was a night owl and something of an eccentric. He made collages of cut slivers of mirrors. He frequently cut himself and feared he was getting quicksilver poisoning from the backing on the mirror. "I'm O.K.," he had said to Reed once. "I got a tetanus shot." Reed hadn't seen Sammy lately, and he was troubled by what Hot Mama had said about him. Reed had never thought of Sammy as "pitiful." Sammy began working at the plant not long after Reed signed on, but after he transferred to utilities Reed seldom saw him.

Sammy was home, watching a movie, and he seemed glad to hear from Reed. They chatted for a while. He sounded O.K., and Reed was uncertain what to ask him. He couldn't bring himself to ask about Sammy's health. He told Sammy about Hot Mama.

"I don't know who you mean," Sammy said.

"Great big woman? Likes Beethoven and cures her own hams?"

"Bettina," Sammy said. "Yeah, I used to go with her. But she's not *that* big."

"Oh, I know."

"Might be a matter of perspective. You know I always went out with big girls."

"But *why?*"

"Reed, you don't know till you've tried it. But big women are—well, *comfortable*. And they're a challenge to make it with."

"Comfortable. Hmm."

"Big women will make good babies."

"I bet," Reed said, picturing a row of corpulent cherubs.

"How did Bettina seem, Reed? I haven't seen her in ages."

"She seemed nice."

"Happy?"

"Hard to tell. She seemed . . . aggravated." Clarence was nuzzling at Reed's arm. Reed patted the dog's head. "How are *you* doing, Sammy?"

"Great, just great, Reed. I've turned a corner, getting my life together, that whole story."

"Good, Sammy. That's really good to hear."

Reed decided not to ask Sammy about his exposures. He went out with Clarence for a moment. The insects outside were louder than the traffic on the boulevard. The night was overcast and humid. He went inside. Something from the church supper had given him heartburn, and as he sought out a remedy from his vintage collection of patent medicines, he began talking aloud to himself and storming around his place. He was angry with Hot Mama and angry with himself for getting into such ticklish tangles with women. He was mad at the world. After locating a plastic shopping bag, he began ditching his expired medicines. Slam, dunk. Cough syrup, antacids, salves, all partially used. A packet of douche powder someone had left, hair conditioner. Tooth whitener, dead. Mouth rinse, dead. Some allergy medicine he had inherited from Glenda. She snored like the devil! He remembered an occasion when he was still married to her—he was throwing things around, cursing and yelling at her. For what? He couldn't remember. It wasn't important. Or maybe it was. Maybe he wasn't paying enough attention to the nuances of her femininity.

39

The digital clock said six twenty-five. The telephone was ringing, not the alarm.

"Reed." His mother's voice was calm and clear, as firm as she
sounded twenty years ago. "I was awake all night thinking things
through," she said. "I'm fully recovered from my stroke. Why, I
could play basketball. I don't need to be in this place anymore."

"Ma. It's six-thirty in the morning. At least I think it's morning."

"Good. That will give us all day to get me moved."

Reed groaned. "Let me get some coffee. I'll come over there
later."

Unhurriedly, he made a pot of coffee and prepared some eggs
and cereal. He read the newspaper. He thought about exercising.
He should take Clarence to the park or the country. He was active
enough on the job, but he needed to work out more. It had been too

hot. A slight midriff pudge had crept up on him. At seven he turned up the radio to hear the news. It occurred to him that he liked for the big things to be simple and clear. He liked for the small things to be intricate and complicated. Wasn't that what Julia was saying to him?

He was reading the editorials when a phrase on the radio news skipped across his consciousness like a pebble on a pond. A headline, innocuous sounding, not elaborated upon, swiftly abandoned for another sensation—a carjacking. He rewound mentally what he had just heard: the administration had announced the start-up of the Strategic Nuclear Armaments Preparedness Program (SNAPP). Ten nuclear facilities were candidates for the new contracts. Reed spilled cereal on the floor. He was barefoot. He stepped in soggy cornflakes. He flung the dish into the sink, but it didn't break.

Nuclear bombs. More nuclear bombs—small ones probably. Suitcase bombs. Baby bombs, what they used to call kitten bombs. Bunker-busters—now named "robust earth penetration mechanisms." Deadly, precise things that could tunnel into rock and sink their hideous light into the dark earth. Baby mushroom clouds. Fast, thick streaks of light. Muffled clouds mushrooming through cracks in rock like easy, silent gas blasts.

Surely he had misheard. Yet he wasn't really surprised. He felt as if a blast of wind had blown a hole through him.

He found nothing about the new plan in the newspaper. On the Internet he located the brief wire-service story. Ten sites were being considered for various phases of bomb processing—including plutonium-pit refurbishment and uranium enrichment. Reed doubted that Congress would stand in the way. The ten sites were not named, but what it meant for the plant Reed could guess: with special centrifuge technology, the fuel could probably be cycled repeatedly until it was enriched to 90 percent—bomb grade. He figured the plant could switch from commercial to military in a sleight-of-hand maneuver, just as a rogue country could slip into bomb making while ostensibly creating electricity for heating up hot-tubs.

Reed telephoned Teddy, who would be getting home from his shift about then, but there was no answer. He tried Jim, paging him on the operations floor. Jim hadn't gone home yet.

"This is happening a whole lot sooner than we thought," Jim said.

"Of course we're one of the ten places," Reed said. "They're going to need our fuel for their new toys."

"We don't know the details, but I'm sure everything will be speeded up now. I knew this was going to happen! You can count on it, Reed. No layoffs. We'll get that centrifuge for sure. We'll see how fast this plant cranks up. I bet the D.O.E. will be here by lunchtime."

"Atoms for Peace!" Reed said, like a sign-off, but he thought Jim lived in an irony-free zone.

The accelerated cleanup would be even more accelerated now, he realized. The universe was accelerating. Everything was flying faster and faster, farther apart.

Reed replenished Clarence's water, pleased that he had the presence of mind to do so. He did not try to call Julia. He felt a slight vertigo, as if the news had made his surroundings wobble. He hadn't finished his breakfast, but he had no more appetite. He set the dishes in the sink and filled them with water.

He found his mother asleep—lying across her bed, her shoes still on. He tiptoed around the bed and stared at her until she woke up. "What are you staring at?" she asked.

"I got here quick as I could."

"I gave up on you." She straightened up and sat on the side of the bed. She seemed agile, her leg stronger.

He helped her to her chair and eased into the sofa. His stomach was still a bit queasy, and his mind seemed to be floating inside his head.

"I can do without these nosy-rosies that work here," she said. "And without their hard-luck cuisine. And without these half-brained people who live here. I'm not one of them. I want to go home."

"If you recall, the Smithfields are living in your house. They bought it. They play volleyball and raise chickens."

"That's so hard to believe," she said. "Sometimes I forget." She fumbled with some letters and cards stacked on her coffee table. "They're going to drive me nuts here," she said. "Norrie Paramor! They're always playing Norrie Paramor's orchestra on the intercom. It never stops. I'd love to hear Fats Waller do 'Flat Foot Floogie With the Floy Floy.' Or anything by Spike Jones. These people have no sense of fun here. They just play paper dolls."

Reed stared at the quilt hanging on the wall by the dining table. It was his grandmother Reed's old pinwheel quilt, its reeling design like drunken galaxies. He shifted his focal point to the bird clock on the wall and felt steadier. It was ten to eight. He wondered which bird would sing. The song sparrow's picture was at eight.

A couple of the cards in his mother's lap fell to the floor. Reed picked them up, a get-well card from someone in Memphis and a card from Shirley.

"Shirley's coming in October," his mother said, taking the cards.

"Great. She can be more help to you than I've been. It's about time she showed up."

Laying the cards on the coffee table, she said, "I've been thinking about all that stuff they've found out at the plant."

"What do you mean?"

"You thought I was in never-never land and didn't have a brain in my head. You're just pretending everything's hunky-dory, but I know better."

"But I didn't want to worry you."

"Well, I *am* worried. I'm afraid of what that plant has done to you."

"You know I'm always careful." He was the voice of reason, clutching at birdsong.

She was silent, wadding a tissue in her hand. Then, haltingly, she said, "They'll never get that mess cleaned up."

He took her hand and held it. He glanced at the photograph of his father on the shelf near the TV. He seemed to have shifted slightly, his face a bit more inquisitive.

"Tell me what Dad's accident was like—and what it did to you," Reed said, putting his arm around her shoulders and giving her a little squeeze. "You never said much."

Reed wasn't in the habit of referring to his father as Dad; for a moment, it was almost as if his father had a life there with them.

Trembling slightly, she turned her face away from him. Reed held her tight until she got over her tears.

"You don't have to talk about it, Ma. I'm sorry."

"Oh, it was bad, real bad. In the hospital he was raw and blistered. All over." She paused and touched her forehead, summoning memory.

"You don't have to tell me."

She shook her head. "He cried," she said. "It hurt so bad. He cried to die. He couldn't even talk to me for the pain. He couldn't form words. And they couldn't give him enough morphine to kill the pain. It went on for six hours." She blew her nose. "By the time you went to work there, they stopped mixing the chemicals the way they did, so I thought it was safe. You wouldn't have an accident like that. And the money was so good. And you were just starting out in life. If I had known. . . ."

"Don't worry about me. I'm O.K."

She clasped his hand. Talking to the bookshelf, she said, "Now I think I was just closing my eyes. Everybody was so loyal; nobody dared to say anything bad about the plant. Your father never knew how bad that stuff was."

"I'm sorry I brought this up."

"I couldn't blame the plant for what they did to him. We were in a war, you know. You couldn't question."

"That's the trouble, isn't it? Things seem different now."

"If you get cancer I think it will purely kill me."

"No, no, Ma, I'm fine. I feel just dandy. My urine's clear and I can run uphill. And I'm still as careful as ever." He grinned. "With chemicals *and* with women."

"I guess I'll stay here and I won't move back home," she said. "I know I'm a burden to you."

"That doesn't sound like you, Mom. Where's your spunk? This morning you were wanting me to come and haul you out of here. Don't play martyr on me."

"Where's the girl who went with us to Captain Mack's?"

"She's gone to Chicago to see her sister. But I'm going up there to get her and bring her back. I can't wait to see her so I can give her a big smack on the puss." He kissed his mother's cheek. "I love her almost as much as I do you, Mom."

His mom laughed. "She's good. She's good for you."

The clock warbled the hour. It was the goldfinch.

"Damn. I have to fix that thing," Reed said, rising and seizing the clock from the wall.

"They still get mixed up," she said.

He worked on it, twirling the knob in the back. "You have to cycle through the songs and stop one bird shy of the one you want to sing next. That would be the cardinal at nine o'clock." He finished resetting the birds and replaced the clock on the wall. He didn't know why it had taken him so long to get around to accomplishing this simple task. It was one more story of his life.

His mother's love gushing over him, he was ready to rip boldly into the fabric of space-time. On his way down the hall, he tipped his cap and greeted a woman pushing a walker—Mrs. Valley! Lindbergh's pal. Preoccupied with the arduousness of her journey, she didn't speak. But the man who said prayers at meals gave him a military salute, and one of the ladies in the sunroom waved and said, "Tootle-oo!" He realized that Norrie Paramor's orchestra was playing on the intercom as he strode down the hall to the exit.

40

$\mathcal{R}$eed filled out forms for the health screening at the walk-in clinic.

"Make a fist for me, dear," said a lab tech in a flower-print smock. "Good. Now you're going to feel a stick."

The tiny woman seemed to be a trainee, but she appeared to be as old as his mother. A nurse in a blue cardigan helped to guide her hand, but the stick into Reed's vein went awry.

"A rolling vein," the nurse said. "Back it up a little."

Reed wondered if senior citizens were infiltrating the medical establishment in order to monitor its abuses. She poked him again. Even though it hurt, Reed stayed silent. The nurse said, "Here, Miss Bonnie, follow my hand. Back it up a little." The old woman seemed frightened. Her rubber gloves were loose. The nurse hovered as the geriatric lab tech drew several tubes of blood. The tubes in the tray tinkled like a distant shattering of glass.

"You're getting the works," the nurse said to Reed.

"I've already had the works."

He got the breathing tests and the chest X-ray; he gave a urine specimen; he scheduled a colonoscopy for one week hence. A physician's assistant examined his prostate. She was unattractive, with frizzy hair and a thick waist. His prostate felt healthy as a peach, she said.

"Did I leave out anything?" he asked. He was covered, ass to elbow.

He drove straight to the cytopathology lab where Julia worked. It was on the third floor in the rear of a nondescript medical building near the Interstate. He ran up the stairway instead of waiting for the elevator. Passing through the hallway of bulletin boards covered with research posters on ticks and viruses, Reed entered the outer office of the lab. There Reed asked the technician on duty if he could speak with Julia Jensen. A personal matter. Urgent, he added.

"I think she's still out of town."

"Can I find out how to get in touch with her?"

"I'll ask Sandra. She may be able to help you."

Sandra appeared, a short-haired woman in glasses. "She went off in a hurry, after her exams were over. She took a course in microbiology, and she'd been talking about going to the University of Chicago." The woman squinted, sizing up Reed. "I think she may have gone up there to see about registering."

"It's molecular, not micro," Reed said. "Wasn't she supposed to be back at work by now? Haven't you heard from her?"

"We expected her back last week, but I believe she called and asked for an extension."

"So you've heard from her? Is she quitting her job?"

"I didn't speak to her myself, and I'm not sure what her plans are."

"Do you know how I can get in touch with her?" Reed jingled change in his pocket.

"I have no idea. Sorry!"

"Could I leave her a message?"

"Well, if she calls I could give her a message. Just write down your name and number." She handed him a notepad bearing a drug ad logo at the top.

"Tell Julia I love her," he sang. Did he really sing that? he wondered later, after he had written down the information and left it with Sandra, who tucked the notepaper in the pocket of her strangely cerulean lab pants.

In the vacant lot, the grass was drying to brown. The sky was clear and blue, with no hint of rain. Clarence was fetching a squirrel toy, his favorite.

"I'm going to Chicago," Reed said to Clarence, who cocked his head and listened. "Burl's going to look in on you at the kennel and make sure they're treating you right. And when I bring Julia back, we'll all go camp out at the lake and watch the meteor showers."

Clarence seized his squirrel toy and began gnawing on it.

"I'm going to Chicago, Clarence," Reed said, easing the squirrel from the dog's mouth. "Forget Atomic Man. Just call me Captain Plutonium."

He threw the squirrel and Clarence ran for it.

Reed rescheduled his shift so that he didn't have to come in until Friday night. Then he called Julia's machine and told it, "O.K., Miss Julia Jensen. It's me again, one last time before I haul my ass off to the Windy City and come looking for you. I know you're secretly checking your messages. Here's my message: I want you to meet me at that sculpture at the University of Chicago. I'll be hanging around there tomorrow, Tuesday, between one and four in the afternoon. I've got a bone to pick with Enrico Fermi. You be there then and we'll have a *nuclear exchange*. You and I together can decide the fate of civilization." He paused, then blurted, "And by the way, I want to see you because I love you."

41

Reed stuffed his good duffel, e-mailed Dalton and Dana, said good-bye to Clarence at the kennel, and tanked up his truck. Riding in the truck was jarring, like driving over speed strips, but his car needed some transmission work. As he headed out of town, he nostalgically recalled the night last summer when he and Julia went in the truck to the cartoon festival at the drive-in movies, like some country couple out on a date after hauling hay on a long June afternoon.

Anonymous on the Interstate, he felt the warm rising of desire for her. He had so much to tell her: the plutonium in the deer, the science-fiction experiments, the night at Fort Wolf, the Celtic warrior, the church pageant. He could leave out Hot Mama. Julia had told him he was being dishonest with her, holding things back. That was true. But he would tell her everything now. She would be glad that he got the physical. His breathing tests were damn good, he thought. She would probably go critical over the plans for renewed bomb production. *We're in this together,* he would say to her.

Once again Reed was hitting the road, letting loose. The astronaut Michael Collins once said that the point wasn't to go to the moon but to leave the earth. Reed thought that was an easy rationalization for Collins, who must have been disappointed that he didn't get to walk on the moon with Armstrong and Aldrin. For as long as Reed could remember, he had been leaving, but never really going anywhere, except in his imaginary Reedmobile. Today, though, he wasn't an intergalactic tourist. He had an earthly mission. He was going to bring Julia back home. He couldn't believe she would enroll in the University of Chicago without telling him. The lab gals must have been mistaken.

He held his breath and swept downhill past the silver anonymous box of an eighteen-wheeler. It could be carrying shipments of shoes. Or toxic sludge bound for Yucca Mountain—to wait in line until Yucca Mountain was approved as the national nuclear-waste dump. Maybe someday it would qualify for the National Register of Historic Places—with a plaque, he thought, so that no one would forget what was there. His mind wandered away then, and melodies surfaced. He wished he could make up a song for Julia. When he was a boy, he formed the idea that men always knelt and sang when proposing. A song could be direct, yet general, without sloppy barbs of reality. A song would go straight to the heart—making love or staying alive or getting by or shuffling off to Buffalo. If he could write songs, he would write about longing, like gases oozing out of the mud of his heart. Better still, he'd write a song about working, to say what he wanted to say to her in a form that embodied feeling more than talking did, with all its evasion and embroidery. A man's work gave him identity, meaning, structure, a fucking raison d'être! He tried to think of some Delta work chants. Tote that barge. How did you tote a barge? Tow? He thought of his grandfather working on the levee, in mud and baking sun. His father heaving greensalt with his bare hands. Surely there was a personal song in all that.

It seemed impossible to think of an original melody. He tried a few lines, but each line he could think of went to the tune of "Eve of Destruction."

Come on, baby,
We're the Atom and Eve of destruction.

He envisioned Julia's mind cruising blithely through the intricate pathways of molecular biology. What would she want with a cell rat? He was only a maintenance engineer; however complex and highly paid his job was, he still was a fix-it specialist, while she was exploring the unknown. It was like the difference between a fry cook and a chef. He remembered eating meat loaf in front of her during their first meeting. But he had made her laugh.

His mind boiled as he rolled down the road. Actually, he was still angry with her. She had wounded him. She was rude in not answering his calls. And she was so absorbed with viruses and her large plans that she wasn't considering him. But his desire for her wasn't just a gonadal flare-up. She was different, just different from all the other women he had known. He would be angrier if he weren't so worried. She had told him so little about her sister's troubles that Reed was free to imagine them. He entertained several scenarios dealing with drugs, guns, hospitals, jails. Something must have happened to Julia. He tried to remind himself that it wasn't her habit to call.

Julia could be either alive or dead in Chicago, and until he knew which, she was both. If Einstein's mind couldn't accept indeterminacy, how could Julia expect Reed to fathom string theory? Physicists had probably thought up strings just in order to tie up loose ends. He wondered if the strings at the itty-bitty Planck level were analogous to the miles of DNA strands inside a cell. He made a mental note to ask Julia if DNA strands, like the p-branes in string theory, could warp in and out of dimensions. Through his windshield the world was commonplace: gray asphalt, broken lines, fast-moving vehicles, speeders zooming around him, green signs, azure sky, emerald corn, and yellow-green wheat. Bugs spattering the glass.

After all that had happened recently, he was surprised that he could add two and two. If he could just burst through his own sub-terfuges and talk straight to her—tenderly—then maybe they could face the darkness together. He would have to tell her about his ex-posures, his numbers, but maybe that would backfire. He felt she was standing in radiant light while he crouched somewhere in a shadowy corner of a dank basement. In recent months he had been bombarded with challenges from all directions, like neutrinos zing-ing through him on the road to nowhere, and his inherent cheerful-ness had deflated. But he believed it would return, as simply as a pop-up on his computer screen, if Julia came back to him.

But what difference would it make? Some dark, mysterious force was pulling the universe apart. The universe was expanding at an ever-increasing rate, like a burst of fireworks shooting into oblivion. Reed's mind jumped backwards and forwards billions of years. How could it be that he was here now? How could it be that the human race existed, and that he was here to observe it? Sometimes he could not distinguish between his imagination and cold, bare facts. Now it hit him more deeply than ever what an unlikely pinprick in the ab-surd fabric of space-time human existence was. He slammed his hands on the wheel. He hated being stuck in his own head.

As he drove past immense cornfields, a thick green rug, he went over and over his situation. Every angle of vision revealed a differ-ent story. Each version was like a cornfield maze, shaped by a vision-ary farmer on a state-of-the-art tractor. You could see it only from afar, the way the pictures etched by Incas made sense only from the air. Either the Incas were trying to guide extraterrestrial visitors to a landing zone, Reed thought, or they could fly and enjoyed Sunday outings in the air to view this art form.

He exited and found gas and a chain restaurant that served baked chicken with brussels sprouts and braised fennel, which befuddled him and made him feel as though he were a time traveler—but from the past or future? He wasn't clear on fennel. He felt better after eating, and he had a second cup of coffee.

When he returned to the truck, he noticed a sign, NO SEMI-PARKING IN THIS LOT. To park or not to park? he wondered. Or semi-park? Indeterminacy abounded. A misty rain had fogged his windshield, but as soon as he reached the speed limit on the highway, the sun broke out.

Reed was grateful when the skyline finally appeared, black towers illuminated in the late sun. The gleaming spires rose out of the prairie like stalagmites—a mutant village, overgrown, hardened from minerals dripping down from the poison sky. A city at a distance conveyed this freakish aspect, its surreal gravestones—underworld thrustings—reaching for the sun as if to pull it down.

Reed could imagine a dirty bomb hitting Chicago—limited fallout, some radiation sickness, more fear than damage. And he could imagine one well-dressed itinerant, wired with a backpack, ambling along Michigan Avenue. But a chain-link security fence shielded the mind from staging expansive nuclear theatricals—a self-protective function for which Reed was immensely thankful. The plutonium experiments had shaken him, but now they were easing into a restful little nook in his memory.

The traffic began to thicken and swirl, like flocks of starlings in an early evening sky. Reed shifted into the new rhythm, alert and slightly crazed. He was tired and hot, ready to have a shower and roam the city. He had always been fond of Chicago, even before he knew Julia. It had authority and pizzazz. It would do him good to have some time here before he met her tomorrow afternoon. As he swooped into the city, he felt hopeful. The complex of towers and tunnels and rails and neighborhoods jumbled together in a million mysteries. He glided along the expressway that led toward the Loop. A couple of years ago he came here with a woman named Frances whose goal in life was to shop at Marshall Field's in her eternal search for the perfect purse. Reed had walked miles in the bitter wind while she shopped. Now he realized how much he had changed since then. He knew Julia would take him to someplace meaningful, like the Museum of Science and Industry, or the planetarium, instead of a department store.

After locating a chain hotel, he instructed the enthusiastic parking valet on driving his truck.

"You have to nudge it a little when it's out of gear," Reed said.

"I never drove a pickup like this," the valet said. "What kind of mileage does it get?"

"Cool," he said when Reed told him.

His beat-up truck was an old friend. He remembered the chartreuse Beetle ride in the rain, how Julia wanted to show him her new car.

His room was on the tenth floor, with a view of a brick wall. He pulled the curtain cords and closed his drama into its own place. The room was comfortable, with large pastels of old-fashioned street scenes on the wall. Exhausted, he stretched out for a nap. It had not occurred to him until he woke up an hour later that the room had a TV set, hidden behind cabinet doors like a prowler in the closet. He did not turn it on, though. He liked the silence. It was quiet enough to hear a mouse pissing on cotton.

At the lobby newsstand, he bought a map and went out walking. It was growing dark, and the streetlights were blazing. Some youths were banging on drums improvised from plastic buckets so loudly the sound hurt Reed's ears. On a street corner he saw a spray-painted man—metallic all over, clothes and skin and all. Jiggly coil springs decorated his cap. The figure, blowing a noisemaker, staggered along—a titanium robot. A woman dropped a coin in his lunch box, and he jerked his hand into his coat pocket and teased out a lollipop.

At a noisy café Reed ordered pan-seared shrimp in a Dixie-beer reduction sauce and rosemary corn bread. Rosemary orzo, he recalled. So many sensations reminded him of Julia. He stayed for the music, a band reminiscent of the sixties, and ordered another beer. The music made him feel he was in a war, heavy artillery surrounding him. He wouldn't have been surprised if a dirty bomb sailed through the door. He didn't stay long. His ears ringing, he meandered through the flashing colors and adrenaline rush of the city. The spectacle of lights spiraled around him, as though he were in the center of a far-flung galaxy. Oddly, a surge of excitement was growing in him about making his pilgrimage to the shrine of Enrico Fermi, a man who, like Julia seeking the eradication of disease, had a dream of figuring out the essence of reality.

After sleeping well in his high-rise cocoon of silence, Reed bought a pocket guidebook and browsed through it while he ate breakfast at a café on LaSalle. Then he walked the city, wondering where Julia had been, where she would go now. He was on the alert for a chartreuse Beetle. He tried to remember places she had mentioned. She had said that a downtown shopping center—with one big store and a string of little ones—was called Fat Man and Little Boy. He had no idea where it was, or what its actual name was. He had asked the bellman at the hotel, who said Reed must be joking.

He walked along the lakeshore, where strips of sand rimmed what might well be an ocean for all you could prove by the view. He passed the pier with its Ferris wheel slowly winding up through the sky, floating down. In a park he saw a woman sleeping face down, her possessions beside her in a bag on wheels. A roller-bag lady, he thought, a witticism to tell Julia. It always unnerved him to see homeless people displayed in public like waste heaps. He glimpsed a tall ship far in the distance, its rigging shining in a trick of light. A cool breeze from the lake felt good. He noticed a man swimming parallel to the shore, a serious swimmer, swimming freestyle as if he were practicing to swim Lake Michigan. The water appeared gray and unforgiving. All of these sights moved Reed as something esemplastic, one interlocking set of sensations. He was thrilled to be alive.

From time to time, Reed was jerked to a standstill by the operations of his own mind. He was a single quark clattering around in an electron cloud, seeking another. He was a strange quark and Julia was a charmed quark. Here he was, in Chicago, alone, knowing no one except the valet at the hotel who had parked his truck, and Julia, who had disappeared. The sun was shining and it was a fair summer day, not too hot. Anything at any time could happen, and until then he was free.

42

At the hotel Reed showered and changed into a royal blue T-shirt and black jeans. He positioned his star-studded leather belt with the silver buckle and checked his look in the mirror. He had dialed up his messages at home three times, and he tried one last time before he left the hotel. Nothing.

Because of the hassle of retrieving his truck, he rode the train to the campus. A Seeing Eye dog, a placid yellow Labrador, sat facing him, with a long-haired young man Reed took to be a student, who was reading a book in Braille. Both dog and student exited with him, and Reed thought about following them to get his bearings, but he didn't want to make the dog nervous. Crowds of young people, dressed in cutoffs and flip-flops, sauntered along with their inevitable backpacks. Like meal portions at restaurants, textbooks must be heavier these days, Reed thought, as he tried to imagine himself a student again. It was gratifying to think of the students' eagerness, their confidence in starting out, bolstered by their privileges. They probably did not think of their privileges, he realized.

With time to spare, he checked his map and detoured through some of the streets of handsome brick houses. Most of the houses had small front gardens enclosed by wrought-iron fences. Reed wondered how people braved the steep stoops when there was snow and ice. He felt uneducated, out of place, probably under suspicion.

As he walked down a residential street toward the library he thought he saw Julia, far ahead of him. It wasn't. He was fooled by a general outline and a motion that evoked her lope and head bob. He knew, of course, that she wouldn't come. Either she hadn't received his message, or she had chosen to ignore it. Or perhaps she wasn't able to reply. Maybe she had been injured or was sick from some exotic disease she was studying in her lab work. Hantavirus or Ebola. E. coli, perhaps, or the Nora virus. Or some new unknown-to-the-C.I.A. strain of Boola-Boola flu. She was just busy, he told himself. She might even be back at work, while he waited for hours at the site of the old Met Lab, where Enrico Fermi, more than sixty years before, had played with plutonium.

It was beyond a group of buildings ahead, on the far side of the library. He drew nearer to the library. Its panels of cold concrete reminded him of a startlingly new nuclear-bomb plant. The style was called the Architecture of Brutalism, the guidebook told him. Staring at the vertical grooves and slit windows of the massive building, Reed contemplated blankly the Architecture of Brutalism. Fermi had split the atom in an underground squash court, under Stagg Field, which was replaced now by the brutal library. Reed walked around the library, anxious about seeing the sculpture Julia had told him about on the day they first met, the day he so crudely wolfed meat loaf in her presence.

The Henry Moore sculpture was a dark spherical blob in the center of a large area of scored concrete. Coming closer, Reed saw that passageways ran through it. He moved slowly around the sculpture. It was a twelve-foot bronze dome, thrusting above him. It was a bald head, a skull, a brain case with an empty face. It was a helmet. It was, also, conceivably—in its smooth roundness—the mushroom cloud. The head and shoulders rested on four shapeless, knobby feet, as if the torso and legs had been excised. Reed leaned against one of the openings. The metal, warm from the sun, was pleasant to touch.

Henry Moore intended it to feel like a cathedral when you poked your head inside, Reed read in the pocket guide. If he said some kind of prayer—some Burl pearl—would it aid him in his quest at all? But he didn't want Julia to catch him here with his head inside this thing saying a prayer.

The design on the concrete paving that surrounded the sculpture was like broken sun rays, lines radiating out from the symbolic fig-ure, or perhaps converging toward it. Little Boy exploded and Fat Man imploded. Hiroshima and Nagasaki. The uranium bomb and the plutonium bomb.

Reed was used to being around atomic energy every day, but being right here at its birthplace jangled him. He could imagine old eager-beaver Enrico below ground here—right here, in the catacombs beneath the soccer stadium here at the University of Chicago—daring to meddle with the basic structure of nature itself. It was terrifying. He felt goose bumps rise on his arms as he thought about the gaggle of scientists huddled over their deadly endeavor. Their experiment was such a tight secret that the citizens of the city didn't have a chance to imagine an uncontrolled chain reaction, a disaster that would have made the great Chicago fire seem like a wienie roast. Maybe, Reed thought, other worlds had consumed themselves by some invasive cracking of their essential building blocks. It could all be undone. A solar system could become a black hole, like the state of nothingness before the big bang. That was one theory of the beginning of time. He glanced at his watch—five to one.

People passed by, unaware of what happened on this spot on a cold day in 1942. Enrico Fermi, charging forth like a medieval knight, had tickled the dragon's tail. In amongst his patchwork pile of graphite bricks and uranium chunks, he placed cadmium rods to cushion the neutrons and keep them from going wild. When the time came, Fermi calmly started the chain reaction by directing the removal of the rods. One by one, they were pulled out, until the pile fairly roared with its energy. Fermi stayed cool. *Put the rods back in*, Fermi said at just the right moment. He had succeeded in controlling a chain reaction. Now he knew how to produce enough plutonium to make atomic bombs.

A man and woman approached, tourists in khaki and sun hats. Reed moved aside. The man said, "The famous story is that they had a test tube of plutonium in the lab down underground here, and they all went to lunch and when they came back it was gone. The janitor had poured it down the drain. They had to go after it with Geiger counters—through the entire sewer system of Chicago."

"Did they get it all?" the woman asked, like someone inquiring about a cancer operation.

"They thought so. Who knows?"

"Do we have time for a drink before we meet Tiffany?"

The man consulted his watch, and the couple hurried away. Reed didn't believe the story. He returned to the sunny dome, which was becoming a buddy. Half-sitting in the sun-warmed seat, virtually inside the skull-cloud, he felt protected, even cozy. He was accustomed to heat. He could imagine the team of scientists toiling below him, beneath the rays scored in the concrete under his feet. He could feel the audacity, the egomania of some of them, the cliquishness of their fraternity—their pride, their rationalizations. He did not know if Fermi was afraid. Probably he wasn't.

Atomic energy was so seductive. Reed's seat in the nuclear-energy sculpture felt warm. He was peaceful. Good old Fermi.

Even though this heavy-metal transuranic memorial seemed as hard as a D.U.-enforced military tank, Reed was growing comfortable with it. He laughed to himself, remembering what Sammy

Blew had said about large women. Then, after removing the guide-book and map from his hip pockets, Reed found himself easing into the niche within the giant head. Pushing himself in rearward, he entered the opening. Curled up tight, he just fit.

In his fortress, he joined with nuclear energy, communing with its monstrous power. He was snug with the sun's warmth, but shaded from its glare. Its stored energy radiated through him. This could be an arthritis cure, he thought.

Realizing his behavior might seem suspicious—he could be stow-ing a bomb—he wriggled out and resumed his position, waiting for Julia. He did a few calf and hamstring stretches to prevent cramps. His knee still bothered him from time to time.

He did not wait long. He could see her coming down the street. She wasn't yet distinct, but he knew her shape, her hair, her walk, even those thick-soled leather clogs, with the floppy straps. Impul-sively, he hid behind the sculpture. Then, as she drew nearer, he crawled inside it again, twisting around so that his head was in the opening that faced her. He was Captain Plutonium in his Helmet of Invincibility. And when she saw him at last, he was grinning.

"May I take your order?" he said.

"This sculpture is talking," Julia said, turning to an imaginary companion. "Darth Vader is flirting with me."

"I've been toddling all over this town looking for you," he said as he struggled out of his nest.

Their reunion wasn't angry. She was glad to see him, and she let him kiss her. Something about her lip gloss was unfamiliar. Had she been kissing someone? Some people walked past, not heeding them. He was so glad to see her, so relieved that she met him at the sculp-ture, that he could not find fault with her. She was alive, and she was here. She was wearing jeans and a gray cropped top with elbow-length sleeves. She was carrying a small, flat bag that hung on her shoulder by a thin strap of leather. There were never any extras with Julia—no artifice, no decoration. She wasn't hidden beneath any distracting frills.

"*So,*" she said. "What have you and Enrico Fermi been up to?"

"I've been trying to figure out if Fermi was just doing his job, or if he should have just said no."

"There's no answer to that."

"I was wondering, would this thing withstand an atomic blast?"

"Who would need to know?" she said.

She was holding his arm, leaning into him. "You're warm," she said.

"From Humpty Dumpty here." He put her hand on the warm metal. "Put some earrings on this guy, and you'll have Buddha," Reed said. Something had shifted inside him. Gas? His knees felt a little wobbly.

"Do we have to decide the fate of civilization?" she said, kidding.

"I don't know if we have time for that. God, I missed you," he said, hugging her. "I need a scintillation counter to keep track of you. You're flitting and flashing around like a firefly."

"Isn't that their courtship method?"

"You tell me."

She shifted her purse from one shoulder to the other, and examined the concrete surface at her feet. "I'm sorry if I caused you to worry," she said. "I was in over my head—so to speak."

They moved away from the sculpture into the shade of some trees.

"Hey, look at me," he said, turning her face toward his. "Tell me, are you going to the University of Chicago? I heard you might quit your job and come up here to go to school."

"Is that what they told you at work?" She laughed. "It's a tough school to get into."

"But you're smart enough," he said, caressing her face.

Suddenly she burst into tears. Uncertain what to do, he wrapped his arms around her and was murmuring, "Hey, what's the matter?"

"I've had a hard time," she said, putting her head on his shoulder. His T-shirt soaked up her tears. "This has been a hard trip."

"What happened?"

"Oh, nobody died or anything. I'm just stressed—family stuff, you know."

"Well, I'm here, I'll take care of you. We'll make it better." He felt rather pleased to discover some vulnerability in her. She needed him to lean on. She needed for him to pet her. She sobbed briefly, uttering sentence fragments about the fate of civilization. She had seriously considered his message on the telephone, he thought. He didn't care about the fate of civilization right now.

"How's your mom?" she asked, breaking away from his hold.

"Dandy. Infinitely better. No worry. I'm here to take care of *you*," he said. "We'll work it out. I don't think it ought to take the grand unified theory to get us back together."

"But we might have to pull a few strings." She smiled and blew her nose with a tissue she pulled from her pocket.

He stroked her hair. It had grown longer since he saw her last. "I don't ever want to be away from you again long enough to see that your hair has grown," he said.

"I'm going to let it grow out," she said.

"Good. I'd like that. I think I'll grow a ponytail again," he said. "You never saw me with a ponytail."

"That would be swell. We'll just let our hair grow until there's some sense in the world," she said, turning away from Reed.

She was walking across the converging/radiating lines past the sculpture to the sidewalk, and he hastened to catch her.

"Hey, how come you stayed away so long? How's your sister?"

"She's O.K. I was worried, but I think she's back on her feet. Feet? In over my head? Why am I speaking in body parts? Anyway, it's a long story. I had to go up to see my parents at their cabin in Michigan. Diana's going to stay with them for the time being. Come on, let me show you around campus." She clasped his hand, leading him.

As he walked along with Julia past huge gray Gothic masses, he felt overshadowed by his own ignorance. He wondered what it would be like to study astronomy here. He remembered his own college days as a long, drunken party, but he had the impression that the students here were suiting up to run the world.

Looking up at the ancient, worn architecture, Julia pointed out goofy, grotesque gargoyles with their tongues protruding and full-feathered angels in bonnets reading books.

"Aren't they hilarious?" she said. "They're keeping an eye on us."

"Spies," said Reed.

They laughed together.

She led him to a spookily postmodern brick building with a security entrance. Julia knew how to get inside with a code on a keypad—from an acquaintance, a boyfriend? He wouldn't ask. The noiseless, sterile white corridors seemed like a futuristic version of a hospital—perhaps an online hospital, Reed thought, where doctors removed gallstones in Oklahoma by remote control from Chicago. Julia paused at a bulletin board, where graduate programs and conferences were posted. A professor of microbiology was lecturing on retrovirus proteolytic processing. And another professor had published a paper on turnip vein-clearing tobamovirus. Along the corridors, Reed saw several white mobile units like miniature labs for weapons of mass destruction. Or perhaps they were only storage carts. Then Reed recognized a yellow radiation-warning sign and an emergency shower for washdowns. The shower was in the hallway, as matter-of-fact as a water fountain. Through a glass pane, he saw a desktop centrifuge in a lab.

"I bet you could dry your underwear really fast in one of those," Reed said. He made her laugh.

As they ate sandwiches and drank coffee at a campus café, Julia chatted offhandedly about the kinds of courses required for a degree in molecular biology. Around them, students were studying and drinking coffee. A young Asian woman was methodically skimming through piles of papers. The students seemed sloppy, nondescript, like laborers. Reed thought he really should shift course—take up astronomy, carry a backpack, drink latte at coffee bars, get to know some intellectuals.

"I'll be right back," Julia said. "I have to go to the restroom."

"I'll be here," he said. She hadn't touched the other half of her sandwich.

Even though he felt he was in a foreign land, he did possess a great deal of experience—even wisdom, he suddenly thought with confidence—that these younger students around him did not have. His technical expertise counted for something. He listened to a couple of students discussing perturbation theory and bounds for eigenvalues. He couldn't decide if they were discussing math, physics, or movies. They kept using the word *matrix*.

"How's your job going?" Julia asked him when she returned. "Anything happening?"

"Finding out that your job has screwed you is hard to take," he said. "It's like coming to the end of your life and realizing you've lived in vain."

"We do live in vain," she said. "I mean, when you consider the larger picture."

"I still think I've done a good job, and an important job."

He was surprised when she said, "I know, Reed. You've done a great job. I never said you didn't."

"If you lived here, would I ever see you?" he asked.

"I told you it's hard to get into the program."

"Suppose you did get in."

She sipped her decaf latte nervously. He thought perhaps he should never have come.

"Do you want another cup of coffee?" he asked.

"No, thanks."

"Don't you want your sandwich?"

She shook her head no.

"You're really serious about going to school, aren't you?"

She nodded. "You know I want to do *something*. Even if I just found some kind of gene match in a BLAST search that would apply in some small way—that would be great! I want to at least help in some way."

"Test tubes and mice?" he said. "I thought you didn't want to kill anything."

"No, you can do a lot on computers. Do you remember telling me that quantum mechanics was more like metaphysics than physics? Maybe there *is* a physics of the imagination. Maybe there's a physics of the soul." Her face was brightening now.

"And maybe Alice went through the looking glass," he said. "Anything is possible. But I'm sure you could figure it out, Miss Superstring. You're dangling me on a cosmic string." He grinned widely. "You've got me so wound up in strings I thought I was going to disappear into a wormhole and come out the other side of time."

"What? You don't get it yet?" She laughed, teasing.

"I've got my shorts twisted in a wad over how many quarks in a quart and how many strings in a p-brane. My mind is worn out. I still can't grasp it. It just seems unbelievable."

"I didn't say you had to believe it." She smiled.

He slapped his forehead. "*Now* you tell me."

She laughed. "You're getting me off track. I'm studying microbes and molecules, not quarks and strings. All that was just for fun."

He nodded and reached for her hand across the table.

"I'm with you," he said. "If you want to study germs, that's what you should do."

"Let's go sit outside," she said, drinking the last of her latte.

They deposited their trash into designated black holes. He followed her outside, and they found a bench.

"Come here." She reached in her purse for her lip gloss and applied it to her lips. "Now I can kiss you better."

"Is it germicidal?"

"No. But it tastes good."

"Yes, it does," he said after sucking her lips. "But you taste better."

Reed wanted to express all his profoundest regrets and apologies, but he knew that would be inadequate. He just wanted to hold her. He felt a long wail arise in his chest. Letting the wail come out, even halfway, almost silently, was a way of translating his painful desire into the long, sustained pleasure of an ending musical note.

"O.K. Level with me," Reed said after a moment. "What's been going on? I know there's something wrong."

They were sitting close together, his hand on her leg, and the western sun was glittering through some shade trees, dappling Julia's complexion. Her mouth started to curl—a grin or a frown? It was a slight frown, he thought.

She said, "I don't know how to tell you this, Reed."

"You're engaged to some other guy."

"No! Don't leap to conclusions."

"You've got cancer!"

"Good grief, Reed. Stop leaping." She laid her warm hand in his lap, sweetly close to his privates.

"What is it, Julia? If you just—"

"I'm pregnant." She clapped her hand over her mouth as if she had uttered a dirty word.

"Heaven and earth!"

"It's true."

Was he grinning? He wasn't sure. "I'll be damned," he said. His heart seemed to be doing some kind of Texas two-step.

"You're the lucky one," she said. "The only one."

He wasn't sure if she was going to cry or laugh. "I'll be damned," he said.

"I didn't want to tell you."

He could feel the blood drain from his head. He was afraid. He felt a hit of aphasia, a moment of self-consciousness that lacked context. On the verge of fading out, he could see himself, stunned, in this moment, unable to grasp who he was or where he was. He could see himself questioning himself. Then he returned.

"How are you going to cure disease if you can't even keep from getting pregnant? That's like not using rubber gloves when you're in the monkey-pox ward."

"I don't have monkey pox. I'm pregnant."

She was irritated, he saw. "I didn't mean to be sarcastic," he said. "I'm just stunned. I'm flabbergasted. Whopper-jawed."

"I really surprised you, didn't I?"

"Heaven and earth."

"You said that."

"What should I say—heavens to Betsy?"

She shifted her legs on the bench and stroked his arm. "I got all your messages, but I was afraid to call back. I had to think it through."

He gave a low whistle. "How did this happen?"

"The presence of initial conditions—of a high order. Unpredictability," she said. "One sperm with a hairy tail wins the race. He can wiggle the fastest and he gets to the egg first and bores a hole into it."

"Aiming," said Reed, nodding. "What did I tell you?"

"It's violent!" she protested. "What did I tell *you*?"

"When did this happen?"

"That morning rush-hour—remember?"

The tender little scene came rushing back. Reed was speechless. His feeling came in waves of mingled breathlessness, glee, horror, giggles, anticipation. Exhilaration and dread. He ran the back of his hand over his eyes. He was frightened, and he was flooded with love. His whole life rushed around him—reconsidered, reconfigured. He was a man reassessing his whole life—let alone the fate of civilization—in light of new information. Atomic Man and Captain Plutonium were just Halloween costumes compared to this.

She was alarmed. "It's O.K.," she said, caressing his face soothingly. "You don't have to feel responsible. I'll handle it."

"I imagine you getting an abortion on your lunch hour the day you found out."

"Do you really think I'd do that without asking you? It hurts me that you'd think that."

"I'm sorry. I'm a horse's ass."

She worried with some strands of hair. "But I haven't ruled out anything."

"This will get in your way."

Reed wanted to ask if she was worried about birth defects, or if some kind of test could tell. Now wasn't the time to tell her about his exposures.

"Have I ruined your life now?" he asked.

"Don't talk that way."

"What about school? All your plans?"

"Shh! Finally it was the fact that you said 'I love you' on the phone. I don't think you ever found that easy to say."

"But you always knew I loved you."

"You never really said it."

"Well, neither did you! I never knew what you felt about me. You were always disappearing."

Impulsively, he issued promises. "I'll take care of the baby so you can go to school. We'll move to Chicago. I'll take my retirement early." She didn't answer. "Or whatever you want to do," he said. "We'll join the circus."

She laughed; together they laughed, like children, at the fix they had gotten themselves into. This was the fourth time in his life a woman had said the words *I'm pregnant* to him. The first was Carol, in high school. She went to Chicago with her parents and got the abortion. And then Glenda briskly announced first Dalton and then Dana, their children, shortly after each conception, as if they were seeds that had come up in her garden, little to do with him.

Some prematurely yellow leaves were drifting down from some tall ash trees. A bell in a stone tower began to chime. Reed felt a preview of mortality, as if he hadn't paid attention all his life, until now, to the tolling bell of his heart.

"Why didn't you call me and tell me?"

"I didn't want to bother you."

"You should have bothered me."

"I had to think about it."

He pondered that, and then he faced her squarely. "The thing is, you should have bothered me. And I don't mean because of my pride, so that I could take charge. It's so you can have somebody with you. A person can't do everything alone."

"I didn't want to intrude."

"You wouldn't have. And maybe all I could do was just be there." She nodded.

"I want you with me," he said. "If you live by yourself, you come home and you're alone. I talk to Clarence, but he doesn't give a shit about string theory, and he's got bad breath. Maybe you can talk to somebody on the phone, or somebody comes over, but whoever it is has his own life and can stick around yours only so long. So you end up online or at some titty bar or god-awful hangout, meeting somebody that makes your skin crawl."

She pushed her hair from her eyes. "That sounds terrible."

"I'm not begging, Julia. I'm just saying that if the human race is doomed to die from nuclear mischief, then that's pretty sad, and the best we can aim for is a giggle and a smooch. How about it?"

She gave a long sigh. "You're like what you said about those transuranics in the pipes. You're in my system and I can't get you out."

He grinned. "That's me, Transuranic Man." He felt hot. "Do I look strange?" he asked her. "I feel like I'm giving off a weird blue glow."

She scrutinized him. "The sun is shining on your T-shirt."

"Wait till you see me in the dark," he said. "I'm a virtual walking criticality. I'm a criticality in your life."

"No, you're not. You're critical to my life."

Something about the scene was like the unreality of a movie ending, he thought—the warm, phony wrap-up. He tried to stop himself from seeing through it, from having the cynical suspicion that the walk into the sunset was an unending descent into flames. For a mere speck in space-time, that warm moment that *glowed* was essential. If you could have one or two in your life, that might be enough, but you had to have at least one before you went cold.

He stood, feeling that they needed to move along.

"Wait," she said, her fingers twiddling a loose eyelash. "I have something in my eye." She plucked the eyelash and then examined it closely, as though she was trying to see all the way past the resident microbes and mites on down into the dark, dancing strings that played the cosmic hum, the imaginary music he always heard in the pipes of the Cascade when he was working.

Acknowledgments

Works I consulted include *Making a Real Killing: Rocky Flats and the Nuclear West* by Len Ackland; *The Elegant Universe* by Brian Greene; *Atoms in the Family* by Laura Fermi; *A Brief History of Time* and *The Universe in a Nutshell* by Stephen Hawking; *Cell and Molecular Biology* by Gerald Karp; *Hubble Space Telescope: New Views of the Universe* by Mark Voit; and *The Plutonium Files* by Eileen Welsome.

I am grateful to various individuals for their gracious help in my explorations: Philip Crowley, Marty Curtis, Mark Donham, Kristi Hansen, Kristen Iversen. Thanks to Judy Krug, my enthusiastic tour guide in Chicago; to Suketu Bhavsar for his thrilling and poetic astronomy lectures; to Dale Bauer for the use of her Twinkie theory; and to Joe Gorline for his inspiration, generosity, and wit.

And I owe my personal thanks to Dottie, Roger, Sharon, and Sam.

BOBBIE ANN MASON is the author of *In Country, Clear Springs*, and *Shiloh & Other Stories*. She is the winner of the PEN/Hemingway Award, two Southern Book awards, and numerous other prizes, including the O. Henry and the Pushcart. She was a finalist for the National Book Critics Circle Award, the American Book Award, the PEN/Faulkner Award, and the Pulitzer Prize. She is writer-in-residence at the University of Kentucky.

ABOUT THE TYPE

The text of this book was set in Janson, a typeface designed in about 1690 by Nicholas Kis, a Hungarian living in Amsterdam, and for many years mistakenly attributed to the Dutch printer Anton Janson. In 1919 the matrices became the property of the Stempel Foundry in Frankfurt. It is an old-style book face of excellent clarity and sharpness. Janson serifs are concave and splayed; the contrast between thick and thin strokes is marked.